Chapter One

The place stank.

Despite regulations, smokers congregated near the door, puffing away and leaving a pall of choking smoke hovering at the entry. Emma wrinkled her nose in distaste before racing through the doorway, head down, not daring to inhale. Inside, a different stench dominated. The sour beer was equally distasteful.

A single sweep of the room was all it took to spot her prey. Greg sat perched on a stool at the bar with one bent leg resting on the foot-rail while the other was planted on the floor supporting most of his weight. She cocked her head to one side. It was the first time she'd really stood back to study the man she'd sort of been dating for the past few months. She snorted and winced at the indelicate sound while wondering if you could call watching a guy play hockey and pool – dating. Hmm, he was more overweight than she'd realised. A small bare strip of pale skin oozed over his belt. So far, she'd never got anywhere near seeing what was under his clothing: even though he'd hinted often enough. Feeling like a voyeur, she lifted her eyes and stalled on his hands, which were long but podgy. One held a cue while the other was rhythmically rolling a block of blue chalk around and around the felt tip.

Clank, clank. Hard pool balls hitting drew her head sideways. A mumbled string of expletives told her the player had pocketed the wrong ball. She recognised him and two more. Oh, no. If they were here, it meant Greg's invitation to a quiet dinner for two wasn't about to happen. On a long, whispered groan, she hefted her shoulders on a sucked in breath. Whooshing the air from her lungs she dropped her shoulders in defeat. They were supposed to be celebrating the end of her university studies, but gut instinct sent a definite message it wasn't going to happen – at least not for a while.

An unbidden sigh slid from her lips. On the cards were another boring couple of hours. As if her thoughts had beckoned it, her stomach rumbled in protest, reminding her she hadn't eaten since breakfast at sun-up. Experience told her she would have to entertain herself until the two teams tired of outplaying each other. Should she turn around and go home? She wouldn't be invited to take part: never was unless one of this regular group couldn't make it or had to leave early.

'Em, you're just in time.'

At the yelled words from the familiar voice, a surge of hope rose. Emma swung her glance towards the source.

STALKED

Tania Park

ISBN: 978-0-6485565-0-3 (Paperback)
ISBN: 978-0-6485565-1-0 (Ebook)

Printed & Channel Distribution: Lightning Source | Ingram (USA/UK/EUROPE/AUS)
Cover Designed—Laila Savolainen, Pickawoowoo Publishing Group
Publishing Consultants/Interior Design—Pickawoowoo Publishing Group

Publisher
Tania Park Publishing
For enquiries, write to: rights and permissions via publisher.

Also by Tania Park

Mistaken

'He never got around to telling me why he wanted me dead.'

When Bella's new boss whacked her across the head and dropped her over a cliff, her life changed in an instant. She became a naïve pawn caught in a very dangerous game.

Retribution

Living with a new identity in a different state on the other side of the country, Amy Masters is stunned and terrified when her ex-husband turns up at her place of work. After almost killing her, he is supposed to be still in jail.

Blind justice

'Panic turned to terror at the sudden onrush of two sets of feet. A rough hand clamped over her mouth to silence her.'

Piano bar pianist, Christine Mears, becomes involved in a murder investigation when she meets Detective Ben Somers. She unwittingly becomes the main target of an unscrupulous gang of drug dealers. To them she is worth two million dollars and the gang goes to extreme lengths to snatch Christine to use as ransom.

Road Trip

'Something inside her broke apart, leaving an intense sensation

of emptiness. It was like he'd taken a huge chunk of her heart with him and he was only her brother.'

Madison Brown, 20 and Gemma Tomas, 17, are complete opposites in almost every way but have a unique bond tying them together. When Gemma lands a job in Brisbane, she sweet-talks Maddie into driving with her across Australia. To save money, they camp along the way. Gemma's impulsive behaviour leads them into some awkward predicaments as they drive through the outback from Perth. Their friendship becomes fractured as Maddie tries to extricate them from difficult and life-threatening situations.

The Swan

'I was seven years old. Do you honestly think I would tell the truth so that I could get beaten again the minute the police left?'

Just as an elegant swan emerges from the gaucheness of a young cygnet, Melanie Jones struggles to escape the darkness of a terrible abusive life. Deep shame and fear are constant companions. Her music is the one haven where she is able to find temporary reprieve from the awfulness of her life. Her mother's tragic murder is the turning point in Melanie's life.

Dedication

This book is dedicated to my dear friend who passed away too soon after fighting a cancer which was determined to plague her despite the best modern medicine could give. Caroline was one of those true friends with a gentle nature, soft heart and determination to do her best at everything. A much loved and dedicated teacher, her loss touched me more than I thought anyone could.

To honour her memory I have named the protagonist's best friend, Caroline, who comes from a beautiful family and whose brother, Nick, saves the day. After what the protagonist goes through, she deserves beautiful people in her life.

There are some amazing people in this world. Caroline was one of them.

Maybe he hadn't forgotten about the promised meal. Straightening her shoulders, she wove a path through the throng, shyly acknowledging each guy she recognised as she went. Only one bothered to repay the greeting but it was with nothing more than a grunt. Typical.

'Hi Greg, how was your day?' She winced at the way her voice came out sounding apologetic but with Greg readying himself for his turn with the cue, she didn't dare interrupt.

'My glass is empty. Get me another beer,' said Greg as he bent at the waist and levelled his eye along the slender tapering length of wood. With the way one shirt tail had escaped belted trousers and was riding up to expose a wodge of white flesh, he'd been there a while, which meant he'd already had more than one lager.

A wave of bitter disappointment washed over her, negating the euphoria she'd felt an hour earlier when she and her two best friends had walked out of the examination room at university for the last time. The three of them had raced around the oval like maniacs, not caring when they got soaked under the powerful surges of huge sprinklers. Study was over forever. It was an amazing feeling.

With her smile at the memory turning to a sigh of regret, Emma neared the bar to order and pay for the lager. She waited until the frosty glass was in her hand before creeping back to the group. To break Greg's concentration while taking his turn with the cue would incur his sarcastic wrath. It wasn't something she wished to repeat.

After completing his series of shots, Greg returned to his seat with a gloating leer at his mates after sinking several balls with the large white spots. From the jeers of the opposition, Emma guessed Greg and his partner were in the lead. Without so much as a word or a glance, Greg took the frothing glass and settled back onto his stool in an almost exact replica of his stance before taking his shot. The only difference was that the chalk was nowhere to be seen. In its place Greg held the full glass against his lips and slurped so loud his mates laughed. Really? Did he have to be such a pig?

Still hopeful they were going to eat at six, Emma searched the humming room for a vacant stool, but all were taken. Typical. Instead, she leant up against the bar to ease the pressure on her feet while pretending interest as the men took turns, ignoring the jeers and shouts of success or failure each time there was a thud. No one bothered to offer her a seat or a drink, so she stayed propping up the bar behind Greg, wishing they were in the lounge bar where there was more comfortable seating and a live band.

Hope faded when six o'clock passed and another game began the moment the last ball was sunk. After a few more rounds with the men playing a round robin tournament, boredom reigned while Emma shifted from foot-to-foot to ease the ache. The sound of the band in the lounge area starting up again tantalised her eardrums and fed up with being treated as a nonentity, she slipped into the room next door. At last, a seat. With a huff, she sank into the worn fabric cushions, turning to face the band as she wriggled numb feet to get the blood flowing. The relief was intense and so welcome. In the time she'd been there, Emma had bought four beers for Greg, but she figured since he'd barely said a word to her, he wouldn't miss her presence, at least not until his glass was empty again.

The band was good, with most patrons dancing to the loud sixties rock songs. Her foot tapped in time to the beat while her fingers drummed the rhythm on the edge of the scarred wooden table. Even though the music was from an era before her time she enjoyed the tunes, especially the slower ballads. They were songs she'd grown up with on the farm, the type of CDs her dad kept running in the utes and tractors.

Emma jumped when a much larger hand grasped her fingers and pulled her onto the dance floor. Alarmed, she glanced at the face of a tall man she'd never seen before.

He grinned, making the small scar on the side of his mouth disappear into the laugh lines. 'Come on, you look so lonely sitting there by yourself, come and dance with me. One dance.'

Afraid of Greg's reaction if he happened to come looking for her, Emma shot a glance towards the next room. From the corner of her eye she caught a frown wrinkle the features of the stranger moments before he leant forwards. 'I promise I won't hurt you. Relax and let yourself enjoy the music. I'm Nick by the way.'

'Emma, Emma Nicholls.' She forced a smile, her body already swaying in time with the music. How she loved dancing, but Greg always refused to dance with her, saying he wasn't a pansy. At the same time, he never allowed her to dance with any other man or even move onto the dance floor by herself, when he was around.

The stranger eased them amongst the writhing couples, none of which were able to do the proper jive movements to the classic rock and roll song. But each managed to contort his or her body in sole interpretations in time to the catchy rhythm. The yelled off-key singing indicated they knew key words and phrases if not the movements.

Trying to be inconspicuous, Emma peeked at Nick from under her lashes, cocking her head to one side to study his face. He looked kind of familiar, but she couldn't recall ever seeing him before. Maybe she'd seen him around the university campus.

'Do I know you?' she asked after a lengthy examination.

He grinned. 'I'm sure I would have remembered meeting someone as pretty as you. I arrived home from the U.K. only this morning and I've been away for five years, so I doubt it. Are you here alone?'

She frowned as she glanced towards the open archway leading to the bar. 'No, Greg is playing pool. I was bored, so came in to listen to the music.'

'Foolish man to leave such a beautiful woman alone. Let's see how long it takes for him to realise you have vanished?'

'I'm not beautiful,' she muttered under her breath before twirling around until she faced him again.

'How can you say that?' He spun her back the other way, catching her hand to stop her spin. 'You're gorgeous. Such a natural beauty.' He indicated with his hand. 'Remarkable eyes which need no make-up to enhance them. Silky soft flawless skin.' A finger ran down her cheek, creating a shiver at the warm touch before the skin incinerated. Embarrassed to the nth degree, she paused, then shrugged her shoulders before relaxing and letting her body move with the music. It was ridiculous to feel so uptight about a simple compliment, but she wasn't used to being on the receiving end of one. She'd never see him again so what did it matter if he lied to keep her attention. It felt kind of good having a man compliment her. Greg certainly never said anything even remotely so nice, never passed comment on her dress or the way she did her hair, but with dead straight mousy hair what was there to compliment?

Nick chatted non-stop about inconsequential topics, which she responded to with reticence, not sure how she was supposed to react. He managed to elicit a few grins from her at his witty comments and gradually she relaxed more and more. He was an excellent dancer: far better than most. He moved with graceful agility and had an excellent sense of rhythm as though he was born to dance.

When the band went for a break, Nick slid into the seat opposite Emma, offering her a drink when the waitress approached.

She flicked another nervous peek towards the next room. 'Err… no. I'd better not but thank you.' Why, oh, why did she say no. She was dying for a drink.

He frowned as he followed the direction of her glance. 'Come on, one drink as a thank you for taking pity on a lonely man. I promise I'll disappear if the boyfriend makes an appearance.'

She paused, mulling his invitation and smiled again. Why not? Greg certainly hadn't cared enough to offer her a drink in the three hours she'd been there. 'Okay but make it a lemon squash.'

While sipping from their glasses, they sat in companionable silence watching couples writhing to a more modern pop tune.

'What the hell are you doing in here?' a loud voice barked.

Adrenalin surged as Emma jerked around, splashing her drink over one hand. Greg looked furious as he strode towards them. He threw a dark scowl in Nick's direction which must have put Greg off balance for he stumbled then struggled to regain his balance. Ah, far out, he was drunk. How could she placate him? Certainly not by lying and how obvious was it with her sitting here drinking with another guy?

'Listening to the music,' she managed to choke out. She couldn't think of anything else to say. Guilt swamped her and she knew she'd gone bright red, she always did and hated it. Petrified Greg would cause an unpleasant scene, she rose and turned towards Nick. 'Thank you for the drink and the dance, it was fun,' she murmured under her breath, hoping Greg wouldn't hear.

Nick nodded in acknowledgement and looked as if he was going to say something when Greg reached them, grabbed Emma's hand, yanking so hard she tripped and stumbled as he hauled her upright. There was nothing she could do but follow as he towed her outside with fingers gripping so hard it hurt.

'What the hell do you think you're doing drinking with a stranger and worse still, dancing with him? You're here, with me!' Greg yelled.

Too scared to look up, Emma peered around under her lashes hoping no-one could see or hear. She caught a glimpse of Nick standing less than five metres away, staring at her. He took two steps towards them. Oh, please don't come, she willed as she shot him a pleading glance before dropping her eyes and backing away from the menacing sensation of Greg. He wasn't touching her but might as well have been for she could feel tension radiating from him in tsunami proportion waves. Her breath hissed out in relief when Nick turned away and strode off with a slightly awkward gait. He looked furious. Well so was she. How could Greg treat her like that in public?

As she dared a peek, tears shimmered across her eyes making Greg's face appear hazy. She fought the moisture back for Greg thought tears were a sign of weakness and couldn't abide them. To not give him an answer would be as bad as using his aggressive tone. Either would inflame his temper as would a sign of tears.

'I'm sorry, but you barely said a word to me in the bar, you were so busy with your friends. In fact, you ignored me except when you wanted another beer. You invited me to dinner at six.' The glance at her watch was deliberate and overacted. 'It's now almost eight. I wanted to listen to the music for something to do.' As her ire rose, her tongue seemed to take on a life of its own and didn't know when to stop. 'I did nothing wrong. It was only one dance. You won't ever dance with me.'

Knowing by the look of fury on his face that she had gone too far, Emma turned away to hide the moisture she'd lost control over. She was shaking so much her stomach muscles felt as though they were going to ping apart. To gain control, she sucked in a long breath and hefted her shoulders high. When she thought she was brave enough she twisted back and eyed him. Enough of being a coward.

'I'll see you tomorrow night. I'm going home.' Terrified there would be reprisals for daring to answer back, she spun around and sprinted across the parking lot to her car.

'Emma, we haven't had dinner yet. Come back, I don't want to have to be the only one eating without a partner. Don't be such a spoilsport.'

Stunned, she paused mid-flight. A spoilsport? Her? And only one without a partner? Dinner was supposed to be with the two of them. And where were the other partners? Or was she supposed to be the only woman dining with a gang of inebriated men? A sudden thought hit–he'd forgotten about his invitation but wasn't man enough to admit it. Her innards clenched so tight she felt as though she was going to throw up. Inconsiderate brute.

As she drove the two kilometres to her unit, Emma struggled to see the road through the haze of salty moisture she was losing the battle in holding back. Feeling more upset than usual over Greg's treatment, it suddenly dawned on her exactly what her two friends meant when they spoke about him. She couldn't recall the number of times Sandy and Caroline had hinted how Greg was not right for her, how he used her as a doormat. She searched the recesses of her grey matter for other comments she'd heard and winced. Bully, inconsiderate, egomaniac and selfish came to mind. Now she realised they were all true.

But the girls didn't understand. All through the four years of university they both had regular invitations to dates and now had steady boyfriends. Not once, until Greg, had Emma been asked out. Not having had the experience of other men, she was grateful having somebody willing to take her out on the odd occasion although, deep down she knew Greg wasn't the nicest of men. But he'd never physically hurt her and had been considerate in not forcing the physical issue when she'd said she wasn't ready for intimacy. So, he wasn't all that bad. He was just, just… She couldn't think of the right words but possessive and uncaring seemed to settle in the back of her mind as she turned into her street.

After pulling into the garage and shutting down the engine, Emma stayed sitting while attempting to calm the churning turmoil in her innards. As she stared at the cream brick wall, she thought long and hard about the way Greg treated her. He wasn't what she wanted in a relationship, but while he was on the scene no other guy was likely to approach her for a date. Could she be brave enough to call a halt to their relationship before she went back to the farm to be with her parents over the Christmas break? It was an opportune time. But darn it, Greg knew she was returning home for a while. She'd been dumb enough to tell him. After the Christmas break she was going overseas to visit Spain and France so she could practise speaking the languages she'd majored in. The farm was far enough away he wouldn't be able to call on her and she hadn't given him the phone number. She grinned. Apart from the nearest town, he didn't even know where the farm was. Maybe she could seek employment and not return to the city after harvest was completed. It would be a great way of ending things.

She shivered at the thought of telling Greg. Having experienced his temper first hand on more occasions than she cared to recall, she doubted she would be able to tell him to his face that it was over. Although he had never physically harmed her, she'd often been on the receiving end of a verbal tongue-lashing. Somehow, he always managed to twist things around to convince her it was something she had done to deserve his wrath. And like an idiot she'd accepted it. How was it she always felt guilty? How did he do that?

Maybe it would be better to wait until she went home, give it a few weeks of no contact and maybe do the coward's thing and tell him by phone or maybe email. There was only a week left before going home with only one date planned – the party tomorrow night. A smile jumped out. All her university friends would be at the party so Greg would have to be civil. He never showed his temper in front of an audience – well, not until tonight. So, the party might not be so bad. For the rest of the week she could plead being too busy packing, cleaning and Christmas shopping. She wouldn't have to see him at all if she organised things right. The days weren't a problem since he worked, although there was this weekend to get through. For the nights, she could pretend she had farewell dinners with Sandy and Caroline. That would take two of the nights. Three if she organised a session at the cinema for there were a couple of new films out which she wouldn't mind seeing. There was late night shopping which she could eke out over another two nights.

Happy she'd solved her problem, a grin split her face as she made her way inside to find something to eat since she'd missed dinner. While dragging the makings of a snack from the fridge, she figured all she had to do was to survive the following night's celebratory party with Greg and never see him again. Problem solved.

Chapter Two

As Emma browsed through her wardrobe, she flicked hangers aside after inspecting each item. The only halfway decent dresses she owned were several years old but had hardly ever been worn. After a close inspection she realised they all looked outdated and way too young. She was twenty-one, for goodness sake, not sixteen. It wasn't often she spent the allowance her father gave her each month, on new clothes, much preferring to save as much as she could for her gap year. She frowned at the entire row of discards. She needed something else for the party, something special. Slamming the wardrobe door shut on her outdated clothes, she grabbed her purse and keys and spent the morning searching the city for something classy. The outfit she found, she loved the moment she saw it, but the price tag shocked her. When did clothes become so expensive? The dress was far classier than anything she owned but it felt right as she swirled around admiring her image in the dressing room mirror. Throwing caution to the wind she handed over the money, justifying the purchase as something she would get good use out of when overseas. There would always be a need for at least one nice outfit, she reasoned, even though she had no plans to hit the high life when she was away, but one never knew.

When she passed a hair salon on her way back to her car, she paused and glanced inside. Why not? She had a fabulous new dress, so why not get her hair styled as well? Inspecting the finished hairdo in the salon mirror an hour later, she was delighted with the way the hairdresser got her layered bob to turn under with a little bounce at the ends. She grinned at her reflection. For once her dead straight, mousy brown hair looked glamorous.

After dressing in the early evening, she couldn't believe she was looking at her own image when she peered into the bedroom mirror. Instead of the casual jean-clad uni student she was used to seeing, there was an attractive young woman she barely recognised, peering back. Mascara on her lashes made her eyes look larger and a hint of blusher, along with a swipe of rarely used lip-gloss, made her look a little older. Awed with the result she felt on top of the world. There seemed to be a permanent grin plastered to her face as she plated the bite-sized savouries she'd prepared earlier.

When Greg Saunders arrived to pick her up, he made no comment about her appearance, not even passing her an appraising glance when she opened the door to his loud thump.

'Are you ready? Let's go,' he muttered as he turned and headed back towards his car. With her heels tap-tapping as she ran to keep up with his rapid loping strides, Emma swallowed her bitter disappointment while keeping her tray of finger-food balanced to prevent the morsels from slipping off. Only tonight and she was rid of him. She could last one more night.

'I'm sorry I was a bit tetchy last night,' Greg said as he fastened his seatbelt.

Emma stared at him in shock. Was he actually apologising to her for something he did? Unbelievable!

'But I had a few too many. You shouldn't have let me drink so much,' he added as he turned the key and the engine rumbled to life.

Her already deflated ego sank even further. My fault again, she thought as she reached out to pull the car door shut but even before the door had clicked, Greg planted his foot and sped off. The jolt sent her off balance, so she shot one hand out to prevent being banged against the glove compartment while the other hand gripped the tray of food tight against her stomach. Regaining her balance, she grabbed the safety belt and hitched it into place, not daring to comment. If she did, no doubt it would be her fault. Biting her tongue to prevent slipping out words she was bound to regret, she peered out of the side window while they drove. If I say anything, she thought, it will all come out wrong and the night will start off on the wrong foot. She snorted quietly. The night was already going down the gurgler faster than water.

The distance was not far, Emma often walking between the two homes for exercise. Feeling dejected, she sat rigid, staring out at nothing, wishing she didn't have to spend the night with Greg hanging around. Inviting him had been a monumental mistake. Despite her earlier thoughts about him being forced to behave, she now realised there was no way she would be allowed to let loose and enjoy the party with her uni friends.

As they turned into Caroline's street, sudden realisation hit. Greg intimidated her, making life unpleasant if she didn't behave the way he wanted. She recalled the only time Greg had been to Caroline's house. He had made incredibly rude comments about the snobbery of wealthy people in front of Caroline and her parents. Emma had felt so embarrassed she vowed she would never again invite him when she visited her best friend. Yet here they were. She sneered at her reflection in the window. How idiotic was she? Why, oh, why did she invite him tonight?

The front door was wide open with Caroline greeting everyone as they arrived. 'You look gorgeous, Mouse,' Caroline exclaimed as she hugged Emma. 'Go straight through to the lounge. Nearly everyone has arrived.'

Caroline raised her eyebrows when Greg wandered in first leaving Emma standing at the door. He didn't bother acknowledging Caroline, but she didn't comment on his rudeness, but boy, Emma could see Caroline was tempted with her lips drawing into a thin line. Emma mumbled an apology as she made her way to the kitchen, struggling with the heavy bag of drinks in one hand and her dish of goodies in the other.

There wasn't much room on the dark granite bench dividing the kitchen from the enormous room which was devoid of its normal dining setting at the near end, while the lounge seating at the far end had been placed against the walls. By moving a few plates around she managed to wriggle her dish among the others. All she needed now was to find a spare space to drop the drinks' bag. Spying a spot in the far corner of the kitchen she lowered the bag to the floor and shoved it between two others with her foot before joining her friends in the large lounge area, avoiding the small group Greg had joined.

'Mouse!' Recognising the effusive voice of Sandy, Emma spun around with open arms to receive an enthusiastic hug. 'I've never seen you look so ravishing. What have you done? I love your hair.' Sandy's voice was so loud everybody stopped what he or she was doing. Emma felt herself shrink back. How she hated being the centre of attention.

To hide her chagrin, she enveloped Sandy in another hug. 'You look pretty stunning as well. I love those shoes,' Emma murmured against her friend's shoulder, ever so thankful the hum of voices rose again. When Sandy's perfume tickled her nose, Emma had to pull away moments before she sneezed. They grinned at each other then laughed aloud before huddling close to discuss the questions in the last exam. They'd only been chatting a few minutes when Sandy heard her name called and she ran across the room to greet a group of newcomers. Left alone and still wanting to avoid Greg who had inveigled his way into the centre of a larger group, Emma retreated to the rear of the room while she searched around for a group she could join.

'So, you're the quiet little mouse Caro always talks about. I prefer Emma. Mouse doesn't suit you at all,' drawled a vaguely familiar voice in her ear. 'Especially the way you look tonight. You look gorgeous.'

Recognising the voice from the night before, Emma spun around. 'Nick! What are you doing here?'

'I live here. Caro is my sister.'

Much to her mortification, Nick lifted Emma's hand to his lips, planting a soft kiss on the back of her fingers. Stunned when his mouth lingered, Emma tugged her hand away and quickly glanced over her shoulder, conscious of Greg spying the interchange. Her fear eased when she noted Greg's back. She turned back to Nick. 'Now I know why I thought I recognised you. You look like Caroline.' She smiled but couldn't stop the rising heat in her cheeks. Not used to being on the receiving end of such compliments, she didn't know how to handle them with any panache. Inside she felt awkward with her innards giving the impression of a quivering mass of jelly.

'Take your dirty hands off my woman!' Emma's hand was grabbed before being yanked hard by Greg. 'What did you do with my beer, Em? I need a drink,' he said as he towed her away.

With an even hotter blush of embarrassment rising from her shoulders up, Emma wrestled her arm out of Greg's fingers and rushed to the kitchen where she hunkered down to remove a beer from the bag, tugging the ring pull to open the can before handing it to him. She was stupid for getting the drink but needed to hide until she could gather her wits. To hide her shaking hands, she bent down to search for the orange juice she always drank instead of alcohol. Darn it. The bag contained only beer. She felt like crawling into some hole with an enormous box of tissues so she could sob her heart out. Instead she shut her eyes, sucked in a huge breath and held it before releasing it slowly as she screwed her eyes tight. It took a few moments before she was happy she wasn't about to burst into tears. A long sigh slipped out as she wondered if she should say anything. But darn the man, he had agreed to bring the liquid refreshments.

She sucked in another breath for courage. 'Greg, what happened to the juice?'

'I didn't bring any. There wasn't enough room with my beer,' he said over his shoulder as he strode towards a group of guys.

Deep disappointment flooded through her, accompanied by a sensation of something she couldn't quite put a name to. As she remained squatting in front of the open vinyl bag her tenuous control snapped and unbidden tears began welling again. Already the night was spinning downhill from awful to ghastly. To hide her face while forcing the moisture at bay, Emma turned to the corner with her eyes screwed tight, daring one single drop to escape.

'Are you okay?'

Emma twisted around. Darn it. Nick was standing on the opposite side of the bench. The way he was looking at her she knew he'd overheard but no way was she going to look like a wimp.

'I'm fine. Thank you.'

'Are you sure?'

To prove she was, Emma stood and forced a smile. 'Yes, I'm sure. I was thinking about something but now it's time to get back to the party.' She didn't dare look in his direction as she rounded the bench and headed for the nearest group after ensuring it didn't contain Greg.

It embarrassed her when Nick slipped a glass of juice into her hand. The second time, fifteen minutes later, he held out a glass of wine, but she refused it saying she preferred no alcohol, so he swapped it for a glass of juice. Deep down, she was grateful for his consideration and even more grateful when he asked no questions or passed comment, but she wondered what he was thinking. Maybe he hadn't heard the exchange. But how did he know to give her juice: which meant he must have overheard the entire conversation. Far out.

It was difficult avoiding Greg, especially since he snuck up behind her each time he wanted another beer. Like an idiot she fetched it, opened it and handed it over. She really, really, really wanted to tell him to get stuffed and fetch his own but even more she wanted to avoid a public put-down or tongue-lashing. One more week – only one more week, she kept telling her brain. Get over this night and she'd never have to put up with his selfish demands again. So, to keep the peace every time he asked, she obeyed. Once he had another beer in his hand, Greg left her alone while he moved around the room chatting to people. But the minute he noticed Emma talking to a guy, he returned to her side to break up the conversation. It was tiring and so darn annoying. These were her mates and he was destroying her night. Fed up, she ended up standing at the back of the room alone, studying a group of family photographs and feeling like a dork.

'Why are you hiding away?'

Startled, she swung her head around to find Nick right behind her with his head cocked to one side. 'Hiding? I'm not hiding.'

He grinned as he shook his head. 'What do you call standing at the back of the room all alone?'

A flush of guilt rose as she sought out Greg. Her breath huffed out when she spied him at the other end of the room. He hadn't seen her.

'How about giving me a hand passing around these plates?' Without waiting for an answer Nick grasped her hand and led her towards the kitchen bench where he removed the plastic wrap from two plates of goodies. As he passed them to her, she didn't miss the cold, angry glare sent in her direction by Greg. She grabbed the plates and immediately moved in the opposite direction to Nick. A sneak peek at Greg and she sighed in relief. He'd eased off his aggressive stare.

As she neared the group Greg was with, she hesitated. No way did she want to go there but a couple of hopeful glances eyed her spicy meatballs and bite-sized sausage rolls. With no choice she stepped closer. It didn't surprise her to hear Greg relating how great he was at his job and how he was going to get the top position within his firm in no time at all. He was nothing more than a dogsbody on the bottom rung having only been in the job for a year. Sickened by the egotistical claptrap, she kept her head down while eager fingers denuded her plates in seconds. She had no idea who had taken what or if everyone had eaten but no way was she staying a moment longer to find out. She raced away to get different platters and spent the next fifteen minutes feeding the hungry.

Suddenly, the serene background music changed to a much louder catchy dance tune. Everyone seemed to stop what they were doing, moved to the centre of the room and began bopping and gyrating. Emma didn't dare. Instead she moved back to the kitchen bench and fiddled with plates, putting odds and ends from almost empty platters onto one, sweeping up crumbs into her hand, balling up bundles of plastic wrap and covering food to keep it moist: anything to make it look as though she was too busy to dance. If she was seen to be busy helping nobody would think it strange she wasn't on the dance floor, for at university functions she was always in the middle, especially if it was a tango. She loved the emotion of tango – in particular, the version from Argentina.

Trying to be surreptitious, she peeked around. Nick was dancing, his slight limp not noticeable, but Greg was making out he was busy by studying the same photographs and pictures on the wall she'd used as a means of hiding. No way would he be caught dead dancing. One guy came up to her and asked her to dance. She hated refusing but shook her head. 'Later,' she said, 'I need to finish this.' He'd been gone for less than a minute when another friend grabbed her hand and spun her around. She bopped for a few minutes but when she noticed Greg glaring at her, she made excuses about going to the loo. The moment she returned, Nick took her hand and gently drew her into the middle of the dancing group where he immediately released her hand and smiled when she began swinging her hips in time to the music.

'I thought I told you to keep your filthy hands off my woman,' Greg growled as he reached out, grabbing Emma around her upper arm with taut fingertips which left a white ring around each as they bit into her flesh. It hurt – a lot–as she dragged her arms away but she super-glued her lips together to avoid a scene.

To her horror, Nick stepped in front of Greg, so close he was invading Greg's personal space. 'No-one was touching Emma. I certainly wasn't. Everyone is doing their own thing in the group. It's obvious she enjoys dancing so why don't you dance with her?' Nick looked angry but his voice was light and amiable while Emma was plain terrified with her heart racing and innards doing a great job of tying themselves into tight tangles.

'I don't dance,' Greg snapped as he tried to step away from the much taller man, making it obvious he was feeling uncomfortable. Well, she also felt downright uncomfortable.

Nick remained still, allowing Greg to move back a fraction. He stepped closer when Greg attempted to further widen the gap between them. 'So, because you are too afraid to show your ineptitude on the dance floor, you figure Emma shouldn't be allowed to dance either when it's blatantly obvious she really wants to join in. Don't you think you are being a bit selfish and overbearing?' To give his words better effect, Nick edged even closer while pulling his taller-than-average frame up to its full height.

The ensuing silence was deafening. In the confines of the small room it was impossible for anyone present not to hear the terse exchange. Conversations and dancing ceased as though it was orchestrated with every single person turning to watch what Greg would do. Emma wondered if they knew what Greg was like. This was her worst nightmare. Had anyone ever had the effrontery to tell Greg what they thought of him before, especially in front of a group of people? Hearing the intensity of the silence, Emma waited for the fallout because she had no doubt things were going to get nasty. Would Greg lash out with his fists? Is this how so many people were hurt by a king hit? Surely, he wouldn't dare.

But by the look of him, maybe he would. The muscles in Greg's jaw tightened and his face reddened with suppressed anger. Not a soul moved or breathed. The tension was palpable.

'Emma, we're going home. Get the bag!' The terse demand broke the suspense.

There was an audible gasp of shock as onlookers breathed out in unison. Greg spun to one side, grabbed Emma's arm and shoved her in front of him, causing her to trip. Horrified, she stumbled and reached out automatically, grasping a hold of the nearest person to regain her balance. Her cheeks incinerated when she saw she was grappling one of the guys around his waist. Far out, what would Greg do now? She didn't dare look at him–she didn't need to. She could feel his anger radiating in sonic waves. He was beyond furious and the last thing she wanted was to leave with him. It certainly wouldn't be a pleasant or quiet journey home. As though an axe had heaved them apart, she instantly released her hold of the startled young man and mumbled an apology.

Suddenly Nick shoved his way between them, twisted around and ended up standing with his hands on his hips in front of Greg, even closer than before. There were mere centimetres between the two alert, tense bodies. Certain there were going to be fisticuffs, Emma slid her eyes shut and stepped back two paces. Her heart was banging so hard she felt it might thump right out of her chest.

'I don't think so my friend,' she heard Nick say. 'These people have worked hard to achieve what they have. This is a special night to let their hair down and celebrate the end of their university life. If you want to go, then go. But Emma is staying with her friends. I'll make sure she gets home safe. If you want your drinks' bag, get it yourself. You would have to be the most selfish, overbearing, disrespectful egomaniac I have ever had the misfortune to meet. This is my home, and you are no longer welcome here, so I would appreciate it if you left.'

Emma's eyelids shot apart. In the intense silence Nick stood unmoving, staring Greg in the eye. Restrained anger simmered from both men, each alert and looking ready to pounce. Being several inches taller and physically a lot stronger, Nick would win if the situation became physical. With her breath held, Emma waited for Greg to take a swipe. She spied a quiver of uncertainty in Greg's eyes followed by a flash of anger.

Finally conceding defeat, Greg turned to leave.

Expelling her held breath, Emma spun around and fled. As she scurried away, she noticed Nick stride into the kitchen, pick up Greg's bag, shove it at him before ushering him out of the door. The last thing she heard was, 'Sorry folks but I couldn't stand by and let him treat Emma with such disrespect. She deserves much better than such an abusive creep.'

Mortified, she fled down the passage as Nick was rewarded by loud applause. In the bathroom with a soaked cold washer held over swollen red eyes, Emma jerked around at a loud tap on the door. Two seconds later she was enveloped in a tight hug.

'Greg deserved what he got,' said Caroline. 'He's deserved it for a very long time only no-one has been game enough to tell him before. I've had to bite my tongue so many times. Don't feel bad. Everyone applauded Nick for having the guts to do what none of us have been brave enough to do.'

Determined to keep further tears at bay, Emma hiccoughed on Caroline's shoulder. 'Now I've got no-one. At least he took me out.' The moment it was out she regretted it. Where was her earlier resolve to end things?

Jolting backwards but keeping her hands in a tight grip on Emma's shoulders, Caroline stared with unblinking eyes. 'You can't be serious. He treats you like dirt. He might pick you up and take you home, but he never treats you like you are on a date. He insists you do everything, and you meekly obey. He never offers to buy you a drink, yet you always buy him one when he demands it. He never dances with you, or lets you dance with anyone else. Has he ever taken you on a romantic date?' Caroline paused and seemed to be holding her breath waiting for Emma to say something, but her mind felt as though a huge vacuum had sucked out her brain.

'I can only recall you going to the pub where you have to watch him play pool and drink himself senseless, or to watch him play his stupid hockey when we have no choice but to listen to him gloating about how fantastic he was with his brilliant moves, when really, he spends most of the game sitting on the bench behind the goal post in time out for abusing the umpire. Sweetie, that's not a romance. You're better off with no-one than a selfish pig like him. Nick was right in what he called him. I wish I'd been brave enough to have said the same things to the bastard ages ago.

Forget about him for a couple of hours. Come and join the party. It's our night.'

'You said your piece?' Emma finally found her voice.

'For now.' Caroline looked serious then burst out laughing. 'Here let me give you a hand.' Caroline took over, delving in the top drawer of the vanity unit and pulling out make-up items. She repaired the damage to Emma's face, grinning as she applied each layer but not allowing Emma to turn towards the mirror until she'd finished. It was a good fifteen minutes before she spun Emma around. 'Tra la,' she quipped as Emma could do nothing but gawk at her image.

'Good grief!' She felt like a harlot. There was dark eyeliner under shadowed brows and far more colour highlighting the bones on her cheeks than she'd ever dared to use before. Her lips were a deep mushroom and so glossy she could see them glinting. 'This is way too much,' she said as she reached for a fresh tissue.

'No way, you look positively ravishing.' Caroline swiped the tissue from Emma's hand before hooking their elbows together. She spun Emma back around before dragging her from the room.

Her mortification hadn't dissipated one iota as they made their way back to the party but when they entered the room everyone was so engrossed in dancing, not a single soul looked up. Emma was more than grateful for the lack of acknowledgement but vowed she would return to the bathroom the moment Caroline turned her back. As though reading her mind, Caroline drew Emma onto the floor to join in. She stayed with Emma for a short while before somehow wangling Sandy's boyfriend, Peter James, to dance opposite her. Peter let out a wolf whistle and grinned moments before he grasped Emma's hands. She couldn't help but laugh when he proceeded to wriggle his body in ridiculous movements. She felt grateful until she figured what Caroline was up to when she noticed Caroline fetch Sandy then pulled Nick on the floor as her partner. Gradually she eased Nick closer to Emma, so they ended up dancing opposite each other. Apart from turning into liquid and seeping under the carpet, there wasn't a lot Emma could do. She was hemmed in making it more than obvious if she attempted to sneak away. Well stuff it. Greg was gone. She could let go and forget about everything except having a darn good time.

As the night wore on, Emma relaxed more and more until by the end of the evening she was laughing as loud as everyone else at the conversations going on around her. She felt so much at ease and was more than grateful Nick had rid her of Greg for without him she could be herself – Emma Nicholls, farm girl, uni student, hopefully with an honours' degree. Emma Nicholls, lover of books, languages and dancing.

It was the wee small hours before anyone made a move to go home. With the party being such a huge success, most were reluctant to leave but finally, one-by-one, the guests departed until only Emma remained. Since she had no transport, she'd not been game to break up the party by asking Caroline to take her home. And no way was she going to walk. She didn't know how she knew it, but Greg would be waiting out there–somewhere. And he would be mad: madder than she'd ever seen him before.

'I promised to see you home, Emma. I hope you'll allow me to keep my promise.' Nick's voice came from somewhere behind her ear. 'Caro has had too much wine to drive.'

'Thank you, I would appreciate it.' Spinning around Emma smiled. 'What time do you want us in the morning, Caroline?'

'Not until after ten at the very earliest, I need sleep.'

Silence ensued until they were seated in a car she recognised as belonging to Caroline's mother. 'Why are you returning in the morning?' asked Nick as he turned onto the roadway.

'Sandy and I promised to help clean up. It was very good of your parents to offer us their house, it is the least we can do to thank them.'

With her eyes drooping, Emma took only a glancing notice of a dark grey sedan as they passed it. For a second, she thought it was Greg's car and did a double-take but realised it looked in the night gloom to be a different colour so at least one other person was out as late as them. A huff of relief blew from the side of her mouth and she relaxed back into the soft comfort of the leather seat. They drove in relative silence with the only conversation being Emma giving directions to her flat, but she was more than aware of the man driving her home. To keep her eyes from straying in Nick's direction she curled sideways with her eyes closed until the car slowed at her driveway.

'Emma, wake up.'

Opening her eyes, she straightened and reached out to open her door. Nick placed his long fingers on her arm to stop her.

'Before you go, let me apologise for my outburst tonight. I'm sorry if I embarrassed you in any way, but I saw red with the way your boyfriend was treating you. Nobody deserves to be treated with such disrespect, especially a beautiful, caring woman like you.'

'I'm not beautiful, why do you think they call me Mouse?' Emma retorted, hanging her head to hide her embarrassment. To her mortification, Nick cupped her face with one hand and drew her face upwards.

'I seem to recall earlier tonight I said the name didn't suit you. They probably call you Mouse because of your shyness, certainly not because of your looks. I also mentioned you are a stunning woman. Well believe it – you are.'

Despite feeling embarrassed about Nick's words, she also felt a tiny thrill of pleasure at the same time. The tiny thrill turned to a shiver of delight when she felt Nick grasp her elbow to usher her to the front door, the warmth of his large hand lingering on the soft flesh of her elbow while she searched for and found her house key. By the time she attempted to unlock the door her hand was shaking like she was in the throes of a serious earthquake. Feeling stupid for not being able to slip the key into what seemed like an impossibly tiny slot, she tugged her arm from his grip to gain some semblance of equilibrium. Sucking in a long, quiet breath, she bent her knees, so her eyes were level with the lock, sending up a prayer of thanks when the key finally fitted.

Embarrassed for feeling so overwhelmed by his nearness, she shoved the door open in a bid to escape inside but she wasn't quick enough. Nick reached out, grasped her hand and lifted it up to his mouth before planting a soft, lingering kiss on the back of her fingers.

Oh, my. Emma couldn't help the quick shiver which started at her head and wove through her body. As though he was aware of her agitation, Nick smiled.

'Goodnight beautiful, Emma, sleep well.' Dropping her hand, he turned and left.

Behind the bushes of a nearby garden, a dark shadow tensed in anger as that bastard cupped Emma's chin and drew her head up. Fury raged as he waited for the upstart to attempt kissing Emma on the mouth. The rage didn't ease when mouth and hand met and stayed way too long. The bastard would pay for his outburst tonight. How dare he interfere! How dare he make me look like an idiot! She would pay as well.

While Emma undressed in her curtained room, he studied her silhouetted movements from under the shadow of a large leafy tree at the side of her unit. The outline of the very feminine naked body she had always denied him sent his hormones on a rampage. As frustration rose, so did his temper. Methods of retaliation flew through his brain. A triumphant sneer shot from the corners of his mouth as he thought of one way he could ensure he left his mark to let her know she belonged to him.

Chapter Three

Pulling into the driveway of the swish Hamilton home, Emma glanced in the rear-vision mirror when she heard a horn blast. She grinned as she shoved her arm out the open window and waved at the sight of Sandy's beat-up red Volkswagen pulling alongside the kerb. A dark sedan turning into the road behind Sandy had Emma's pulse thrumming. For a moment she thought it was Greg's car but after scrutinising it she realised it was the same model and make, but the colour was different; this one was definitely blue. She shook her head as she willed her heart to settle. To make out everything was normal, she plastered on a smile before easing from her seat. After hugging Sandy in greeting she took her time to relinquish her hold in order to gain some semblance of being able to utter friendly words. Chatting about the previous night's events was safe as they linked arms before heading up the paved drive.

From the corner of her eye, Emma spied the sedan passing them. A frisson of fear snaked down her spine as she watched it pull up against the kerb at the end of the street. She couldn't make out the occupant but didn't want to be caught staring so looked away. A nervous rage broiled the contents of her stomach. She had to stop imagining every dark sedan contained Greg, but after his phoned threats waking her earlier, she felt edgy. Then she realised the same car had been parked in the same spot last night. Far out, the owner probably lived there. She was such an idiot. Shoving the thoughts away she broke into a run, dragging Sandy up the porch steps where both rapped their knuckles on the door at the same time.

It took a few minutes before the door opened to reveal a dishevelled Caroline, still in her cotton shortie pyjamas. She stifled a yawn with one hand. 'How can you two be so bright and chirpy?'

Sandy grinned at the disgruntled frown on Caroline's face. 'You go and get dressed while we start.' Together, they moved into the entry. 'Boy, what a mess. Looks like we'll need some garbage bags before you disappear.'

Side-by-side they stood in the wide opening of the lounge, casting their eyes around the littered room. Searching a couple of drawers in the kitchen, Caroline found a packet of plastic garbage bags and handed them over before filling the electric jug. She reached into an overhead cupboard and took out four mugs.

'Coffee first, I need a kick-start to wake me up. Nick is still asleep. I think jet lag has caught up with him, but he'll still appreciate a coffee. The party was fun. I'm going to miss our uni mates and the great times we've had. I'm especially going to miss you, Mouse, when you go away. Have you organised your trip yet?'

'Not yet, I'll wait for the results. There's no hurry. First, I'm going home for Christmas to help Dad with the harvest. I was even thinking of finding a job back home until I go away.'

'Well make sure you come back to visit us before you leave,' said Sandy as the trio sank into kitchen chairs.

They lingered a while, sipping on coffee and chatting about the party. When Caroline went to shower and dress, Sandy and Emma started what looked like a mammoth task. After gathering up the rubbish, they deposited it in the garbage bags then collected empty bottles and cans, placing them in the recycle bin they found on the back patio. With the rubbish gone, the job didn't seem anywhere near as huge. Dirty glasses and dishes were stacked on the kitchen sink. Emma tackled the washing up while Sandy wiped down the surfaces in the rooms they'd used. When Caroline returned, she dragged a vacuum cleaner behind her. She began denuding the carpets of the party remnants, using a can of spot carpet cleaner to lift any marks.

'How is a man supposed to sleep with this racket?'

Emma squealed at the whisper in her ear. Unnerved, she dropped the mug she was washing back into the soapy water, which splashed up into her face. She screwed her eyes while feeling around for the tea towel she knew was on the other side of the sink.

'Allow me,' said Nick moments before Emma felt her face being patted dry.

When she was able to open her eyes, she gasped. Nick was clad only in a pair of jeans riding low on his hips, the brass stud not secured. She shot her eyes upwards only to find them settling on bare flesh and a smattering of dark chest hair. Far out, those muscular arms and bare chest looked so hunky despite the scar slashed across his left shoulder. Now she remembered Caroline telling her about the car accident her brother had been involved in, but she couldn't recall the details. It must have been earlier in the year, she thought.

Nick chuckled as he indicated the blush rising her face. Mortally embarrassed, Emma turned away to concentrate on the dishes, giving the mugs an extra hard scrub to cover the wild thoughts she felt must show on her face.

Without another word, Nick put the tea towel to use by drying the pile of dishes draining on the sink. 'Why didn't you use the dishwasher?' he asked.

Lord, she wished she had. 'There are too many dishes and I always find it quicker in the long run to do them by hand. I don't mind washing up. I use it as time for reflection. I'm sorry if we woke you. You must be tired.' Even though her words were for the half-naked hunk standing next to her, her avid attention was on meticulously scrubbing the prongs of a fork.

Laughing, Nick reached over to remove the fork from her hand. 'Any more scrubbing and there won't be any silver left.' He grinned as though he was highly amused at her chagrin. 'I'm not tired. I stopped off in Singapore for a couple of days. They have the same time zone as us in Perth, so most of my jet lag was gone by the time I arrived home. I'm not used to these all-night parties though. You are remarkably alert and bubbly this morning. Care to give me your secret?'

Thankful the conversation was heading to a safer place, Emma concentrated on the rest of the cutlery. 'Force of habit, I guess. Being brought up on a farm I was always up at the crack of dawn. Plus, it's not often I drink alcohol – only on special occasions. Nor does Sandy as it interferes with her performance in gymnastics.' She pulled the plug and began wiping down the sink. 'But I did sleep in later than normal this morning and I'll probably be in bed early tonight to catch up.'

With the four of them working together, the house was soon spotless. Caroline insisted the two girls stay for lunch by producing a pile of toasted ham, cheese and tomato sandwiches and coffee, which were consumed under the shade of the patio by the pool.

Nick disappeared to have a shower and returned dressed in a clean pair of jeans and collared T-shirt. The spicy aroma of his after-shave wafted over Emma when he wandered past, pulled out the chair next to her and lowered his body.

'Emma, you mentioned a farm, do your parents still live there?'

Her heart was palpitating by his closeness causing her brain to forget how to formulate words for a few seconds. She shifted in her seat before answering. 'Yes, I'm going home next week to help out with the harvest and spend Christmas with my family. Dad says they have a bumper crop this year.'

'Is the boyfriend spending Christmas with you?'

Emma jerked at the mention of Greg. She glanced at Caroline who was shaking her head at Nick as though telling him he was on dangerous ground. Mortified, Emma dropped her eyes.

'No. He wouldn't fit in and I would never ask him. Besides, he's not my boyfriend.'

She didn't impart how Greg had woken her earlier in the morning, shouting a tirade of abuse down the phone, which only ceased when she had shouted back, 'I never want to see you again,' before slamming down the receiver. At the time she felt proud she'd found the courage to do so. She recalled the foul threats, the memory bringing sudden, unbidden moisture to the surface of her eyes. To hide her distress, she shot from her seat to gather the plates without daring to raise her eyes. After carrying them inside she began the next round of dish washing while fighting for control.

She had been there barely a minute before Nick wandered back into the kitchen to refill the electric jug. Again, he picked up the tea towel to dry the few plates Emma was washing. 'We're all having another coffee; will you join us?' Nick asked.

Not game to look at him she nodded.

'What happened, Emma?'

Unbidden, Emma's head jerked up and noticed Nick frown. Darn it, he must have seen the unshed tears she was fighting back. 'How did you…?'

'It's pretty obvious from your reaction. Did he come around to see you or did he ring?' Dropping the tea towel in a crumpled heap on the cleared sink he turned Emma to face him.

It took a while before she had enough command over her see-sawing emotions. She swept a fist over her eyes to brush away any moisture. 'He phoned this morning.'

'And?' Nick cocked his head to one side.

'He was pretty irate. No, he was more than furious.'

'I take it he gave you a mouthful of abuse and blamed you for his own inadequacies as a man.' She couldn't help it but when she glanced at Nick in utter surprise her unshed tears began to tumble down her cheeks. She felt so stupid.

'Can I ask what you said in return?' asked Nick.

Emma gulped down a deep breath to gain control. 'I shouted back at him, told him I never wanted to see him again. I hung up. I've never been so rude before.'

'Good girl! And how did it feel?' There was a smile teasing the corners of his mouth.

She thought about it for a moment before letting a grin slide out. 'Truly, it felt pretty darn good.' Emma's voice sounded a lot more confident, even to herself. She gave Nick a big, teary grin before she was pulled into his arms and held against his chest. Her screwed emotions were overwhelming her, but she sure enjoyed the warmth and security of Nick's embrace. No man, not even Greg had held her like this before. Nick had a firm yet gentle touch while Greg was always groping and harsh. And Greg's hands! They were never smooth and warm but were cold and damp, like a slimy slug.

'Normally, I wouldn't be this bold or forward, but you said you were going home next week.'

'Yes.'

'Which doesn't give me a lot of time to get to know you better before I ask you out.'

Her head shot up of its own accord. 'Ask me out?'

He grinned. 'Yes, I'm asking you out. You have intrigued me from the moment I saw you sitting in the hotel lounge two nights ago. Please, will you allow me to take you out to dinner tonight? I know its Sunday, but I'm sure we can find some kind of eatery open for a decent meal.'

Emma pulled back in surprise. With the back of her hand, she rubbed away the last traces of the tears she had managed to force under control. 'I don't want you to feel sorry for me.'

'Emma, you are sadly mistaken if you think I feel sorry for you. I'm asking you out because I want to get to know you better, because I think you are a beautiful woman and not only physically beautiful. From what little I've seen and what Caro has told me, you have a beautiful heart and soul which is far more important than physical beauty. Emma, I'm asking you out because I really like you and I really want to take you out. Please say yes?'

There was a stunned silence while Emma fought to find her voice, which had suddenly abandoned her. 'I… I feel like I'm dreaming and this isn't really happening but yes, I'd very much like to go out for dinner with you.' She couldn't believe the range of emotions flooding through her body and to make her even more startled, she suddenly found herself engulfed in Nick's arms again.

'Fantastic but since I'm not up with Perth eateries I'll ask Caro where she recommends and let you know. Let's get this coffee made or the girls will be curious as to why I'm taking so long and knowing Caro, I'll be getting the third-degree on what we've been up to in here.'

With hot flushed cheeks at his teasing comment, Emma gave Nick a hand. Five minutes later all four were sitting on the patio again, with Emma doing her best to ignore Caroline and Sandy's inquisitive glances. She drank her coffee as quick as she could so she could make her excuses and leave.

Not even bothering to finish her coffee, Sandy stood at the same time. They both said their goodbyes and left together but as soon as they reached Emma's car, Sandy grabbed her. 'Okay, Mouse, what happened with Nick? I'm not letting you go until you spill the beans – all of them.'

'He asked me out,' Emma replied, feeling sheepish.

'Wonderful, but Greg is going to be furious.'

'You may not believe this but I told Greg I never wanted to see him again.' Emma surprised herself with the confidence she felt. What stunned her even more was the sudden sensation of a heavy black cloud being lifted from her shoulders.

'This has to be the best news I've heard in a long time. Congratulations and don't think I won't be pestering you for all the details of your date with Nick. When are you going out?'

'Tonight.'

'Wow, he is a fast worker. I'll ring you first thing in the morning and if you don't answer your phone, I'll bang on your door. I can't believe you've finally seen the light. Oh, this is fabulous.' Grabbing Emma, Sandy hugged her tight before releasing her and waltzing down to her own car.

Emma's exit was a little more subdued, but she couldn't wipe away the smile plastered across her face all the way home. After pulling into her drive, she stayed in her seat for a moment with the engine still idling. She was going on a real date with a nice guy. Unbelievable. But what was she going to wear? Making an instant decision, she changed gears, revved up the engine and reversed out, speeding past the dark blue sedan parked at the end of the street. She whipped her eyes around for a second look. Surely it isn't the same car which had been in Caroline's street. Worried, she glanced into the rear-vision mirror. The car looked the same but there were hundreds of the popular make and model on the road. Even Greg had one similar. A gasp escaped. But Greg's is green and this one a dusty blue. Man, she was getting paranoid about a simple common car.

The tension eased when she figured Greg's earlier words must be playing on her mind or maybe her conscience was sending her the guilty verdict. But the day was too special to let him spoil it. It was the first day of Sunday Christmas shopping. She was going on a real date. Determined to make the night extra special, she went in search of her second new outfit in two days.

Anger surged, firing every filament of nerve in his body. Where the hell was she going now? How dare the bitch not ring him back?

Only waiting long enough for Emma to turn the corner so she wouldn't spot him following, Greg managed an awkward U-turn, flicking a finger at the old bag who dared to toot her horn at him. The tyres squealed as he planted his foot and shot around the corner then swore and slammed the foot on the brake pedal when a car reversed onto the road from a driveway forcing Greg to swerve around the intruder to avoid T-boning the idiot.

Swinging back into the lane, Greg searched the road ahead but couldn't spot Emma's silver Mazda. He sped up, weaving onto the wrong side to pass two cars before squeezing into a spot barely long enough for him to fit but the driver behind would pull back. If he didn't want his car bingled he had no choice. After ten metres of crawling, the cars banked up. Glancing up, he spied the cause: damn red lights. Curses echoed around the inside of his brother's car as he thumped the steering wheel. He had four choices; turn left or right, drive straight through the intersection or go home. With his luck, he would go the wrong way and spend hours searching for the bitch. Easier to go home for a few hours then stake out her house and wait. Emma would have to come home sooner or later.

Chapter Four

The flashing red light on the answering machine caught Emma's eye the moment she swung in the door after a successful shopping expedition. Her jaunty swagger slowed while her happy smile turned to a frown. One finger hesitated over the play button. The only reason she jammed her finger down was maybe there was a message from Nick.

She was almost afraid to listen to the third message after hearing the two abusive tirades from Greg, threatening her with all sorts of dire consequences if she didn't call him back. Well, no way was she going to call back.

The third message was far more pleasant, giving her details for the evening. A smile broke out at Nick's words; her new outfit would be perfect. She'd already figured Nick wouldn't be the type to take someone to the local pub to watch him play pool on a first date, or any kind of date. She wasn't wrong. They were going to an upmarket place she'd heard about but never been fortunate enough to visit.

Not wanting her night spoiled by being too tired to enjoy it, Emma set her alarm before lying on her bed to catch up on lost sleep. As an afterthought she unplugged the phone. No way would she allow more angry words to mar her feeling of euphoria.

The same exhilaration was still with her when her alarm summonsed her from a deep sleep. Shooting out of bed and straight into the shower, Emma shampooed her hair and lathered her body in her favourite body wash; the smell of lavender always lingering on her skin. Her simple hairstyle was easy to blow dry, so it wasn't long before she was dressing in her new two-piece outfit of flowing skirt and top. Gold strappy sandals along with her favourite gold earrings with matching chain and pendant completed her ensemble. After a splash of perfume and final flick of her hair she stood back from the mirror, staring at her reflection. What she saw made her feel like a brand-new person.

When she heard the knock, Emma glanced at the clock. She plugged in the phone as she walked past with a sense of expectant euphoria and ran the final few steps to open the door. It was shoved with undue force the instant the lock turned. Utter shock hit. Greg stood there with arms folded over his thrust-out chest. One glance at his face told her he was fuming.

'You didn't ring me back. Why not? I told you what would happen if you didn't.' He paused as his eyes ran up and down her body several times. A shiver snaked across her shoulders at his screwed mouth. It didn't need his look to remind her the outfit she had on was far dressier than he'd ever seen her in before.

'Where the hell do you think you're going?' Fisted hands reached out and barrelled into her ribs, shoving her backwards.

A squeal escaped at the pain as she staggered to maintain her balance and hit the wall.

'Emma is going out for dinner and I'm taking her.'

Greg spun around with his face contorted in fury. He shoved at the door but thank goodness, Nick had planted his foot inside the opening. Terrified, Emma crept backwards.

'Oh, no she's not,' Greg spat. 'She's my girl and she's not going out with anyone but me.' He shoved at the door at the same time he stamped on Nick's foot with the heel of his boot.

Ignoring what must have been incredible pain to the arch of his foot, Nick shoved back harder, flinging the door back so hard it hit Greg on his shoulder and pushed him into the wall. Everything rattled: the pictures on the wall, the little hall table and everything on it.

'I don't see a ring on her finger, which indicates she belongs to no man.' Stepping into the tiny entrance, Nick looked alert, ready for retaliation. 'Could I suggest it might be a good idea if you returned to your car and left Emma in peace?' One hand wavered in her direction.

'Emma, move back a few paces.'

His words were well timed because as Greg spun around towards her, he lifted his arm.

'You bitch!' Greg spat as he swung his clenched fist towards her head.

Instinct had her duck as she jumped back with her hands over her head. Her heart was hammering as she waited for the impact. When it didn't happen, she peeked up to see Nick had Greg's arm in a vice-like grip.

'That's no way to treat a lady.' Nick sounded so calm – way calmer than Emma felt. Her innards were pounding, and her legs felt like liquid gloop. She managed an unsteady step backwards when Greg staggered to regain his balance. He stumbled again when Nick jerked one arm up behind Greg's back. Greg grunted as his face screwed for a few seconds before reddening. Emma wasn't sure if it was in anger, agony or embarrassment.

'Now, are you going to leave peacefully or are we going to do this the hard way?'

'You have no right, Emma is mine.' There was a hesitancy in Greg's voice. Was he more scared than he let on?

'It appears we are at a standstill,' said Nick. 'Why don't we let Emma decide? I understand she asked you to never see her again. To me, when a woman says no, she means no.' He turned to Emma. 'It's your decision. I'll leave if you tell me to.'

Pressed up against the wall, Emma's head shook furiously from side-to-side. There was no way she was going to be left alone with Greg so angry, especially after all his threats. 'No, please, I want you to stay.' But how to get rid of Greg? Terrified but knowing she had to face him, she turned towards him, her nerves thrumming with tension. Summoning up the courage she felt sure had fled forever she sucked in a couple of breaths. She felt so petrified but figured now was the time to make a stand, to make her wishes public and with Nick as a witness, Greg could never say she hadn't told him to go. It was the only way Greg couldn't use her words and twist them around to suit himself. 'I told you this morning, over the phone, I never want to see you again. I meant what I said. Please leave?'

When Greg didn't move, Nick edged closer to Emma as he shouldered the door wide open. Using force, he shuffled Greg away from the wall towards the open door.

Emma cringed at the scuffle of pushing and shoving between the two men. Despite the grunts, groans and hard breathing she could see Nick had the upper hand, but she was still more than worried Greg would start a more serious fight.

'The lady has spoken and we both heard her words, so there can be no misunderstanding,' panted Nick.

More scuffling ensued.

'Emma, it appears he didn't hear you. Would you mind calling the police?' Nick added over his shoulder.

She spun around but could only manage a wobble down the passage. Her legs seemed to have forgotten how to work properly, or maybe the floor was made of three feet of soft foam sponge. She skidded as she reached for the phone but shook so much, she had difficulty making out the numbers written on her emergency list stuck to the wall above the phone. The numbers had taken on the appearance of wavering lines. Focussing hard she began dialling.

'All right, I'm going.'

Her finger paused on the second last number.

'But don't think you've seen the last of me. I'll get you for this – both of you,' Greg yelled seconds before Nick finally succeeded in spinning him around and gave a final shove.

'Sound like a threat to me,' Nick said but he sounded so calm while Emma could feel her entire body shaking like an upturned jelly.

'So, if anything happens to either of us, we'll be pointing our finger at you and to make sure, I'll let a few people know of your threats so they can go straight to the police. Now get lost!' Nick slammed the door so hard the bang echoed around small entry passage and the two pictures on the wall rattled in response.

'Hell, you're shaking,' said Nick as he turned around.

Her legs giving way, Emma slumped against him as he slid his arms around her and drew her close. Still panting from the scuffle, he lifted one hand to cradle her head against his shoulder. 'Relax, he's gone. He is nothing but a belligerent bully. I'm sorry I didn't get here soon enough to prevent him from knocking on your door. When he sped past me, I tried to ring to warn you, but your phone was engaged. Are you all right?' He pulled his head back to study her and smiled. 'You look stunning in your outfit by the way.'

'How can you be so calm? I can't stop shaking.'

'Bullies like him only deal in aggression and anger to get their own way. They can't handle it when you don't lose your cool. Your calm is more of a threat to people like him than anger. Underneath all his bluster, I think you may find he's really a coward. I wouldn't have let him harm you even if I did have to resort to physical violence, which I abhor.'

'That wasn't physical?' Emma pulled away as she swept her eyes all the way up Nick's body. 'Look at you.' One button had fought its way free of its opposing hole and his shirt had parted company from his belted trousers.

'I meant really physical as in exchanging blows,' he said as he tucked in his shirt and straightened his tie and leather jacket. Emma pointed to the loose button.

Nick grinned as he slid the recalcitrant button back into place. 'Unfortunately, I doubt he got the message and I'm afraid he might be back.' Leaning one arm against the wall he smiled. 'Now, are you still up to joining me for dinner? Let's forget about him while we enjoy a pleasant evening getting to know each other. I've been looking forward to tonight.' Not giving her a chance to reply he sought out her hand and entwined their fingers. As he ushered her outside, he glanced around to ensure Greg had departed and tugged on the door to ensure it was firmly secure.

The restaurant was a well-known establishment in one of the more exclusive sections of the city. Awed at the elegant décor, Emma paused as they stepped inside. The only eateries she'd frequented were the more casual ones, when she went out with a group of friends. Greg had never bothered to take her anywhere near so upmarket and rarely with only the two of them. In fact, now she really thought about it, she could recall only one occasion where he had taken her, alone, to a restaurant soon after they'd met. Since that one meal, his dates consisted of a meal at the pub with his group of cronies.

Nick nudged Emma as eyes lifted and watched while they were shown to their table. 'I told you, you look stunning,' he murmured close to Emma's ear so only she could hear. 'All those eyes are on you with everyone wondering who this gorgeous newcomer is. I imagine the women thinking how ideal you would be for their unmarried sons.'

Even though Nick was teasing it still made her feel all squishy inside. 'I think the women are stabbing me in the back with daggers, wishing they were in my place,' she shot back. 'You look pretty good yourself. Aren't you every woman's romantic ideal–tall, blond, broad-shouldered and handsome? Or do they prefer dark haired men?'

Nick chuckled. 'I doubt they think I'm a hunk with this scar,' he pointed to the corner of his mouth, 'But, you tell me, you're a woman.'

Emma sat as the waiter pulled out a chair. 'I've never really thought about it. To me, what is on the inside is more important than how a person looks. My Dad is not the greatest looking person in the world, but you couldn't want for a better man and your scar looks kind of rakish.'

Sitting opposite, Nick cocked his head, 'I know I shouldn't bring this up, and I'll probably regret doing so, but if that is what you think, how on earth did you get tangled up with Greg Saunders?' To soften his words, Nick reached across the table and lifted her hand up to his lips, brushing a gentle kiss on her knuckles.

Feeling all quivery at his kiss and not knowing what to say, Emma took some time to answer. She lifted her eyes. 'I guess it was more loneliness than anything. I've been away from home for over nine years, first boarding school and then uni. I miss the closeness of my family. Caroline and Sandy are the best friends anyone can have, but they have boyfriends and were often out at night so there were many times when I felt plain lonely. Greg was never really a true boyfriend, we never had any kind of, you know, physical relationship.' Finding discussing intimate things with a man difficult, especially someone she'd only recently met,

Emma knew she was blushing. She could feel the heat rising all the way up her neck and cheeks. 'But it was somewhere to go and there were always other people around to whom I could chat,' she added before clamping her mouth shut when the waitress arrived.

After the meal was ordered Nick glanced at her with a puzzled frown. 'Why didn't you date other men? Caro said she had never seen you with any other guy.' When Emma raised her eyebrows, Nick smiled. 'Yes, I asked her questions because I'm interested in you and, no, she said nothing to embarrass you. Caro has nothing but high praise for you, but she did mention she couldn't abide Greg Saunders, so why no other men?'

'That's simple. No other man, until you, has ever asked me out.' Emma sank back into her seat while Nick leant forwards looking stunned.

'You have got to be kidding me! I find it almost impossible to believe. You would have to be the epitome of every man's dream. You are gorgeous to look at, kind, gentle, generous of heart, obviously intelligent and Caro tells me you have a wicked sense of humour. I look forward to discovering these things for myself. Personally, I think it's your shyness preventing all those lovesick men from daring to make a move on you. It gives you an aura of aloofness. But, I could imagine you were deliberately waiting for me to return home. Such a thought boosts my male ego somewhat.' Brushing his fingers down the side of Emma's face, he smiled at her heightened colour. 'I like it when you blush.'

The last comment caused Emma to redden even more. She buried her face in her hands while attempting to control the redness she hated so much. When she looked up again,

Nick was watching her with a quizzical but smug smile on his face.

'Can we change the subject?' she asked. 'For instance, tell me about yourself. What have you been doing overseas and why have you come home?'

'I've come home because, like you, I was homesick and wanted to spend time with my family, especially after my accident,' he pointed to the scar. 'I went overseas because I was offered an excellent job when I left university. I've worked hard, established my own consulting business in computer technology and have decided to take a six-month sabbatical to see if I want to go back or stay here. Since I work with computers I can work almost anywhere in the world. And in case you're wondering, there is no wife, partner or lovesick girlfriend left behind. I've had a few girlfriends along the way but never found anyone I wanted to spend the rest of my life with.'

Nick was silent while the food was being served but then he asked question after question as they ate, eliciting information about Emma's family, farm, hobbies, likes and dislikes. When Emma figured he knew almost everything about her while imparting very little about himself, he had a smug look on his face. To get back at him she clammed up, refusing to say another thing about herself. Nick laughed every time she made the motion of zipping her lip when he tried to slip in another question.

They lingered over a second cup of coffee, but eventually had no choice but to leave as the restaurant had emptied. Upon arrival at her flat Nick remained seated at the wheel. The silence was unnerving until he looked up. 'What day are you going home?' he finally asked.

'Saturday morning.'

'Which doesn't give us a lot of time does it? Have you got many plans for the rest of this week, because I would very much like to spend as much time as I can with you?'

Turning to look at her, his blue eyes seemed to search her face seeking answers.

'I want to go Christmas shopping for family gifts and I need to clean my unit. I had nothing else planned, except for a meal with the girls on Friday night. Sandy asked if we could get together for our own Christmas celebrations before I go away. I believe you are going to be invited to join us and I strongly suspect it was planned to get us together. I know how the pair of them think.'

Seemingly unabashed, Nick laughed. 'And the rest of my question? Are you going to allow me to spend most of the time with you?' Nick's voice had dropped to a whispered plea.

'Sounds good, but I thought you said you had come home to spend time with your family?'

'I have, but I only have a week to get to know you better. Mum and Dad aren't home from their holiday yet, so I've got plenty of spare time and what better way to spend it than with a beautiful woman. I've really enjoyed your company tonight.'

'I've enjoyed tonight as well even though I have to be honest and say I was petrified, because I've never been on a date like this before.' She couldn't believe she said those words. How stupid. 'Thank you for a wonderful evening and a special thank you for giving me the courage to stand up to Greg, or should I say, for standing up to him for me. You don't know how much I appreciate it. He intimidated me and I guess I was always afraid of him and what he would do. Now I know.'

'Much as I hate spoiling our evening by talking about him, be careful. He's not the type who would give up easily. Bullies don't like losing and I guess since I took you out and it was me who showed him up in public, could make it harder for you. I'm not frightened of him. He'll get a shock if he tries to attack me, but you need to be particularly careful. You know Caro's phone number – ring any time if you even remotely suspect he's hanging around. Would you mind if I came around in the morning?'

Would she mind? Not likely but not for the reasons he was thinking. With Nick there, Greg couldn't do anything horrible. And somehow, she knew any meeting with Greg wouldn't be of the warm fuzzy type. 'I was going to go Christmas shopping, but you're welcome to join me if you like. You might be able to give me some ideas on what to buy my Dad and young brother.'

'Wonderful, I'll be early.' After alighting Nick opened Emma's door for her before ushering her up the pathway. He waited behind her while she unlocked the front door. Before she could scamper inside, he grasped her hand and once again planted a kiss on her fingers, before turning her hand over to give her another seductive, lingering kiss in the palm of her hand.

Her senses were rocked by the warmth and touch. A strange tingle spiralled up from where Nick's lips brushed her palm. The heat coiled up her arm then through her body, resulting in her legs feeling suddenly weak.

'Goodnight, Emma, and thank you for a terrific evening.' He dropped her hand and left without turning back, leaving her heart beating a furious tattoo in her chest.

Chapter Five

A shrill ringing startled Emma awake. Still in the twilight zone of semi-awareness, she struggled to free limbs from tangled sheets which didn't seem to want to release their hold. She managed to get upright on the floor before full awareness brought her brain alive. She yawned, remembering how hard it had been to fall asleep. Thoughts about the chain of events over the past few days prevented her swirling mind from relaxing enough to slip into unconsciousness. Her emotions had swung from desperate feelings of unhappiness and fear to deliriously on top of the world. It must have been the latter thoughts when she had yielded to oblivion for Nick's kiss into her hand had been the last thing she recalled, and oh, how many times had she relived the moment.

Smiling, she groped around before finally finding the offending instrument which was still shrieking. She lifted the receiver to her ear, wincing at the exuberant demands from Sandy.

'It was great. I had a lovely time,' Emma managed to get in.

'Give me the details, where did you go? What did you talk about? Did he kiss you?' The loud questions ran into each other without giving Emma a chance to respond until Sandy paused to take a breath.

'Sandy! We went to *Esmereldas*, talked about everything in general. The rest is none of your business.'

'I'll take that as a yes. Are you seeing him again?'

Emma laughed at Sandy's persistence. 'Yes, since we are going out on Friday night together. Your idea I believe, and you can take things anyway you like, it doesn't mean it's true.'

'So, he didn't kiss you. I'm disappointed and Friday was Caroline's idea.'

'Sandy, I never said that either. Whether he did or didn't is none of your business and there is no way in this wide world I would tell you either way. Think what you like.' A grin broke out at her friend's moans and groans.

'I'll ring Caroline and she'll get the details out of her brother.'

'Go ahead, so I can get back to bed. I'm tired. I'll see you Friday.' Emma hung up, laughing at her friend's frantic pleas but was too wide-awake to return to the warmth of her recently vacated bed. Instead, she dressed, straightened the knotted mess of bedcovers then began the tedium of spring-cleaning. The unit was going to be empty for a couple of months, so she didn't want any microscopic remnants left around to grow into obscene balls of mould. Her brother was moving into the unit to begin university life and he would give her heaps forever if it wasn't fit for his fastidious habitation. For a guy, he was obsessive about cleanliness. Not like her young sister who was a slob.

Not long after she started scrubbing, she answered a second phone call: one not so pleasant. She slammed the receiver down moments after Greg uttered his first words of filth, starting off the conversation by calling her a slut and whore. She frowned. What did he mean? He knew she'd never slept with anyone – well maybe he didn't for she'd never had the guts to tell him. It was something she'd never told anyone. It was ridiculous to feel awkward about being a virgin at twenty-one, but she wasn't going to succumb to peer pressure for the sake of bragging rights. She'd been a party to plenty of smutty girl-talk, heard all the gross and not so gross details, the oohs and aahs of hot experiences but deep down she couldn't think of anything worse than regaling private intimacies with anyone let alone the entire group. Not even Sandy and Caroline would hear of her sexual encounters. She'd never had the opportunity so far. Well, she had but the thought of being intimate with Greg Saunders gave her the creeps. Now, what did that tell her? She snorted. Emma Nicholls was an idiot for even going out with him. So why did he call her those names? To avoid any other unpleasant phone calls, she switched on the answering machine, deciding she would only pick up when she knew who was calling.

Still shaking at the abuse, she returned to the laundry where she began spraying and wiping every surface but only managed one swipe with the cloth when she heard knocking at the front door. Fearing Greg had turned up, she crept down the passage to the entryway and called, 'Who's there?'

'It's me, Nick. I told you I would be early. Please let me in?'

Far out, he said he'd be early, but she hadn't expected this early. When she opened the door, Nick gave her a cheeky grin as he waltzed past her.

'It's a good job I'm up. So, did you escape before the Spanish inquisition started?' After closing the door she turned around, almost barrelling into Nick's still body. Embarrassed, she pulled up a few centimetres from him.

'Pardon?' He reached out to steady her which did nothing to lessen her hyper-awareness.

She sucked in her breath at the feel of the warm, soft skin on her bare arms. It made her realise her previous feelings were as sensuous as she recalled, even after convincing herself during the night, it wasn't possible to feel such a way about a guy after so short a time.

'Sandy woke me, demanding to know every lurid detail of our night out. When I wouldn't say anything, she reckoned she would ask Caroline, who, she said, would be able to wangle everything out of you. I was wondering if you managed to escape before you were given the third-degree.' Desperate to regain some equilibrium she swung around Nick and led the way down the short, tiled passage into the small but adequate kitchen where she pulled a stool out for him from under the Laminex bench. She held up the electric jug in question. At his nod, she filled it and plugged it in.

'Ah, no, not really. Caro was waiting up for me. All I told her was where we went. She wasn't happy and kept hounding me with a barrage of questions. What questions were you asked?' There was a curious look on his face telling her exactly what question he had been asked.

'Never you mind. I didn't answer them except where we went. I think they may have been conspiring together. Maybe we should play them at their own game. How about we make up some whoppers and both tell them the same thing?' she asked as she pulled out the makings of coffee.

'I'm beginning to see what Caro means about your sense of humour. I'm game. Now, more important matters, have you had breakfast?'

Emma didn't get a chance to answer. Her phone rang again, the message going to the answering machine but still audible. There was no way she could prevent Nick from hearing the foul words of abuse and threats.

Her nerves were zinging while Nick listened intently to the entire message. He turned to her with a scowl. 'How many times has he rung?'

It was stupid to feel embarrassed, but she did. 'Only one before this one, which is why I turned it onto the machine. I hung up on him as soon as he started.'

'Don't erase the messages. I have an old school friend who is in the police force. I'm sure he can do something about this if he has the proof. You could unplug your phone and use your mobile.'

'I don't have a mobile.'

His jaw dropped. 'Everyone has a mobile.'

'Not quite everyone.' Somehow her embarrassment level soared and sent her in defensive mode. 'I survive very well without one and all my friends know they can only reach me at home, so it has never been a problem and besides I won't be here for a while and he doesn't have my parents' phone number. And maybe it's a good thing I don't have a mobile for now he can't contact me. No surly text messages, no abusive calls, no slutty messages on my Facebook or Twitter pages because I don't have them.'

'It will take him two seconds to find your parents' phone number by ringing directory assistance or look it up on the internet but let's not think about him now. How about we find somewhere to have breakfast before we hit the shops? I have some shopping to do as well, although I did bring a few gifts home from London.'

The day was as enjoyable as the night before. Never had Christmas shopping been so much fun. The heat of the day was waning by the time they returned home. They'd had a good laugh after Caroline rang her brother to see where he was, complaining how she had crept around the house thinking he was still asleep and miffed when she discovered he was missing. During Caroline's barrage she asked if he was with Emma to which he was evasive. When asked if he knew where Emma was, he replied, 'She mentioned something about Christmas shopping. I won't be home for dinner tonight.' At those words he hung up and turned to Emma. 'Care to join me for dinner?'

She laughed but his invitation gave her an idea. 'Let me cook dinner so we can eat in. I've got food which needs to be used up. I'll ring Caroline from home and drop hints about eating at home. If I don't mention who I'm dining with I won't be lying.'

'You are a bit of a devil, aren't you? Sounds fine by me.'

When they arrived home, there was a message on the answering machine from a very curious sounding Caroline. Grinning, Emma returned the call.

'Did you go Christmas shopping with Nick?' was the first question before even saying hello.

Emma grinned across the room at the smiling Nick. 'Why on earth would I go shopping with Nick? It's bad enough shopping on my own. I still couldn't find everything I needed so I'll have to go out again tomorrow.'

'Are you going out to dinner with Nick again tonight?' was the next question.

'I'm too tired to go anywhere tonight. I'm eating in then having an early night. I need to catch up on some sleep.' She finished her conversation with Caroline only to be confronted by Nick standing slap bang in front of her.

'I'm not sure I like the early night bit. I hope you're not going to throw me out too early. If I go home Caro will be suspicious, and I would be very disappointed.' Nick reached over to playfully tap Emma on the end of her nose.

'When Caroline pumps you for information, maybe you could tell her you met up with a friend and had a casual dinner with them. It would be more or less the truth.'

'You are a sneaky little devil, aren't you?'

Emma rummaged through her fridge, pulling out a heap of vegetables to which she added diced chicken to turn them all into a curried stir-fry.

A dark sedan drove past Emma's house, the occupant thumping his hand against the steering wheel when he recognised the car in the driveway. Driving to the end of the street, the car came to a standstill around the corner. Dressed in black, an amorphous shape emerged then slithered from shadow to shadow until it reached the garden opposite Emma's unit. The shape merged with the branches of a dense tree and settled down to wait.

He watched the two people eating on Emma's small back patio while the sun dropped below the horizon of a few trees and grey fence sheeting.

Only the murmur of muffled conversation was heard across the road, but every time the sound of laughter drifted through the air, intense anger surged, causing the dark hump huddled on the ground against the gnarled trunk of fir tree to squirm

The sound of scuffles and chair legs grinding across concrete was followed by the rumble of glass doors sliding. Then silence. By shifting a few metres, he could make out the two figures at the kitchen sink indicating intimacy of shared dishwashing. She'd never invited him to eat with her. The woman disappeared while the man looked to be fiddling with things on the sink. Coffee? Lights were doused. Through the hanging branches, the flickering light of the television incensed the itching man even more. With pine needles and resin dropping down his neck, his scratching intensified. He wasn't visualising the television screen; all he could see in his mind was a naked Emma engrossed in different kinds of activities with another man: activities denied to him.

Later, too damn much later, there was movement. One stood, then the other. Blue lights went dark. The passage light flicked on followed by the one on the porch. Greg scooted back to the other side of the street and hid behind a tree trunk. The front door opened. They'd better not make out on the porch. Only the bastard Nick stepped outside. No Emma. Was she still naked?

Nick hurried to his car and drove off. Greg raced to his car and followed.

Why was he going to King's Park, the high hill of natural bushland overlooking the river and city? When the car pulled into a parking bay, Greg slowed, drifted past to find a parking spot further away but within sight.

After twenty minutes of nothing, he figured now was the time for payback. He slithered from his car, leaving the door unlocked and slightly ajar for a quick getaway. Keeping to the shadows he circled around through the bush, ensuring he could rush to the driver's side, yank the door open and mete out suitable punishment. There was no-one else around.

He wouldn't be seen.

No-one would know.

Only ten metres to go.

The engine rumbled to life. Before he had a chance to run, the car reversed, swung around and drove off.

Chapter Six

Awake soon after sun-up, Emma tackled the cleaning with a vengeance, accompanied by continual thoughts about the night before. Nick had kissed her. Very gently at first, his tongue had explored the outline of her mouth before his lips settled on hers and the kiss deepened. It was so magical and so different from any other kiss she'd had. She could remember every single one including the first behind the local hall when she was twelve. Glen Paterson, whose kiss had been nothing more than a puckered peck of inexperience. It was probably Glen's first kiss too. But Nick – oh, wow. His mouth was smooth and warm which was nothing like Greg's, whose kisses were cold and slobbery.

But suddenly Nick had jerked away, fisted his hands in his pockets and left as abruptly as she had been kissed. It had taken too long to sort out her confused mind, by which time Nick's car had reversed down the driveway. She remembered plonking back down on the lounge in wonderment, trying to make sense of what had happened. Making her way to her bedroom on unsteady legs, she'd readied for bed in a daze. She didn't recall climbing into bed but remembered lying for a long time, reliving every moment of the kiss, repeatedly.

Still confused this morning, she tried to assuage her thoughts by working at a furious pace so by mid-morning she had completed most of her tasks. The flat was not large, nor dirty, as she always kept her place clean and tidy, but she liked to have it spick and span when she went away for any length of time.

Pausing for a bite to eat gave her time to think, wondering why Nick hadn't rung when he'd promised he would and worrying why he had left so suddenly the night before. Maybe he regretted kissing her.

Maybe he didn't like the experience.

Maybe her inexperience turned him off.

The longer she sat, the more her lack of self-confidence reared its ugly head. Her thoughts became more and more negative until she was convinced Nick didn't want to see her again. She checked her phone messages to make sure she hadn't missed one from him, erased the half dozen threats from Greg and decided to finish her Christmas shopping alone. After a quick refreshing shower, she changed her clothes into something more appropriate than a dirt smudged holey T-shirt and frayed shorts. Checking she had everything she backed out of the front door, locking it as she went.

Twisting the knob to ensure the door was secure, Emma turned around and squealed at the sight of Greg standing five metres in front of her, half-way along the path, hands akimbo, his face devoid of all emotion, eyes unblinking.

'What do you want?' Emma squeaked, her fear mounting from the menacing look spreading across Greg's face.

'You. You're my girl.' Greg took one step closer, a cold look set on his face, his voice harsh.

'I don't belong to you or to anyone. I'm not someone's piece of property. I've asked you to leave me alone. I don't wish to see you any more so would appreciate it if you left.' Although she found it difficult to maintain control, Emma attempted the tactic Nick had used – keep calm. Great theory, Nick. Inside, she felt terrified, a surge of adrenalin flooding through her veins as her entire innards tightened like they were trapped in a vice.

'I'm not going anywhere. You're my girl and I'm going to make sure you know it. Open your door, we're going back inside and I'm going to do what I should have done ages ago. We're going to your bedroom and I'm going to enjoy stripping off every single item of your clothing nice and slow, one-by-one. It will give me great pleasure to make you mine.' With every word, his voice increased in volume, scaring Emma witless but she was determined to hide her mounting fear.

When he took another step towards her, she glanced around in the vain hope of spotting a neighbour outside his or her home. Bile rose in her throat as she frantically tried to think of what she should do. Swallowing down the rising acid, she took a few small steps away from the door to clear the edge of the tiny portico even though she knew she was moving closer to Greg, but instinct told her she would be in far more danger if they were inside. At least out in the open she had the chance somebody would either hear or see and outside she couldn't get trapped.

Noticing her glance, Greg darted furtive looks around to make sure no-one was nearby. Somehow Emma knew he had deliberately waited until most people had gone to work before approaching, knowing not many people would still be at home. It was insane to be thinking such thoughts at this time, but she wondered why he wasn't at work.

Greg took one step.

Emma sucked in a breath as a shiver wound its way across her shoulders. She had to do something.

Now.

She jerked sideways when he raised his hand as though to strike her, but instead he held his hand out with his palm open. Emma winced, unsure whether he was going to do her physical harm. Some innate feeling told her he would be none too gentle if he got her inside. The same gut instincts told her she had to get away, soon and fast.

'Give me the keys, Emma, or open the door. There's no-one around, they've all gone to work. You can't escape. I'm going to enjoy the next hour or so, destroying your precious virginity. I should have forced the issue months ago.'

Emma's thoughts were frenzied while she tried to figure out what to do. There was no way she could allow Greg to get a hold of her keys. She needed to run. But first she needed to distract him somehow. An idea hit. 'Bill, call the police,' she shrieked out at the top of her voice while staring over Greg's shoulder as though talking to someone behind him.

In the instant Greg turned his head Emma lobbed her keys in a large arc over the top of her roof at the same time as she dashed to one side and bolted; gaining a few precious metres before Greg turned back.

He swore profusely, made a grab for her but missed. He panted and cursed as he chased after her. Emma was fit and agile and much as Greg bragged about his sporting prowess, his heavy consumption of alcohol and fast foods had taken its toll. She hoped it was more of a toll than she imagined but she'd seen the extra weight he carried and how puffed he got on the hockey field.

Emma was able to increase the distance between them, centimetres at a time, as she flew past the front of her unit and leap-frogged the low fence into the neighbour's yard. Chasing after her, Greg made to grab her legs when she went over the fence, but she was too quick.

He missed.

Emma grinned when he couldn't leap the fence as she had, losing time clambering over, and even more time, when he had to pick his overweight body off the crushed plants on the other side.

Popping quick glances over her shoulder she ran diagonally across the front of the neighbour's house to reach the road, where she turned down the pathway along the road, having made a deliberate decision to run in the opposite direction to which Greg's car was parked.

Not hearing him behind her, Emma dared to twist her head around. He was headed towards his car. In the time it took him to return to his car, unlock it, start the engine and turn it around, she had reached the end of the street, turning right, which sloped down the next one, desperately seeking someone to help her or somewhere to hide.

While she raced full pelt along the empty bitumen, her eyes darted from side-to-side. With curtains drawn, all the houses looked as though there was nobody home and most had their backyards sealed off with fences and gates. Please, please, please, let someone be home, she whimpered.

All of a sudden, a few houses ahead on the opposite side of the road, Emma noticed a middle-aged lady emerging from her front door. 'Rape, rape – he's trying to rape me!' she screamed as she hurtled diagonally across the road towards the lady.

She was halfway across the road when Greg rounded the corner. She heard the roar of the engine as he planted his foot on the accelerator. Daring a glance, she baulked when she saw he was aimed directly for her. Sheer anger took hold as she heard a squeal and the engine roar.

The car sped faster.

The tyres squealed, causing smoke to billow from the rubber at the sudden rapid increase in speed. The car gained momentum and was almost upon her, closing the gap, still headed directly for her.

Adrenalin surged, giving her an extra spurt of speed moments before Greg reached her.

Missing her by what felt like a hair's breadth she heard him slam on the brakes with a grinding squeal, causing the car to spin around then fishtail down the road. As he spun, Emma noticed the elderly lady standing on the edge of her porch watching. She heard foul words spew from Greg's mouth as he fought for control of the slewing vehicle.

Still she ran, across the verge and over the low rock wall, barely missing the flowers in the garden bed. The engine revved again. Reaching the startled lady, she grabbed her around the shoulders and pulled her back into the house, slamming the door after them. Gasping for breath, Emma bent over, her hands leaning on her knees.

'You have to help me,' she puffed out in between rasping breaths. 'I need to call the police. He was going to rape me.'

Realisation hit as to how close to being run down she had been. The woman's arms wrapped around her shoulders.

'Now, now dear, you'll be safe in here.' Hearing another squeal from the tyres the lady released Emma and shot back to the window, tweaking back the curtain a fraction to see what was happening outside. 'He's gone now, dear. You come and sit down and calm yourself.'

'May I please use your phone? I need to call someone to come and get me. I'm not going out there again. He might be waiting for me.' Distraught, Emma felt her mind rambling and hoped the words came out right.

The lady led her into the kitchen, handing Emma the telephone receiver before filling the kettle. 'I'll make you a soothing cup of tea,' she said.

Emma dialled Caroline's number, her nerves creating havoc with her innards as she waited for what felt like forever, for the phone to be picked up. Caroline answered. 'Caroline, its Emma.'

'What on earth is the matter? You sound upset.'

'I need help. Can you come to get me?' Emma's voice rose with each word, unable to hide her desperation.

'Emma, what's happened? Are you all right?'

'No, I need help.' She shuddered at the way she was shouting at her friend. 'Greg attacked me… wanted to rape me... he tried to run me over but barely missed. I'm so scared… I can't go back home. He might be waiting for me.' She gulped between sobs but heard Caroline ask where she was. 'I'm not sure – I ran for my life, hang on, I'll get the address.'

'Address, I need your address,' Emma gabbled to the woman.

'I ran in the opposite direction than we usually go from my flat, turned right at the end of the road and I'm at number thirty-six. So, if you drive past my flat and keep going to the next road, turn right. Please hurry?'

'I'll be as quick as I can. You stay put. Have you got someone with you?'

'Yes, I half frightened this poor lady to death and she's looking after me very nicely, but I can't stop shaking and I'm so scared. What if he comes back? Oh, Caroline, please hurry?'

'Have you called the police?'

'No, not yet, I called you first.' As her terror began to ease, logical thought started returning. 'I need to call the police, don't I?'

'Leave it to me. I'll do it. Try to relax. I'll be there soon. Emma, did he harm you in any way?' Even though her voice softened she heard a distinct tremor in Caroline's words.

'No, I managed to get away. I was so frightened.'

There was dead silence.

'Caroline?'

'I'll be there soon.'

After Caroline hung up, Emma stood leaning against the wall for a few moments. Her saviour offered her a chair, begging Emma to sit and only after she had complied, was she offered tea or coffee.

'Coffee thanks, white.' Reaching out she grasped the woman's hand. 'I'm really sorry about this and thank you most sincerely for your help. I'd hate to think what would have happened if you hadn't been here.' She shuddered as she released her tight grip. 'I'm Emma Nicholls and live around the corner, halfway along the street.'

'Mary Booth. I'm so glad I was here for you.' Mary stirred the coffee, clanged the spoon on the side and handed the mug to Emma. 'Now you get this inside you and relax. You didn't half give me a fright when I saw the man deliberately trying to run you down. My, I was scared. You need to call the police, dear.'

'My friend, Caroline, said she would ring. She's coming to get me.'

The pair sat on either side of the Laminex kitchen table, sipping their drinks, Emma trying to make sense of the past few minutes of terror. Every now and again Mary reached out and patted Emma on her hand. It was such an inane action, but it sure felt good. They were still sitting in silence when they heard a knock at the door. Emma looked up in alarm then crept over to the door, asking who was there in a quivering voice.

'It's me, Nick.'

Far out. 'Nick!' She flung the door open and threw herself at him.

'It's all right, you're safe now.' Nick managed to free his hand from Emma's tight grip and introduced himself to Mary. 'I'm Nicholas Hamilton. Thank you so much for helping Emma. The police are on their way and they may want to ask what you saw. Can I give them your name and address?'

'Most certainly. What I saw was him try to kill her with his car. It was so close … I feared the worst. I'm Mary Booth. You take care of her now. She's had a terrible bad fright.'

Mary stood in the open doorway while Nick assisted Emma to his car. Her legs seemed to haven taken on the consistency of custard. She was shaking so much he had to bundle her in but once she was settled, he knelt on the verge next to her. Taking a clean handkerchief from his pocket, he gently wiped the moisture from her face. 'Are you all right?'

Emma nodded but said nothing then realised her eyes were leaking like a colander. Talking was beyond her.

'I'll take you home. Steve is waiting for us. He's the policeman friend of mine. He was off duty but insisted on coming since he lives close by.'

'Home? No way,' she managed to stutter.

'Greg's not there, I looked as I drove past. I doubt he'll be easy to find. He'll probably go into hiding. He must know he was seen. I won't let anything happen to you I promise.' Rising from his cramped position, he shut the passenger door, raced around the other side and climbed in. He drove the short distance back to Emma's flat where two cars, one a marked police sedan, were pulled into her drive with two police officers, one in plain clothes, waiting at her front door. After forcing her legs to work she managed to alight and stumble to the porch where her drama had begun. Nick introduced the two officers.

'Can we go inside?' asked Steve.

Emma paused. A weak grin crept out as she turned to face them. 'We could have a bit of problem there. I'm not sure where my keys are. When Greg demanded I open the door so he could get me inside, I threw them away.' Three sets of eyes followed the direction Emma pointed–upwards. 'I don't know where they landed, but I think I heard them hit the roof as I raced away.' The three sets of eyes shifted to look directly at her. Sheesh, she felt like an idiot.

'Well, I guess we had better go and have a look,' said a bemused Steve. 'Clever thinking.' He walked around the side of the unit to find the best place to climb up onto the roof. With the other two men giving him a leg up, he scrambled up to search, first the front and then the back, finally retrieving the keys from the rear gutter. Climbing down was a bit more difficult but Steve managed with nothing more than a torn shirtsleeve, scratched arm and smart comments from the other two men.

Once inside, Emma related her story while the uniformed officer, Mike Dean, jotted down notes. After the day's activities had been related, Nick detailed the background story. Emma felt her cheeks heat in shame when she admitted wiping all the abusive messages from her answering machine. But who needed such filth contaminating her home?

She was asked to retrace the route she took when she fled. While they walked along the road, her eyes and ears were alert for any sign of Greg returning. She was more than thankful when Nick kept his arm around her shoulder, holding her close. Without his physical support she was sure she would collapse in a heap. They left the two policemen at Mary Booth's door so her version of events could be gained.

She knew it was ridiculous to do so but Emma kept to the very inside of the pathway while they walked back to her little home.

Once they had the privacy of her lounge room with no onlookers, Nick prowled back and forth before pausing. He glanced up. 'I'll never forgive myself for causing all this,' he muttered.

'I certainly don't blame you, Nick. I should have listened to the girls months ago and walked away from him. I never imagined he would be this aggressive. The scariest part was when he tried to run me down. I think it was my adrenalin which made me move faster at the last moment.'

Nick shuddered. 'We need to talk. Are you up to it?'

'Talk about what?'

'Several things, the first one–you can't stay here alone. You have four days and nights before you go home to your parents. If Saunders isn't caught, he could come back, probably under cover of darkness and I doubt he would be unarmed. You would be much safer away from here so why don't you stay with Caro and me? There's plenty of room. Mum and Dad are not due back until next week but that doesn't matter. We've got several spare beds always made up and there would be two other people to watch out for you. You don't really have the room here for anyone else and I'd rather not put your reputation at risk by me staying here alone with you.'

He was right. Staying home would be asking for trouble but she hated the idea of being babysat – by Nick. 'Can I think about it?'

'You can think all you like, but I'll do my utmost to twist your arm and if all else fails I'll commandeer Caro and Sandy to get you to agree and you know how persistent they can be. Also, I want to apologise for last night. I'm embarrassed to say I was on the verge of losing control. I should never have kissed you like that, nor left you so suddenly without explanation.'

'What do you mean?'

He brushed a hand through his hair. 'After I left last night, I spent a few hours giving myself a hard time while mulling things over in my befuddled brain. I couldn't sleep, hence I failed to ring you this morning when I said I would. I slept in. Emma, I'm confused. There was something about you which intrigued and attracted me the moment I saw you sitting in the seat at the hotel. I had this desperate need to meet you, to get to know you. It was fate you turned out to be Caro's best friend. I've heard a lot about you, as Caro was always writing emails or talking to me on the phone about the wonderful Sandy and Mouse and the things you got up to.

'I was absolutely delighted when I saw you at our house the next night and I have to tell you the sight of you had my heart beating far too rapidly than is good for my health. Things seem to have escalated at an enormous pace. I mean, it has only been four days, and look what's happened. I feel responsible for today and all your grief, because if I hadn't been here none of it would have happened. It pains me to know I have been the cause of all your hurt. But on the other hand, I'm delighted to have met you. I want to know you better and be with you as much as possible. Meeting you has changed everything. All I can think about is you. The dread I felt this morning when you rang and told Caroline what happened, was something I don't ever want repeated. I don't know what has come over me, but I do know you have crept into my heart and I would very much like for us to take time to see whether we have a future together. I know you're going home to your parents for a while, and I'll be spending time with my family, but I'm going to miss you like crazy.'

Stunned, Emma plonked into the nearest chair. 'I have no idea what to say. I'm so confused. I'm glad you got rid of Greg for me and don't blame you in the slightest for his appalling behaviour. He's the one who is acting like some crazed maniac where-as you've done nothing but treat me with the utmost respect and gentleness and to be honest, I've never experienced anything like it before.' Pausing, a shy smile spread across her face. 'Nick, I liked the way you kissed me. I was surprised, but I really enjoyed it.' Her eyes dropped. 'I thought I had done something wrong when you walked out afterwards though, and when you didn't ring this morning, I convinced myself you had decided you didn't really like me and I wouldn't see you again.'

Pulling Emma from her chair Nick enveloped her in a warm embrace. 'Oh, I like you.'

Chapter Seven

Even though it took Nick and Caroline quite some time coercing Emma to pack they managed by dragging out a couple of overnight bags and filling them with her clothes. Bags packed, they shoved her out the front door, giving Emma no option but to move out of her unit until she returned to the farm. Still November, she would be gone for at least six weeks, probably closer to eight, and since she needed her car for the long drive, Caroline bundled her into said car amid remonstrations then laughter when Emma saw how ridiculous they must look. By the time they reached the Hamilton home, Emma was resigned to be staying there. Deep down she felt relieved there would be no more unpleasant confrontations with the odious Greg. The shock of his aggressive actions still rocked her every time the memory surfaced, which seemed to be every few minutes. It was almost impossible to erase the visions from her mind.

After being shown into a room next to Caroline's, Emma was left to settle in. She sat bouncing on the edge of the bed, her mind going over her reason for being there, recalling in detail the terror of her flight down the street. After a big shuddering sigh and a severe talking to, to get over it since nothing bad happened, she went in search of her friend, needing the company to keep her mind away from the day's scary events. She was safe and Greg probably wouldn't be game to show his face again.

After enjoying a quiet barbecue dinner on the patio, they sat chatting late into the evening until Nick suggested a quiet amble around the neighbourhood. Emma didn't miss Nick's glance at his sister when she suggested she join them. It was obviously a blatant request for her not to accompany them. She took the hint, but her grin told Emma, Caroline knew exactly why she wasn't wanted.

At first, Nick held Emma's hand while they strolled. It felt right. Nick chatted about a lot of the characters from his childhood who had lived in the various homes as they wandered past each. Somewhere along the line, his arm slipped around her waist while he related some of his more daring exploits with his mates in his school days. Emma couldn't help but laugh, certain he was exaggerating the mischief he had been involved in. But it felt so good to laugh and even better when his arm rose to her shoulders and he tugged her a little bit closer.

'What have you planned for tomorrow?' Nick asked as they turned the last corner before home.

'I have to finish Christmas shopping. I won't have a chance once I'm on the farm. I'll be busy helping Dad with the harvest and there are no shops for miles. What are you doing?'

Stopping, he stepped in front of her. 'I hope I can spend most of my time with you. Would you allow me to take you out for dinner tomorrow night? I'm thinking of some place where they might have dancing, my type of dancing, where I get to hold my partner in my arms.'

Before she had a chance to answer he began walking again without taking her hand. 'I suppose I should ask if you do dance?' he said over his shoulder.

Feeling the loss of his touch it took her a moment to find the right words. 'I'm a country girl. We were brought up with regular dances in the local hall,' she said as she quickened her pace to catch up with him. 'All the kids learn to dance from an early age. Every time someone in the town has a big birthday, engagement or anniversary the whole district goes. There's always a bush band and plenty of dancing. I would love to go dancing. Are you coming shopping with me or are you doing your own thing?'

'I'll go with you, but I would also like to go off on my own for a while. We could meet up for something to eat.' Linking elbows, he guided her into the driveway then through the front door where Caroline met them with a smug grin. Feeling self-conscious about being caught so close, Emma pulled away and hurried to her bedroom.

Emma was surprised she slept so well after her ordeal but was up at dawn, eager to be at the shops the moment they opened since she needed time in the afternoon to prepare for her night out. Much to her disgust, Nick slept on. So, did Caroline. When the wait became too much, she did what she used to do with her young brother to get him out of bed. Searching the freezer, she found a tray of ice-cubes. After emptying half a dozen into a mug, she crept down the passage to Nick's room. His door was slightly ajar, so she pushed it open a bit more, her heart in her mouth, praying he didn't sleep sprawled on the top of his bed stark naked, because if he did, she was in for more of a shock than he was.

A quick glance showed he was under the covers lying on his stomach: with no top on. She watched his naked muscled back rising and falling in a steady rhythm. Heavens but he was a hunk.

She crept over to his bed, took three ice-cubes in each hand and ran all six over his bare back and shoulders. The moment he began to stir, she turned and fled full pelt across the room.

'God, almighty!' he roared. 'What the? Strewth, that's cold. Emma, get back here,' he yelled.

Emma was doing no such thing. She scarpered back to her room and jumped into bed, fully clothed, pulling her quilt up around her ears, and shut her eyes pretending to be asleep.

Mutterings came from Nick's room, followed by striding footfalls down the passage. Emma bit her tongue to stifle her giggles. She heard him whack her door then there was silence, she hoped because he thought her to be asleep and Caroline was the culprit. She held her breath but her body began shaking with suppressed laughter.

All of a sudden, her quilt was yanked but she had a tight hold of it. She buried her face in her pillow so he couldn't reach any of her bare skin.

'My sweet little innocent, you will pay for your little escapade,' he said from the foot of her bed. He grabbed hold of the bottom of her quilt and swiftly yanked it up.

She squealed when he rubbed the remains of the melting ice on the bottom of her bare feet and up her calf muscles.

'What the heck is all the noise about?' called Caroline from the doorway.

'It's called shocking a man awake with a tray of ice-cubes,' Nick growled.

Caroline laughed. 'I seem to recall telling you Emma had a wicked sense of humour. Maybe I forgot to mention all the pranks she gets up to. She is nowhere near as shy and innocent as she portrays to the general public.'

'Something I discovered to my detriment,' Nick said as he stalked out.

Hearing him go Emma emerged from the safety of her blankets, unable to suppress her grin. She climbed out of the bed and remade it while Caroline stood watching.

'What was your little prank in aid of?' Caroline asked.

'I've been up for ages and Nick was coming shopping with me. I needed to wake him so we could leave. It worked,' Emma said, unable to suppress her grin.

'Have you ever tried taking in a cup of coffee to gently rouse a person?'

'It's nowhere near as much fun.'

Having succeeded in getting everyone up, Emma raced to the kitchen to prepare breakfast, not to make amends, but to hurry Nick. She had scrambled eggs and coffee waiting and as soon as each arrived in the kitchen, she handed them their plates. She had eaten earlier but joined them for coffee. The minute each plate was emptied Emma gathered, washed and put them away.

But Nick dallied, a serene smile on his face which told her his actions were deliberate, probably to pay her back. At last he was ready to leave.

'Hurry up, Emma or we'll be late.' He dared to laugh at her raised eyebrows.

After reaching the city they went separate ways, agreeing to meet for coffee. With the list she'd made the previous night Emma flew around the shops making her purchases, allowing time to find a third new outfit. She had seen one the last time she had tried on clothes and had been in two minds about buying it before. Pleased to find it still available, she purchased the dress leaving her with only enough time to race down the street to meet Nick on time. Arms laden with parcels she sat at the table, re-organising everything into two bags while she waited, tossing the superfluous packaging into a nearby bin and there seemed to be more wastage than items.

'You have been busy,' said a voice from behind, causing her jump.

Her heart thumping, she turned. 'You scared me.'

'Sorry, I didn't mean to.' He looked concerned before a grin broke out. 'Have you got everything yet or do you need more time?'

It took a few seconds before she could catch her breath, her heart was beating so hard. 'I think I'm about done, what about you? I only need to call into my local Post Office to have my mail redirected but I can do that tomorrow.'

'I have all I need. Coffee?' he asked.

'Yes please.' She needed more than coffee. For a moment she'd thought Greg had found her, which was ridiculous because it was the middle of the day and he would be at work, although he'd thought nothing of skipping work yesterday. Oh, please don't let him be on annual leave? No, couldn't be because he would have said.

They didn't linger over the coffee, which was lukewarm and bitter. Once home, each disappeared into their own rooms to dispose of their parcels. There was a knock at Emma's door as she finished hanging up her new dress in the wardrobe. Not waiting for a response Caroline wandered in.

'Have you got your bathers with you, Mouse? I'm going for a dip in the pool. Justin's coming over for lunch and Nick's cook today. Come and join us.' Her eyes rose as she spied the new dress. 'What a gorgeous dress. It's good to see you finally buying some classy clothes. Are you wearing it tonight? Nick said you wouldn't be home for dinner.'

'Yes, yes and yes, to answer all your questions. Give me a couple of minutes to change.' Emma rummaged through her bags to find her bathing costume. A few minutes later she dropped the towel she had wrapped around her body to hide it and dived straight into the pool, giving a brief shudder at the sudden cold. To warm up, she swam several lengths, floundering at a sudden splash followed by a tidal wave which filled her mouth and nose.

'It's not as cold as the ice this morning, little witch,' Nick said as he shook the water from his hair and face, deliberately splashing her. She was still spluttering when he grabbed her around her waist, turned her around and planted a seductive kiss on her mouth. The kiss deepened, sending her senses on a roller-coaster ride. Just as suddenly, he released her, swam to the side of the pool, hoisted himself out, wrapped a towel around his waist and disappeared back into the kitchen.

Emma was left floundering for a moment while she regained her equilibrium.

'Don't let me interrupt. That was some kiss.' She spun around at Caroline's voice. Mortified, she sank under the surface not to only hide but to give her incinerating cheeks a chance to cool off. When a need for oxygen was on a desperate level, she rose to see Caroline entering the pool more sedately, shivering as the cold water gradually washed over her. Caroline edged closer. 'I've always thought you two were made for each other. He's a great man, even if he is my brother.'

Much to Emma's relief, their conversation was interrupted by the arrival of Justin. Caroline climbed back out of the pool to greet him while Emma swam a few more laps before leaving the water to warm up on a sun lounge, making sure she wrapped her towel around her torso the moment she stepped onto the paving.

At that moment, Nick opened the servery and called for assistance. Emma changed direction to carry the items from the window to the already set table. The last platter, Nick didn't release straight away. While he held it back, he caught her eye. 'I think I might have mentioned this before, but you are a very beautiful woman, Emma Nicholls.'

Her eyes dropped as she felt the tell-tale blush rise on her face. Her hand trembled so much she almost tipped the food off the plate and would have done so if Nick hadn't gripped it tight.

'Even more attractive when you blush,' Nick added. 'Don't you dare drop that on the ground.' The heat intensified as she spun around and somehow managed to reach the table without being incinerated by her mortification. It defied logic to be so self-conscious about her body, she never was back home or with the girls. It was just… just… she didn't have a clue.

Lunch was a lingering laughter-filled affair while the four chatted. A brief swim followed with Nick being on his best gentlemanly behaviour, much to Emma's relief. She couldn't understand why she felt so up-tight about being kissed. It wasn't as if she'd never been kissed before. But with Nick it was different. As she observed Justin kissing Caroline, she wished she could feel so at ease with a public display of intimacy.

To ease her thoughts, she collected an armful of dishes, carried them inside to wash them.

Nick followed with another pile of plates. 'We'll put this lot in the dishwasher and I'm cleaning up. You go and have your shower. Dinner is at seven, by the way, so we'll leave around six-thirty.' Removing the dishcloth from Emma's hands he gently pushed her out of the kitchen. 'Go and relax, because tonight I am going to dance you off your feet.'

Hours later there was a gentle tap at her bedroom door. 'Are you ready?' called Caroline.

Emma was ready but her stomach wasn't. It felt as though it were being tumble-dried. 'Almost,' she called, 'come in.'

The door opened and Caroline's head appeared. Her eyes boggled before she emitted a shrill wolf whistle, twisting Emma's already knotted stomach even tighter.

'Wow, I want to see Nick's eyes when he sees you. You look gorgeous. Come on, this I have to see.' Caroline took two steps, grabbed Emma's arm and tugged.

Emma tripped then laughed nervously as she straightened. There was no point in resisting as she knew darn well Caroline never gave up when an idea entered her head. She was virtually dragged across the room and shoved out of the door. Caroline followed behind giving gentle nudges all the way down the passageway. Emma could feel her blush rising while she tried to escape her friend's jostles. There was one last, not so gentle shove as they reached the doorway to the lounge room. Emma stumbled forwards and had to fight to regain her balance, coming to a sudden halt when she spied Nick on the other side of the room.

His eyes were staring as he rose ever so slowly from the chair.

Even though she felt terrified, Emma loved the way Nick's blue eyes softened with admiration. But he appeared to have difficulty breathing and for a moment Emma thought there was something wrong with him.

'Are you all right?' she asked as she took a step forward.

'Not really,' said Nick on a croak. He coughed to clear his throat.

Alarmed, Emma took another step. 'What's wrong?'

Nick smiled. 'Oh, nothing is wrong. In fact, everything is perfect.'

'Then why do you sound so…?'

'As though I can't breathe?' Nick finished for her.

'Yes.'

'Probably because I can't. You took my breath away.' He closed the gap and brushed the tips of his fingers down the side of her face while he openly admired her. 'I am truly at a loss for words to tell you exactly how I feel right now, but you look exquisite.'

'Oh,' was all Emma could get out. She didn't have a clue as to what else to say. No one had ever reacted to her in such a way before or paid her such a compliment. She so didn't fit into this circle of wealth with its social status and etiquette. Heavens she was a simple farm girl with no experience.

'Oh, indeed.' Grasping her fingers, he planted a kiss on the back of them and smiled again.

'Doesn't she look gorgeous,' said Caroline from the door.

Nick slid an arm behind Emma's back and began guiding her towards the door. 'Gorgeous doesn't cover it,' he said. 'Don't wait up for us,' he added.

The restaurant was so new, Emma had never heard of it before and it was so unlike any she knew about. A real-life trio of musicians played key-board, guitar and violin at one end of a dance floor situated at the far end of the room with the tables set around the remaining walls. The dance floor was not large but would accommodate ten or twelve couples. They sat without speaking, listening to the soft background music while they perused the menu. After ordering, Nick invited Emma to dance. This was something she felt confident about. Dancing was one thing she could do with ease. And so could Nick, she soon discovered. His movements were lithe and fluid, something she wasn't used to. Most men at university could do little more than shuffle around when it came to traditional ballroom type dances. Sure, they could wriggle and bop to funky modern tunes but rarely since moving from the country had she found a guy who could really dance. Countless dances in the local hall meant she had mastered many complicated steps with the older generation being excellent teachers, but Nick seemed to be able to match her and it wasn't long before they were soon the centre of attention while they waltzed around the floor in complete unison. When the music ended, Emma was shocked to hear applause and even more disconcerted when she realised she and Nick were the recipients. Feeling mortified she dropped her eyes as she blushed in embarrassment.

'I told you I would have to fight the men off. It's not often I can find a partner who really knows how to dance. You continue to surprise and delight me. Our first course has arrived.' Placing his open hand in the small of her back he guided Emma back to her seat, for which she was more than grateful. Even after he took his hand away her back burned from his touch.

Once she had regained her composure, she was able to relax enough to enjoy the light repartee between them while they ate. After the starters of delicious, fat, juicy garlic prawns, they returned to the dance floor to join in with the small group of fellow dancers with a quickstep, remaining on the floor until their main course was served. When the dishes from their main course had been taken away, the band started up with a provocative tango.

Emma caught Nick's glance. 'Tell me you can tango,' he said.

Oh, she could tango. It was her favourite dance. She stood, offering her hand to him while placing, what she hoped, was a sexy seductive smile on her face. Nick was about to find out exactly how well she could tango. She let loose, laughing at the stunned look on Nick's face. Then she concentrated on making her movements sinuous and went all out to seduce her partner. Falling into step, he played his part in the erotic dance to perfection. The emotional tension building up was palpable. They kept their eyes glued on each other, allowing their bodies to do the seduction. The atmosphere was mesmerising. When the music ended, there was silence while they stared at each other. Emma felt overawed, her innards burning with the tension of blatant sexual arousal.

All of a sudden applause erupted. Stunned, Emma glanced around the room. Standing patrons were clapping profusely. Oh, God! Why didn't she notice? She wanted to flee but her feet felt as though they had been super-glued to the floor. She felt Nick wrap his arm around her waist. Thank goodness, for she needed the support to remain standing. To increase her mortification he kissed her, and not only a light peck. The kiss was long, hot and mind-frazzling.

He suddenly released her. 'That was some tango. You surprise me. For once you don't seem to be in the slightest bit self-conscious about being the centre of attention. Maybe I should get you to seduce me more often.'

Not self-conscious? She was dying, especially since his words brought on a heat which incinerated not only her cheeks, but her entire body.

'Don't ever change, Emma. I like you exactly the way you are.'

Chapter Eight

'How was the dancing?' Caroline set her plate on the bench behind her then licked the crumbs from her fingers, as though pretending the question wasn't important but Emma could tell her friend was dying with curiosity.

Wondering how he was going to reply, Emma glanced at Nick who stood next to his sister, leant up against the kitchen bench, munching on toast.

'Excellent, the band played great dance music,' said Emma to break the tense silence.

'And did they play a tango?' asked Caroline.

Emma caught Nick's surprised glance. 'You know about her tango?' he asked as he swung his eyes towards his sister.

'Oh, yes, Mouse is famous for her tango. They used to deliberately have tango music at uni functions for her. I've seen her dancing with six different men at the same time and she seduces every single one of them.'

'Caroline, keep quiet,' Emma implored as Nick straightened, a half-eaten piece of jam-laden toast held in mid-air.

'She did a damn good job of seducing every male in the restaurant last night, including me, I might add. They were all squirming in their seats.' The toast moved into Nick's mouth while he set his plate down and lifted his mug of coffee from the bench.

A squirm of embarrassment shimmied across Emma's shoulders at Nick's blatant nuance. Well, she could be as blatant. 'And who had every female drooling into their desserts when he gyrated his hips towards them and showed off his muscles as his shirt drew taut across his chest?' Emma retorted with a sly smile. 'I think every woman present wished she was up on the floor dancing with the most handsome hunk of a man.' She paused a moment while eyeing Nick, who was choking on the mouthful of coffee which had gone down the wrong way. 'I do believe you are actually blushing, Mr Nicholas Hamilton,' she added. 'Maybe I should tell Caroline what the second standing ovation was for.'

His eyes watering, Nick stared at Emma sending her the message she would be wise to keep her mouth closed, but she couldn't suppress the grin spreading across her face as she strutted out of the kitchen on her way to collect any mail from her letterbox and visit the Post Office to arrange a mail diversion. Before she'd taken two steps, she heard Nick's voice.

'Caro, why is Emma so withdrawn and shy most of the time and yet she showed not a skerrick of timidity last night when she was the centre of attention?'

Oh, boy, this was not good. Emma stalled, in two minds about listening in. Knowing eavesdropping was impolite she took one step away, but curiosity got the better of her and she crept back and hid behind the door.

'Oh, if she was the centre of attention she would have been dying inside but she loves dancing. She's reticent with anyone she doesn't know well but with Sandy and me, she's outgoing. She's confident dancing, because she is so darn good at it and knows she isn't going to embarrass herself. She's brilliant at languages, being able to speak fluent Spanish, French and Mandarin. On the farm she's a different girl from the one you see in public. Her mother would die laughing if you said Emma was shy. With other things, she isn't so confident and shies away in case she makes a gaffe. She doesn't believe she is gorgeous to look at and has no confidence at all when it comes to men or romance, mainly because it is all new to her. I'm certain Greg never treated her in a romantic sense; he wouldn't have a clue how to treat a woman nicely. You might see a more outgoing Emma on Friday night, because she knows everyone who will be there. Give her time, even this morning she was more open and daring with you. You're in love with her, aren't you?'

Emma eyed the ceiling, mortified but keen to hear Nick's answer. How did he feel about her?

'I've only known her a few days but she sure as hell plays havoc with my insides. How am I supposed to know exactly what love is? Does anybody really know?'

'You'll figure it out if it's right. See how you feel next week when she goes home. I know I'm going to miss having her around. By the way, what was the second standing ovation for?'

Oh, heavens, please don't tell her, Emma willed.

'I kissed her.'

'A kiss warrants a standing ovation, there's got to be more. How did you kiss her?' Caroline sounded way too amused.

'She'd just seduced me in the tango, how do you think I kissed her?'

Emma cringed. Far out, this is so embarrassing.

'In the middle of the dance floor?' asked Caroline with a definite chuckle. 'How did Mouse handle that?'

'A great deal better than I thought she would. She hardly batted an eyelid at the time, but her cheeks were flaming when I came up for air.'

'I can imagine they would, but she must have enjoyed it. I think she might like you quite a lot, dear brother; something which pleases me a great deal. I'm off. Justin has a couple of hours free today so I'm going to meet him for lunch. Enjoy your day.'

Oh, God, Emma thought as she turned and scampered on tippy-toes to the front door, grabbed her keys and purse from the little china dish on the wall table, snuck outside and raced to her car.

When she reached her street, she slowed to a crawl and studied every drive and yard for any sign of Greg. So she didn't have to risk getting out of the car, she drove onto the verge to collect any mail without alighting. It took half an hour at the post office filling out forms and pay a ridiculous fee to redirect any mail, not that she received much other than everyday utility bills.

When she returned to Caroline's house, Nick was working on a laptop at the far end of the open plan lounge area. 'Everything sorted?' he asked without looking up.

'Yes, all done.'

'Did you check for messages?'

'Umm, no.'

'Maybe you could leave me a key to your unit so I can check for any while you are away? I could also make sure nobody breaks in.' Setting his work aside he crossed the room to Emma. 'One other thing concerning me is whether or not Greg knows you are going home to visit your parents, and does he know where home is?'

She screwed her eyes, trying to remember what she had told the cretin. 'He knows I'm going and knows the name of the town but not exactly where the farm is, which is about fifty kilometres from town, but I guess he could ask around.' She glanced at Nick. 'You're putting the wind up me.'

'I didn't mean to, but we need to cover all bases, so I'll talk to Steve and see what he recommends. Now I want to make a suggestion. Is your farm in mobile range?'

'It is now. They've put up a few towers around the place over the past few years. Dad uses one on the farm now and Mum has one. Why?'

'Good. I think it would be wise if you carried a mobile with you for safety's sake.'

'I hardly think it's worth the money.'

'I do, especially after what's already happened. You wouldn't have to use it a lot, but have it with you all the time, in case you have an emergency. How about we get one today? I'm not really asking your permission because I intend doing it in any case: my Christmas present to you.'

'Nick, no, you don't need to buy me a gift.' Emma protested.

'Sweet Emma, you don't get any say in what I choose to give you as a Christmas gift, so save your protests. Come on, we're going now.' He grasped her hand, not giving her a chance to say no.

Once in the shop, the technological language Nick and the shop assistant used, bamboozled Emma to the extent she held her hands up in submission. 'I don't have a clue what you guys are talking about so leave me out of this. I don't even want a darn phone.'

'I insist – but only to keep you safe. I promise I'll get something easy for you to use. Do you want me to choose?'

She sighed. 'Go ahead while I'll amble around the store.' What she saw stunned her. She was adept at using computers although her laptop was six years old and worked on an outdated system. She didn't care since it worked well enough to carry out her studies and her internet worked perfectly to do research. What more did a person need?

When Nick retrieved her to choose what colour she preferred she stared at him as though he'd grown two heads. 'They have different colours, isn't a phone just a phone?'

'Is she for real?' asked the techno-head salesman.

In return, Emma glared at the man while Nick slung his arm around her waist and drew her closer.

'Emma has never had a need for a mobile phone before so isn't up with what's available.' He pointed to a large glass case full of different phones on display. 'Choose a colour,' he said to Emma as he moved his head closer to hers.

Her mouth gaped at the range she had to select from. Stunned, she turned her head so they were eye-to-eye. 'Dad has a black one. I thought they were all black and people put them in those fancy cover thingummies. I'm so not with it am I?'

'Why should you know if you've had no interest in owning one? It's a bit like computers these days. The day after you buy one, they come up with something new and what you bought is out of date.'

'Are you inferring I'm out of date?' she muttered as her mind pictured her laptop – black of course and oldish. Maybe it would be a good idea to not let Nick see it, especially since he was one of those computer techno geeks.

'Hell, no.' Nick straightened and placed his hands on her shoulders, tugging her around so they were face-to-face. 'Emma, do remember what I said last night about me never wanting you to change?'

She nodded, but her thoughts didn't agree with her head actions. She felt so out of place.

'I meant it. You are perfect the way you are right now. You not knowing the latest fads in this kind of technology is the same as me not having a clue about speaking in Mandarin. I earn my living through technology, so I need to keep up. Your forte is languages.'

Oh, heavens, she wasn't supposed to know how he found out. Her conscience slammed her around the ears for eaves-dropping. 'You know I can speak Mandarin?'

'Caroline mentioned it.'

'I need to have words with her.'

'Go ahead but first let's choose a colour so we can go home and you can chew her ear off, something I will relish seeing.'

Not having a clue what she was looking for, she pointed to the first one which caught her eye. The silver sparkled at her. 'Silver will be fine.'

After the purchase, they were sitting at a table in a shopping centre eatery, having ordered a light lunch, and Nick was showing Emma how to use the phone. He told her what he was doing as he punched in and stored his own mobile number, Caroline's number as well as those of her parents so she could speed dial them at any time. Not realising her phone was already connected she was stunned when her mother answered while she practised using various features. Nick sat back, grinning at her while Emma chatted to her mother.

'See, it's not so hard, is it?' he said when he showed her how to hang up. 'Practise using it over the next couple of days so we can iron out any problems you may encounter before you leave. The battery is new so won't have much charge yet. I'll show you how to charge it when we get home. The important thing is to make sure you keep it charged. The last thing you need is to be trying to make an urgent call only to find your battery is flat. Also, when I call you in the middle of the night when I can't sleep because I'm thinking about your seductive movements in the tango, the last thing I'll be needing is for the battery to run out, sweet seductress.'

He reached over and tapped Emma on the end of her nose with one finger. She was grateful her club sandwich arrived, giving her an excuse to drop her head and hide yet another bout of pinkness.

They ate in relative silence until their hunger was sated. Nick settled back in his seat, removed his own mobile phone from the top pocket of his shirt and fiddled with it. This was one reason she wasn't a fan of the gadgets. Social conversation was almost non-existent nowadays. Miffed, she sat back and concentrated on the people around her. A nearby phone rang, which she tried to block.

'Emma, your phone is ringing.'

Startled, she picked it up and searched for the correct tab she was supposed to touch and slide as she tried to remember all his instructions. Her eyes flew across the table when she heard his voice. 'Good afternoon my little temptress, how about taking in a movie while we are here?' He laughed at the glare Emma shot at him.

After a quiet evening meal with Caroline, Nick spent time catching up on work on his computer while Emma sat curled up on the lounge on the other side of the room, engrossed in a book. Every now and again she glanced up to spot him looking at her, which sent her nerves on edge. It was difficult to keep her head down, so he didn't think she was peeking. It was also impossible to concentrate on the words so she kept going back to the beginning sentence and must have read it a hundred times before she heard him call her name.

'Emma, come over here and see this.' He indicated the screen she couldn't see so she rose, crossed the carpet and watched as he typed.

'You speak French!' she exclaimed.

'*Mais ouis, Madamoiselle, certainement.* I spent two years working and living in France. I had no choice but to learn the language, although I did study French in high school, so I knew the basics. I also own a small unit in Paris, which I bought to live in while I was there. Caroline tells me you hope to go there some time next year, so you are welcome to use it. I also have one in London you can use.'

'But what about you?'

'I've not made a decision yet and won't for a while. I work for myself, tendering for contracts. This work is for a company I still do small contracts for.' He gestured towards the screen. 'I might take on a local contract while I'm here, to see how things work out. I'll keep the units regardless, as investments. Come for a quick walk before we go to bed.'

Nick slung his arm around her waist while they ambled around the block. When she asked him more about his time in France, he obliged by telling her about some of the best things he had seen while offering suggestions about what she could do when she visited the country. He even suggested he could help her find employment through some of the companies he had worked for.

They were crossing a road not far from the house, when there was a sudden revving of a car engine followed by the squealing of tyres. Still in the centre of the usually quiet suburban street, Nick tugged Emma to a stop and turned to see what was making such a racket.

Her heart shot to her mouth, back down to her stomach then yo-yoed when she spied a dark sedan bearing down on them. Emma froze. The brilliant headlights blazing into her eyes blinded her. Instinct told her exactly who was driving the car.

Nick swore at the same time he grabbed her around the arm and made a Herculean dive back the way they had come, dragging Emma after him. Hitting the ground, her chest and abdomen took the full brunt of the impact as she skidded along the ground, her legs dragging behind. There was a searing sting as her skin tore underneath the thin cotton of her slacks and top. Landing spreadeagled across the footpath, all breath whooshed from her lungs leaving her winded. Gasping out aloud to suck in some oxygen, she twisted her head to see Nick sprawled across the kerb, his feet still on the road.

Glancing sideways, she noticed the dark looming shape altering course. It zigzagged from side-to-side as though out of control until it came to a screeching halt. There was a stench of burning rubber followed by a squealing of tyres as the car spun in a doughnut and faced them head on. A second surge of adrenalin shot through her blood vessels when she realised the car was coming back for a second attempt. Scrambling to his feet Nick hobbled the short distance to her, grabbed her under the shoulders and hauled her onto her feet. She screamed at the pain and knew she was hurt; but there was no time to stop to investigate how bad.

'Run,' Nick gasped as he flung one arm around her waist and dragged her with him as he headed for the nearest house with lights on.

'Matt, its Nick Hamilton, for God's sake open the door,' he yelled as he pounded on the door.

Nick kept banging and yelling while Emma swung her eyes from the rapidly approaching vehicle, back to the door. It seemed like an eternity before the door opened. With the car heading straight for them Nick flew inside, knocking the occupant to the floor as he pulled Emma after him. She squealed in agony when her hip landed across the hard door step but managed to glance at the speeding vehicle as it mounted the kerb and was halfway across the lawn before brakes were applied. The wheels spun in the soft lawn, spewing sods of grass and black dirt across the pavement and towards the house. Finally finding traction, the car reversed out of the garden back onto the bitumen. Brakes squealed as they were jammed on. Tyres screeched as the car tore down the street, leaving deep gouges in the front verge and the acrid smell of burning rubber filled the air.

Nick staggered upright and leant against the wall of the foyer with his head resting on his arm while trying to regain his breath. Emma was desperate to get up but felt as though she had been super-glued to the cold hard tiles. She really, really, really didn't want to move any time soon.

The owner of the house picked himself up off the floor. 'What the hell is going on, Nick?'

'I'll explain in a minute,' Nick gasped. 'I need to make a phone call first.' Pulling his mobile from his shirt pocket, he inspected it for damage, nodded with a grunt of satisfaction then scrolled and pressed the call button as he knelt by Emma's side to see if she was all right. 'Emma…' was all he got out before he turned his attention to the phone. 'Steve, its Nick, the same idiot just tried to kill us by running us down, and almost succeeded. We're around the corner from my place. Yes, the same car I believe. I'll be home when you arrive. Thanks mate.'

Turning to Emma, Nick leant over and ran his hands over her heaving body. 'Emma?'

A long moan was all she managed for she was beyond formulating words.

'Are you all right?' He eased her over onto her back. 'Dear, God, what a mess!' He swept his eyes over her, groaned and squatted beside her. It was a struggle to get upright but with Nick helping she managed. As she stood on legs which felt as though they didn't belong to her, Emma glanced down, noting the shredded cut-off slacks and ripped blouse held together by two buttons, all the others having been torn from their anchors. There were cuts and grazes almost everywhere she looked. Blood was beginning to ooze from several different places, soaking through the fraying fabric of her clothes.

'I've never been so terrified in all my life,' she managed to stutter out. 'He must have just missed us. Are you all right?'

'I think I'm alive,' Nick gasped on a wince, 'but I hurt all over.'

Emma couldn't hold it together any longer, bursting into tears while grasping a firm hold around Nick's waist for support. Great tremors wracked her body as Nick assisted her into a large room, easing her down into the soft leather of the sofa. The other man followed, rushing forward to pull a couple of cushions out of the way.

'Let me see the damage,' said the man, Emma presumed was Matt, as he knelt in front of her and reached out to touch her.

When Emma recoiled, Nick laid a hand on her arm. 'Emma, Matt and I went to school together. He's a doctor so let him check you over.'

Matt felt her limbs to ensure there were no broken bones. Even though she felt as though every single one had been crushed into dust, all seemed to be intact. He called out to his wife to bring towels and a bowl of warm water. She came out in her dressing gown, took one look at Emma and promptly disappeared again to gather all her husband asked for.

Nick perched on the edge next to Emma, grasping her hand as he leant towards her. With utmost gentleness, he wiped the tears from her eyes with the corner of his own bloodied and torn T-shirt. While Matt worked, Nick rang Caroline to pick them up. All Emma could think of while he talked was, thank God, because there was no way she was going out there again to become a bullseye target for the maniacal Greg.

Matt worked from the top down. Emma's face was unscathed, but her bare arms were badly grazed on the tender underside where they had skidded along the concrete pavement. Matt bathed, patted her skin dry and plastered the worst of her cuts to stem any bleeding. Moving to her midriff, he asked permission to inspect those areas hidden by the remnants of her clothing.' She winced when she noted the number of nasty areas already darkening to the colour of deep bruises, but she couldn't see any major damage requiring surgery, even though it felt like she needed a skin transplant and being knocked unconscious for about a week.

Wincing in pain, Emma stood to remove what was left of her tattered slacks while Nick draped a towel around her as she sat again. The front of her legs looked like they had been gone over by a cheese grater but nothing deep enough to require stitches, although it looked as though there weren't any solid patches of skin for sutures to hold onto. She ended up looking like a patchwork quilt with different sized plasters stuck to her multi-coloured skin.

A gasp of shock from the open doorway broke the intense silence. 'What on earth happened?' asked Caroline.

'Saunders tried to run us down. How he didn't kill us I don't know,' Nick said while still holding Emma's hand clutched in his as though he didn't dare let her go. She wasn't going to complain about the tight grip for it seemed to anchor her.

'He didn't kill us because of you, Nick. You saved my life. I froze, too scared to move,' Emma replied, her voice quivering. 'Can we go home? I need to lie down; I ache all over.' She tugged her hand back and stood, swaying at first before finding her balance. She groaned at the first step towards Caroline as she tugged the towel tight around her waist. Far out, she was wearing nothing but underwear and a shredded shirt which revealed more than it covered but she was too sore to care.

After thanking Matt, Nick assisted the jelly-kneed Emma outside to the car. Every step felt like the pavement was made of springy goop. After settling her in the front seat he waited for Caroline to fold into the driver's seat before clambering into the back. Once home, he settled Emma on her bed. 'You can't shower yet, because I'm sure Steve might want photos of your injuries. I'll send Caro in to help you dress in clean clothes. I'll be back in a few minutes.'

When Caroline arrived a few seconds later, she carried a pair of soft tracksuit pants and a T-shirt. Every movement while Caroline assisted her to change, had Emma wincing in pain. She was more than glad when she was able to lie down to rest her stinging body.

When Nick returned, Steve accompanied him. Going over the sequence of events took ten times as long as when it happened. A few seconds of reality took a long time to relate, after which the police photographer was called in to photograph the injuries. At last they left her in peace to shower but first she needed to lie down and not move a single millimetre for ever. The front of her legs stung, her muscles ached, her scrapes smarted, and the rest of her just plain hurt.

She was still there when Nick returned about half an hour later. As he knelt by her side, his sucked in breath indicated his own agony. He gently traced the outline of her face with two fingers. 'Have a shower. You'll feel a little better. I'll get Caro to help you while I make you a warm milky drink. Matt said a couple of painkillers would ease the pain and help you sleep. Personally, I need someone to hit me with a sledgehammer to make sure I'm out to it for the next twenty-four hours. My body is protesting but yours is in far worse condition.'

The shower was what she would describe as agony and ecstasy at the same time. The flowing warm water running over her skin felt amazing while every tiny movement sent stabbing pain shooting along every damaged nerve fibre and there must have been millions of them. She ended up standing still while Caroline gently dabbed away grime and blood. After turning off the taps, Caroline patted Emma dry with a soft towel before easing a cotton nightgown over her head and carefully shimmied it into place. Emma's elbow was held while she shuffled to the bed where she sank onto the cool sheet and stilled, willing her mind to switch off so she could slip into unconsciousness.

Chapter Nine

Waking, Emma peered through the gloom of the darkened room, not having a clue where she was. She twisted her head, groaning when the sudden movement reminded her about the previous night's activities in no uncertain terms. Hearing a sound, she turned over carefully, slowly, to avoid the agony of stiff, sore muscles. Her eyes settled on Nick sitting sprawled in a chair across the room. He was watching her.

'Good morning, sleeping beauty. You had nightmares during the night and screamed the house down, so I stayed with you. How do you feel? I'm as stiff as a marble statue and feel like I've been run over by a very large bulldozer, so I imagine you must feel worse. I assume you need the bathroom, so I'll help you up then leave you in peace for a few minutes.'

Moaning under his breath as he moved over to the bed, he gave Emma his arm to hold on to while she pulled herself up. She winced at every movement but held back her groans. After assisting her to the bathroom door he continued down the passage towards the kitchen. Emma took her time, sucking in her breath when she shuffled towards the sound of chinking china coming from the kitchen.

'Nick,' she called.

He turned from the bench. 'Emma, go back to bed and rest.'

'No, I'm up now and I'm sure my muscles will stiffen even more if I don't keep moving. Can you hold me for a while?' she asked.

Nick gingerly walked across the tiles, reached his arms around then eased her close. 'Go and sit on the lounge. I'll take a coffee into Caro and then bring ours in there.'

They sat together on the lounge while sipping hot coffee, saying nothing. Nick took the empty mug from her hand, placed both mugs on the coffee table and edged up one end of the sofa. He eased Emma down, so she was lying stretched out with her head on his lap. It felt good when he brushed his fingers through her hair. 'Show me your stomach and legs.' Edging up her top, she revealed the dark bruises and streaked red grazes on her abdomen.

'Pretty colours which match mine. I guess there won't be any more tangoing for a while. Pity.' Nick's attempt at a joke hit its mark, eliciting a smile from Emma.

'We need to discuss a few things. What about tonight? Do you want to cancel it?'

After thinking for a moment, she shook her head. 'No. We might as well be sitting in a restaurant as here and we need to eat in any case. It's going to ache regardless of what we're doing or where we are. I'll take a couple of painkillers and take it easy. Definitely no dancing though. Justin rearranged his shifts at work especially for tonight and it's the last time I'll see Sandy for ages.'

'The other thing is you going home. I spoke with Steve and he doesn't think it will be safe for you to drive such a long distance alone. You are in no fit state to be undertaking such a long drive in any case. How about flying? A lot of farms have their own landing strips – do you know of any near your farm?'

'Yes, there's one on the place next door. They use it mainly for crop dusting.'

'If I can organise a private flight for you, can someone pick you up? But it may not be tomorrow. We may have to wait a couple of days.'

It took a mammoth effort to sit upright but Emma managed. She turned towards Nick, the sudden movement causing her to suck in her breath when pain hit. 'Yes, of course, Mum or Dad would pick me up, but you don't have to organise a flight for me. I can wait a few days until I feel a bit better and drive.'

'You are not driving. You have, how many hundreds of kilometres on quiet country roads? Five, six? Greg knows where you are going and when. Since Steve can't find any sign of him, it's possible Greg could be on his way there now, setting up an ambush. He was deadly serious last night, and I mean deadly and I don't think he's going to walk away now. Steve feels the same. Regardless of how you feel, it's not safe for you to be driving around by yourself until this cretin is caught. For your information, Steve is sending someone down your way to talk to townsfolk and show around a picture. Caro found a photo of you all at some function. If anyone asks after you, they are to ring the police.'

'I hardly think it's necessary to go to such extremes.'

'I do and so does Steve. This is very serious. He's tried to kill you twice now apart from the attempted rape. Personally, I'd prefer it if you stayed here, but I know you need to be with your family. You'll have to tell them what is going on so they can be alert.'

'I'll be helping Dad with the harvest, so I'll either be out in the middle of a huge paddock driving an equally huge harvester or at home asleep.'

'The very thought of you doing anything alone scares me witless. One other thing, Steve wants us at the scene of the crime to walk through what happened so they can fill in the finer details. Do you feel up to it? We could walk to Matt's place but quite frankly, I don't have the gumption to be putting my body on the line again. I don't mind admitting how petrified I was last night. We'll drive around the corner when Steve calls.'

Emma settled down again with her head on Nick's lap. 'Nick, did you get any sleep last night?'

'Yes, I slept on and off. Every time I shut my eyes, I saw that flaming car heading for us and I figured it was what you were seeing in your sleep. You kept calling out and thrashing around. Don't be alarmed when I tell you this, but I slept with a gorgeous tango dancer in my arms.' His smile was enigmatic. 'It was all above board. I was wrapped up in a cocoon of my quilt to keep you safe.' He smiled at her blush. 'Emma, I would never, ever do anything to harm you in any way. You needed comforting so I held you. You were literally screaming at the top of your voice in your sleep. Caro will back me up although she did raise her eyebrows when I told her I was sleeping with you, but she knew I wouldn't hurt you. Now how about the breakfast I promised you?' Easing upwards he retreated to the kitchen to prepare breakfast, his awkward cautious steps the only indication of his discomfort.

It took Emma ages to dress, with every slight movement agonising. She was shuffling back down the passage to rejoin Nick when Caroline emerged. The three sat at the kitchen table chatting about the night before. They had barely finished eating when Steve rang.

At the scene, a shudder travelled from the top of Emma's body down to her feet when she eased out of the car. She didn't really want to be there but figured she had little choice. Steve had them walk through last night's events. Standing in the middle of the road facing the direction from where the car had come caused Emma to tremble. She was amazed at the distance Nick had pulled her when he leapt out of the way. There were several sets of tyre marks on the road and on the verge in front of Matt Jones' place, which enabled the police to take measurements and do calculations as to speed and directions.

Nick kept his arm around her the entire time, giving her a gentle squeeze of encouragement every time she shuddered. When Steve had completed his investigations, Emma was more than thankful to be able to return home.

Entering the kitchen to take a couple of painkillers before going out for her farewell dinner, Emma found Nick doing the same. He looked at her in admiration, removed two tablets from the foil and handed them to her. It wasn't often she took medication but this time she welcomed the two painkillers.

The restaurant was packed. It was not so upmarket but was always popular because the food was good and affordable to uni students. Sandy, Peter and Justin were already seated when they arrived. Justin stood to greet Caroline with a hug and kiss before settling her down beside him. Being the last to arrive, Emma and Nick were forced to take the last two chairs opposite each other at the table set for six. As the night wore on, Emma's inhibitions vanished. The only times she felt self-conscious were when she glanced up to see Nick watching her.

They stayed longer than intended with Nick having to coax Emma away, leaving Caroline with Justin to return home together. Once home Emma perched on a bench stool while Nick prepared a nightcap of milky hot chocolate. 'I'm going to miss you, more than I care to admit. If Mum and Dad weren't coming home on Monday, I'd drive you to the farm myself, but I would still have to leave you and it would be just as difficult.'

Placing his mug on the eatery bench he cupped his hands on either side of her face, staring into her eyes. Her heart soared when he bent his head and brushed his lips against her mouth. It felt so wonderful until he stood back. It was ridiculous the way she felt the loss although he didn't remove his hands, keeping a tiny thread of connection.

With a curious warmth spiralling through her, causing her hands to quiver, Emma settled her mug on the bench to avoid spilling her hot chocolate. With a mind of their own, her arms crept around his neck as she rested her head on his shoulder. She felt Nick's arms move around her, tightening his grip, drawing her closer. They remained in the embrace, giving her heady sensations which thrilled her. This is what a real relationship felt like. Lord, but what a fool she'd been to have even gone out with Greg one single time.

She felt confused by seesawing emotions. Standing in the security of Nick's arms she very much wanted to stay exactly where she was forever; it felt so amazing. She knew for certain she was going to miss Nick a great deal. At the same time, she felt concerned about the rapidity in which they had grown so close. Niggling doubt began gnawing away. What if this was only some infatuation? What if Nick sought out someone else the minute she left? Maybe, as soon as she was gone, he would do the same with someone else; go to the pub, pick up some girl sitting alone, ask her out. They'd only known each other a week, nowhere near long enough for either of them to know if this was a lasting attraction. And she would be gone for at least six more weeks–possibly longer, depending on how long the harvest took and whether she found local work. There was no way in this world a gorgeous wealthy hunk of a man like Nick would wait so long for a nonentity like her.

Nick couldn't possibly only want her. In the blink of an eye, her confidence took a nosedive. It would be far better to say goodbye now and not let the night linger. Much as she wanted more, she couldn't allow things to go any further. It would make it so much harder to let go. It was already too hard.

Lifting her head, she felt so much tenderness as she stared into his eyes but surely he didn't feel the same. He couldn't, especially since she was way out of his class. Stretching up she planted a soft kiss on his mouth. Goodbye, Nick, she thought. Before he had a chance to deepen the kiss, she dropped her hands from his waist, ducked under his arms and shuffled to her bedroom, moisture brimming in her eyes. Once she reached her bed, Emma let her tears flow, having convinced herself there was no future for them together.

She heard him tap at the closed door but ignored the knocks as well as the repeated calling of her name.

Up before dawn, she stripped her bed, shoved the linen into the washer and locked herself in her room while she finished packing until all she had left was a pile of gifts. She peeked down the passage to ensure Nick wasn't around before carrying the carefully wrapped gifts to Caroline's room where she knocked, waited and entered at Caroline's husky call.

'Can you put these under your Christmas tree?'

'Sure thing. How are you feeling?'

'I'm fine,' she lied. Embarrassed, she spun around and scooted back to her room where she latched her bags and tugged them out into the passage. She heard Nick when he picked the bags up to take them out to the car. A few minutes later she held her breath when there was a knock at the door. She prayed it wasn't Nick but at the same time hoped it was, then cursed herself for being such an idiot. A sigh escaped when Caroline stuck her head in the door.

'Come on, Mouse, why so sad? You'll be seeing your parents in a couple of hours, but they'll send you straight back with your long face. What's wrong?'

'I'm fine, truly. I'm looking forward to being with the family for Christmas. Let's go.' She forced the brightness to her voice, but Caroline's look told her she hadn't done such a good job. She spied Nick straighten from leaning against the wall at the end of the passage. The moment she caught his eye, she turned away, avoiding eye contact with him.

The silence during the drive to the airport was profound, only broken when they neared the terminal. 'Drop me off and keep going so you don't have to find a parking spot,' Emma insisted.

By way of answer, Nick kept driving until he reached the car park. He carried Emma's bags, leading the way to the counter where she was to meet the pilot of her small plane. After her bags were weighed, the pilot waited while Emma said her goodbyes giving Caroline a long hug while she figured a way to escape without getting close to Nick. As she pulled away and turned to flee, Caroline gave her a little shove into Nick's arms, laughing as she strode away to give them privacy.

Resisting Emma's struggle to free herself from his embrace, Nick held her close until she gave in. Head hung low, she felt him place his fingers on either side of her face, forcing her to look at him. 'Emma, please listen to me for a moment. I have no idea what I did last night to cause this impasse between us but my heart is already aching for you. I'm going to miss you a great deal. I never believed it was possible for this to happen and have always scoffed at people who have told me it could, but the other night when I thought I was going to lose you, I knew I was in love with you. I know it sounds crazy, because we only met a week ago, but please believe me when I tell you, I love you, Emma.'

Everything inside her lit up like she'd been struck by a lightning bolt. Maybe this could work. She flung her arms around his neck. The kiss they shared was intense and passionate continuing on until a loud clearing of the throat from the pilot to hurry them up was heard. Emma jerked away with her cheeks flaming.

'For the first time ever, I don't want to go home. I'm going to miss you too.'

She turned away, her eyes brimming with tears. Even though he called after her as she limped across the polished tiles, she didn't dare glance back as she followed the pilot out to the small plane.

Chapter Ten

A raft of emotions flooded through her while Emma flew southwards. Finding it hard to believe Nick's amazing words, she wished they'd had more time together to talk. Despite what he'd said, she still had misgivings. What concerned her the most was the short time they had known each other. It had only been a week – but so much had happened in those seven days, much of it ghastly so maybe she was over-reacting to the good bits. Was it only infatuation they felt for each other? Was it possible for two people to fall in love in such a short space of time? Joy turned to sadness at the thought of them having to spend so long apart but feelings of ecstasy followed, knowing she would soon be home with her parents.

When the plane landed Emma alighted to see both Mum and Dad standing arm-in-arm along the edge of the rough gravel runway. They'd always been close, never hiding the physical joy of touching each other and the sight gave Emma more to think about. It was the same type of love she yearned for, when she found the right man to marry but could Nick be the man? How would she know?

Agonising pain in her legs made it impossible to run towards her much loved parents but she forced as normal a gait as she could, attempting not to show the pain she was in; pain which was forgotten the moment she was enveloped in long tight hugs. It felt so darn good to be home.

The pilot handed two bags to her father who carried them while Emma strode alongside her mother to the waiting car. It was only a short journey home before Emma was back in her old bedroom, which her mother had kept unchanged. The last time she had been home was six months earlier but only for a short stay because she needed the facilities of the university library to study for her final exams and complete all her assignments. Sinking down onto the side of her bed, Emma stared at all those familiar items of her childhood, a sense of warmth tingled from deep inside, happiness filled her heart – she was home.

Her joy was short lived. Over a much-missed home cooked dinner, Emma felt her heart turn to a lump of lead when told the farm had been sold due to her father's ill health–a heart condition requiring a lot less work with no stress. They were to harvest the year's crop, while the bulk of the sheep had already been sold and her parents were retiring to the city. Feelings of anger because she hadn't been told of her father's condition, swept through her.

'We only kept the news from you until after you'd finished your exams–we didn't want there to be any distractions,' Jeannie said as she sat between her husband and daughter, a hand on each person's arm.

'You still should have told me, Mum.'

'Normally we would have, Em, but in this instance your final exams were more important to us.' Bob Nicholls smiled. Emma knew it was to soften his words, but she felt anything but happy. 'It's done now, so there's no point in labouring over our decision. I'm happy to have you home for a while.' He leant over and hugged her, which felt downright wonderful but didn't ease her chagrin one iota. She should have been told.

Sucking in the familiar aroma of her father, Emma wallowed in the comfort of his hug. I can't tell them about Greg, she thought. They don't need the added stress of my problems–not now. He won't find me here.

'What's this?' Her mother's alarmed voice brought Emma's head up at the same time as she felt her arm being lifted. Guilt suffused her.

'Err, I slipped over in the street a couple of days ago.' She forced a laugh. 'Tripped over the kerb.' She dragged her arm down to avoid closer inspection. It's not really a lie, she added in her mind as she crossed the fingers of one hand behind her back. If they can keep important information from me so my mind doesn't wander from my studies, I can do the same so Dad doesn't worry.

By spending twelve hours on the harvester each day, Emma took on the bulk of the work to lighten her father's workload to the extent he didn't spend any time harvesting. Spending every day out in the paddocks, she refused to take a day off. The work exhausted her; her fatigue giving her one upside–she was so darn tired each night, she was ensured of a deep sleep, keeping her nightmares at bay. Despite the summer heat she wore jeans all the time to keep her other injuries hidden.

Much to her delight, Nick rang every evening. But to avoid explanations, she carried her mobile phone outside to chat to him in private. Each time she hung up, she sat in quiet contemplation; missing him so much her heart physically ached.

After the first week, her very astute mother caught her when she returned inside from one of her long conversations with Nick.

'What's his name, Em?' Her mother's quiet voice from the shadows startled Emma.

'What do you mean, Mum?'

'Sweetheart, you can't hide it from me. Who is the man who has stolen my daughter's heart?' Grasping Emma by the hand Jeannie steered her into a kitchen chair. 'I've never seen you look so forlorn. He rings you every night, your face lights up when you hear the phone ring. You sneak outside looking over the moon but come inside looking like the end of the world has arrived. It can only be a man.'

Although she felt embarrassed, Emma knew her mother would keep at her until she had all the details, especially since they had never kept things from each other. 'It's Caroline's brother, Nick. He recently arrived back from overseas, where he's been since before I met Caroline at university. Mum, I only met him about a week ago and yet I feel like I've known him forever. He makes me feel so special and treats me as if I am special and yet I'm not. I'm just ordinary.'

'You are very special. How does he feel about you? Sorry, it's obvious he feels quite a lot since he rings you every night.'

Emma didn't answer. How could she tell her mother what Nick had said the last time she had seen him; words he repeated every time they spoke? She only knew for sure how much she missed him–so much it physically hurt.

'How can you be sure you love someone, especially if you have only recently met them?' she asked, feeling embarrassed but she didn't know why she should: this was her mum.

'I guess you can never be a hundred percent certain, but I fell in love with your father almost the moment I met him. I had a lot of dreams and aspirations on what I wanted to do with my life, but the moment I met Dad, none of those dreams mattered. I would do anything, if it was with your father. I wasn't wrong. I still love him as much now as I did when we met. You don't have to know a person a long time to know they are right for you. I knew it was right between us. I guess I was as confused as you to start with. I wasn't even as old as you are now and I hadn't had many boyfriends to compare Dad with, but it didn't take me long to figure it out. You don't have to stay here you know. If you think it important to go back, we would understand. Your happiness is important to us and we'll be in the city soon in any case. Why don't you go back?'

'I came home to help out and since Dad isn't well, I'll stay till the crop is off and help you pack everything. I'm staying until after Christmas. If it's right between Nick and me, he'll wait, but I do miss him so very much.'

Emma drove across the low tan stubble of the back paddock, stopping to shut the gate on the remaining flock of sheep. She swept across the fallow home paddock around into the large open-fronted shed to park the old utility. Too tired to move, she sat for a few minutes, fighting for the energy to go inside. The day harvesting had been long, dusty and hot. She itched from the bits of chaff which always seemed to find a way between skin and clothing no matter what precautions you took, including spending most of the day cocooned inside the air-conditioned cab. Emptying the grain into the bins was when the heat and dust crept into her pores and ever-present flying scraps of dried stalks snuck down her back and front, even under the tightness of her underwear. Knowing she had to find the energy to walk across the yard and get inside, she clambered out of the utility carrying a thermos and small polystyrene cooler box then began striding towards the house.

She stopped mid-stride when she spied a familiar looking car parked near the house. It had to be Greg. Oh, God, no!

Her parents didn't know about him so he must have inveigled his way in. What lies did he tell? Oh, Lord. Not knowing what else she could do, she spun around and returned to the car she'd been driving. She ran the final few steps, flung the door open and sped off. When her mobile phone rang, she was in two minds about answering until she realised Greg didn't know she even had a phone and he certainly wouldn't know the number. It had to be Mum or Dad. Snatching it up, she slid the green marker and planted the instrument against her ear.

'Dad?' she asked.

'Emma, come back to the house. It's me, Nick. The car is a hire car. Sweetness, I'm dying to hold you in my arms.'

It was the endearment which stopped Emma in her tracks. She slammed on the brakes, sending a huge cloud of red dust billowing into the air, then sat for a moment, hardly daring to believe her ears. Only Nick called her Sweetness. Spinning the wheels in the gravel, she turned the utility around one hundred and eighty degrees and raced back to the way she had come. Not bothering to put the car away, she drove as far up to the house as she could before slamming her foot down hard on the brake pedal, bringing the car to a sudden halt and creating another enormous dust cloud. Sitting perfectly still she stared through the windscreen, waiting for the dust to settle before climbing out. She took a few tentative steps.

'Nick,' she whispered while she stood staring at the tall, blond man waiting under cover of the back veranda, her parents each side of him.

'Nick,' she yelled louder. Her steps quickened as she ran towards the wide-open arms.

'Oh, Nick,' she whispered when those strong, welcoming arms wrapped around her and she was lifted off her feet while his warm lips ravished her mouth. As her feet touched the ground again she flung her arms around him, hugging tight.

When at last, the kiss ended and they came up for air, Nick kept Emma held close. 'I've missed you, Sweetness, much more than I ever thought I could.'

'What are you doing here? You never said anything last night. But I'm so glad you are here. I've missed you so much.'

'Your mother invited me to stay for a week, so I said yes.'

'Mum invited you, have you been talking to Mum on the phone? A week? You're staying a whole week? Oh, Nick,' she rambled on, still in a state of shock, still held firm against his hard chest.

He eventually released her and held her away from him while his eyes roamed over every centimetre of her body, absorbing every detail. What must he think with her hair tied in two tiny bunches on either side of her face and she was covered in grime and dust? She stank of fresh wheat grain which clung to her hair and clothes and there was probably a stench of sour sweat along with putrid body odour.

'You look so beautiful, Sweetness,' he said as he pulled her back into his arms.

'I'm filthy dirty and itchy from the straw. Let me have a shower and then I'm going to have severe words with Mum, and with you.'

Nick laughed as she swung her arm around his waist and together they walked inside, stopping only long enough for Emma to remove her scruffy old work boots at the back door. She showered in record time, emerging dressed in a clean pair of jeans and a more respectable T-shirt than was her normal attire in the evenings after a hard day's work. Jeannie was busy serving up the evening meal at the large kitchen table, while Nick and her father were standing, leant against the wall chatting when Emma walked into the roomy kitchen. A long arm snaked out capturing her when she tried to walk past the two men. Pulling Emma close, Nick planted a quick kiss on her lips.

'I have two weeks of being without you to make up for, Sweetness. Don't think I'll be far from your side for the next week.'

'Might be a bit hard on the harvester. There's only one seat,' Emma quipped with cheek.

'He's got you to himself tomorrow morning. You're taking the morning off. I'm going out on the machine,' she heard her father say from behind her left ear.

'No, Dad, you need to rest,' protested Emma as she wrenched free from Nick's tight embrace.

'I've done nothing but rest since you arrived home. You need a break. Half a day isn't going to harm me.' He turned to Nick, who was reeling Emma back into his arms. 'Emma has been harvesting twelve hours a day, every day since she came back home.'

Nick glanced at Emma with a quizzical frown. 'You still haven't told them, have you? How did you manage to climb up the harvester ladder when you could barely walk?'

Emma sent him a startled and irate look.

'Well, Sweetness, your parents have to know so either you tell them–or I will. If Greg turns up here, they need to know.'

'Sit down, Emma,' ordered her father in a tone brooking no refusal. 'I want to know exactly what is going on. Now, and don't spare me the details because of my heart. I'll worry more not knowing everything.'

Emma sent Nick looks of ice as she obeyed her father. She started talking but glossed over the details to make light of the situation, for her father's sake.

'Enough, Emma,' Nick interrupted as he slid two fingers over her lips. 'You're not giving any details.'

'Dad's heart.'

'The only stress my heart is under at this moment, is knowing you are keeping things from me. Maybe, Nick, you should relate all the details – implicitly.'

For the next five minutes Nick explained everything in vivid detail while Emma sank back into her seat with her head down, eyes closed and an increasing sense of mortification.

'Those bruises on Emma's arms were nothing compared to the ones on her legs and body. The police are still looking for Greg and Madam here—was supposed to tell you all this because she is still in danger. Greg knew she was coming down here and knew what town, but he didn't know the exact location of your farm.'

Nick placed two fingers under Emma's chin and tugged so her head was at eye level, but she refused to open her eyes. 'I think I've given most of the detail. Anything you want to add, Miss Nicholls?'

The tone of Nick's voice indicated she was in trouble, so she simply shook her head, not daring to look.

'That explains something,' interrupted her father. 'Bill Thwaites rang me to let me know there was a stranger in town asking details about Emma.'

Those words did cause her eyes to take on a will of their own and fly apart.

'I believe the police have spoken to all the shopkeepers in town as well as shown them a photograph of Greg,' said Nick. 'If he asked about Emma's whereabouts, they were to let the police know and plead ignorance about her. I need to ring Steve. It seems I have come in time.'

He turned towards Emma. 'You are not to drive anywhere alone, even on the farm. In fact, you don't step outside at all without someone else.'

'And you carry a loaded rifle with you at all times, Em,' added her father.

Nick looked startled; his gasp of shock very audible. 'Rifle!'

Emma grinned at the same time as her father said, 'Emma is a crack shot. She's been using a gun since she was a youngster. We always keep a rifle locked in each farm vehicle to kill aggressive snakes or put down an animal in distress. They are always unloaded but we keep a few bullets in the glove box. I wouldn't want her aiming at me – she wouldn't miss. She can drop a wild dog in flight from quite a distance and would outshoot me in a competition.'

He turned to Emma. 'Lock the harvester door from the inside and keep the rifle by your side. I'm not asking, take it as an order. Someone else is to drive you out to the paddocks and bring you back each time. And remember the distress signal – use it.'

He twisted to face Nick. 'Emma is safe in the harvester. It has a lockable door and it takes a lot to climb up to the cabin. You can see anyone coming for quite a distance when you sit up there. The signal is three long blasts from the horn. It's a loud horn. Sally and Brian will be home from boarding school next week. They can take over the harvesting and you can take Emma back with you. I want her safe.'

'Dad?' begged Emma, feeling more than a little stunned at the turn of events. 'I'm home for Christmas.'

'We'll worry about Christmas later. Your safety is far more important than a family Christmas dinner. Maybe by then this creep will be caught. Thank you, Nick for enlightening us. I have one question, Em. No, make it two. How could you get tangled up with such a character and what sort of relationship did the two of you have?'

Emma knew she was blushing bright red as she squirmed in her seat. 'We went out together a few times, never anything more.'

Bob Nicholls turned his eyes to look at Nick, seeking more to Emma's answer, as though he knew she wasn't telling everything.

'From what Caro told me, they saw each other for about six months, but he never really took her out on any meaningful dates. Usually to watch him play hockey followed by several hours at the pub. Caro feels sure it was never a physical relationship and Emma tells me she only went out with him because she was lonely and no one else ever asked her out on a date.' His voice softened, 'I find it hard to believe. Such a beautiful woman not being pursued by a bevy of men. Caroline tells me it was her intense shyness preventing men from asking her out.'

'Emma, shy?' asked her bewildered mum. 'We can't be talking about the same girl.'

Nick grasped Emma's hand in his and looked as though he was enjoying her embarrassed, pleading looks. 'No, Caro said you wouldn't believe it, but I'm rather glad Emma has kept her horde of admirers at bay by pretending to be shy.'

Emma had had enough. 'Do you people mind if we eat and change the subject from talking about me as though I'm not here? I'm starving.'

Laughing at her daughter's discomfiture, Jeannie went to the oven to retrieve the meals she had kept warm. After the food had been consumed, Bob went outside and didn't come back for so long, Emma began to worry until she heard him on the veranda.

Left alone, Emma did her best to chastise Nick, but was soon silenced when his kisses melted her resolve and her words.

Chapter Eleven

Up at her usual crack of dawn, Emma urged her father to stay at home while she went out to the paddock, but he insisted she have the morning with Nick, and re-iterated repeatedly that either Nick or her mother was to drive her out to the paddock when she relieved him at lunchtime. After moping around the house waiting for Nick to rouse, she finally decided to do what Caroline had once suggested. She made him a cup of coffee. After carrying the steaming mug down the passage, she hesitated before opening his door. What if he was naked? To make sure, she stuck one eye around the door frame.

'Good morning, sweetness,' said a voice, causing her to almost drop the coffee.

'Nick, you frightened me. Since you're awake you won't be needing this,' she retorted as she turned away.

'Ah, but I need something to really get me going so I'll have the energy to get up and spend time with my gorgeous girl. Otherwise I might need to linger here until lunchtime.'

'I could always find some ice cubes,' Emma quipped with a cheeky smile as she pushed the door open wide and stepped inside.

'Coffee and the sight of you are far more gentle ways to wake me up. I still owe you for your little prank, don't I?'

Emma handed over the coffee, which Nick took in one hand, grasping her arm with his other. He placed the coffee on the bedside table, sat up and pulled Emma onto the bed against his bare chest. She was trapped while he kissed her but the sensuous feel of his skin and warmth of his kiss sent her head spinning until she was suddenly released.

'You need to get out before I lose control.' The strained huskiness of his voice had her step back in confusion. As she lifted her eyes, she noticed the covers had slipped down to his waist only barely covering the bulge of his arousal. Unable to handle the intense inner responses her body was making, she fled from the room seeking somewhere to hide. The nearest room was the bathroom where she leant against the back of the shut door, her chest heaving. Even drowning her heated face under running cold water didn't seem to make any difference, especially when he chuckled as he passed her in the passage as he made his way to the bathroom while she headed for the kitchen.

Slow sips of coffee gave her the time needed to cool her ardour before daring to face another soul, especially her parents. Her mother would be able to read her like a book. To ensure she wasn't caught with a sappy look on her face she set about preparing breakfast. At least concentrating on not burning scrambled eggs would push the vision of Nick's state of arousal from her mind. It worked until he arrived.

'Even a cold shower didn't work so well, my sweet.'

Her face flamed again while he had the gall to laugh. She kept her back turned while plating up fluffy eggs on toast. It took several sucked in breaths before she was game to turn around to place the loaded plate in front of him. To ensure she didn't so much as touch him, she plonked her plate on the other end of the table.

'It's a good job you're keeping so far away,' he said after swallowing his first mouthful.

Emma choked. 'Please don't.'

He laughed. 'Sweetness, surely you're not so innocent you don't realise exactly what the sight of you does to me? You come from a farm. What happens when you put a ram into a paddock of ewes, or a stallion in with a herd of mares?' His smile was devilish. 'You've had the same effect on me since I first saw you in the hotel.'

'Far out, please give it a rest?' Emma stood and fled the kitchen, sucking in great lungsful of cool morning air as she leant against the veranda wall. The sun had barely risen above the horizon so hadn't had the chance yet to rid the ground of the layer of moist dew which sparkled like precious gems. She shivered as the cold settled onto overheated skin. The fly-screen door squeaked as it opened. Emma dared a peek to her side. Nick stood there looking mollified.

'Sorry, come and eat your breakfast. I promise to behave.'

She didn't dare say a word but eased her stance and followed him back inside where she was overjoyed when he took his plate to the sink, rinsed it off and left so she could eat in peace.

The morning was fabulous, exploring some of the more attractive parts of the farm. It saddened her knowing she probably wouldn't see any of the beauty spots again since the farm was changing hands on New Year's Day. She was thankful she had grabbed her mother's digital camera and used it to take a raft of photos so she could make up an album of memories. She had been taking photos for the past two weeks but now she could include Nick in her shots.

Back at the house, Emma changed into old jeans and a long-sleeved cotton shirt, covering as much of her body as possible to avoid the itch from the cut stalks. Well it would do as an excuse for it was more of a need to keep her exposed skin out of Nick's sight. After an early lunch, Nick drove her to the paddock they were in the process of harvesting. She had tried to sneak away by herself, but Nick had caught her and insisted she be driven.

Nick dropped her off at the top of the paddock next to the portable wheat bins where Emma would pick up the harvester when her father completed his round, stopping to empty the wheat into the bin. His utility was parked between the rusty wire strands of the fence and the huge galvanised metal bins, which afforded the car little protection from the searing sun. Leaving Emma sitting in her father's car with the door wide open to let the heat escape, Nick drove away. She picked up the rifle from behind the seat and settled it across her lap.

A smile hovered as she leant against the back of the seat with one foot resting on the doorsill and the other on the ground. Seeing Nick again only reinforced her surety about how deeply she felt for him. Basking in euphoria it took her several minutes to realise something was wrong. She sprang out the door of the utility listening with her ears attuned to every sound.

Something wasn't right.

The sounds she heard didn't bother her – Nick driving around the edge of the paddock behind her, a small flock of colourful parrots squabbling over spilled seed under the wheat bin, a plane high up in the sky on its normal route from the Eastern states – all those sounds should have been there. But there should have been another sound, and it was the absence of the header rumble which sent a wave of fear shuddering through her body. She scrabbled into her jeans pocket and slid out her mobile phone, dialling Nick's number.

'Nick, come back,' she yelled when he answered. 'Something is wrong. I can't hear the harvester and it is never turned off during the day. Hurry. Drive around the paddock until you find me. I'm going to look for Dad.' Not wanting to waste a single second, she slammed the phone shut, jumped back into the utility and reached over to the passenger seat, her fingers curling around the barrel of the rifle as she jammed her foot on the accelerator. Following her father's last cut up to the top of the small rise, she crested the top of the hill where she stopped, scanning the vast paddock until her eyes rested on the harvester, which had cut a large snaking swathe through the middle of the unharvested section of the crop.

'Oh, God,' she muttered and planted her foot back onto the accelerator, speeding down to the harvester which had gone on a wild ride down the slope and was now leant on an angle against the raised bank of the paddock dam. Her heart lodged in her mouth as she slammed on the brakes, skidded to a halt, grabbed the rifle and clambered up the ladder of the harvester. She had to jump up to the first step because of the angle, and after reaching the top had trouble pulling the door open.

Tears poured down her face while she grappled with the heavy door. It was one thing opening the door when the machine was standing upright in the paddock, it swung easily on well-oiled hinges, but on this angle, having to pull the door open at forty-five degrees while she could see her father slumped against the other side was a different thing entirely. The darn door was too heavy for her. Unable to tell if her father was dead or unconscious, panic set in. Her heart shot to her throat before rebounding like a yoyo several times.

'Dad, Dad!' she screamed as she tugged and tugged and tugged. All of a sudden, hands grabbed her around the waist, and she swung around with a tensed elbow to dislodge the interloper. A grunt blew into her ear as bone punched into hard flesh.

'Damn it, Emma, it's me.'

'Sorry,' she huffed as Nick hoisted her out of the way. He grasped the door handle, twisted and wrenched, his strength making a much easier job of it than Emma could manage. Reaching in, Nick stretched out to feel for a pulse on Bob's neck.

'He's alive but his pulse is weak,' Nick yelled while easing into the angled cabin, seeking footholds so he didn't squash the unconscious man. 'Phone your mother to get some medical assistance to be on its way while we get your father home. He may have had a heart attack.'

Tears flowed unchecked as she grappled for her phone. It was almost impossible to focus through the bleary moisture for her mother's number. Finally finding it, she jabbed down and waited what felt like forever before her mother answered. She gabbled what must have sounded like nonsense while she watched Nick struggle to lift the comatose man from behind the side of the seat. He managed to get Bob's upper torso onto the open doorway.

'Hold on tight,' Nick ordered, 'So he doesn't slip back in.'

Even though she was lean, Emma was strong, and didn't dare relax her hold until Nick was able to get some leverage with his shoulder under her father's body. With an almighty heave, Nick forced Bob up until most of his body was leant over the edge of the door. Emma grabbed her father's arms and gripped tight while Nick fought to untangle arms and legs so he could climb from the cabin. He pushed Bob's feet out while Emma did her best to ease the impact as her father rolled onto the running board.

After scrambling out of the cabin Nick swung his eyes from man to the ground and back to Bob, assessing the next move. 'Emma, maybe it would be best if you move the utility tray as close to the harvester as possible.'

Instead of scrambling down, she jumped, grunting at the impact then tumbling onto her backside. She swore as she stumbled upright and scrambled into the utility. After carefully easing the side of the utility tray against the harvester, she stood on the flat metal tray to guide her father down. Her breath held while she watched Nick. With a tight grip on Bob's hands, Nick used one foot to roll him off the edge. It took all his strength to take the brunt of Bob's fall. He straightened, bracing himself against the side of the cabin on the harvester. Bob's body shuddered while Nick absorbed the weight as it dropped down the side of the machine.

Emma guided her father to a lying position while Nick eased him down before releasing the tension on his muscles and let go. He clambered down from the harvester and dropped to his knees against the comatose man to check his pulse.

'Dear God, I can't feel a pulse. Quick, you drive while I tend to your father but take care and don't go bouncing us off the tray.'

Panic-stricken, Emma scrambled into the cabin of the still idling ute, jammed her foot on the accelerator and steered along the ruts rather than over them, while Nick knelt over Bob's abdomen, a knee each side and began CPR.

The drive back to the house was traumatic as Emma took a lot longer than normal to travel the few kilometres to avoid the worst of the bumps through the paddocks by driving along the firebreaks and keeping her speed down. She fought the desperation to plant her foot to get her father home sooner but knew she had to keep at a slow pace so he wasn't hurt, and Nick could continue with the CPR. All the while, she kept swinging her eyes to the rear vision mirrors, watching Nick work. She was sure she wouldn't have known what to do but if he was still pumping on Dad's chest, he must still be alive.

Noticing her tear streaked face in the mirror, she swept one forearm across her eyes, a little shocked she hadn't realised she was crying. To get rid of the rest of the moisture she lifted the hem of her T-shirt up and scrubbed at her face. Far out, she was being a wimp and tears were a waste of energy. She needed to be strong for Dad… and Mum.

When they approached the house, Emma spied her mum pacing backwards and forwards and knew how she felt. She drove around to the front of the house, going straight through the wire-mesh house-fence in order to get her father as close as possible. Multi-coloured chickens scattered in all directions as Emma bumped her way over the flattened fence and across the two garden beds, taking no heed of the few rose bushes her mother had nurtured for years. She heard Nick's muttered oaths as he bounced around the flat tray on his knees.

'Why don't you drive us right into his bedroom, while you're at it?' Nick yelled.

At his words, Emma jammed on the brakes, causing Nick to lose his balance, the momentum hurtling him over the edge of the tray. He glared at her while she helped him up from the destroyed garden bed, full of apologies. Jeannie helped Nick hoist Bob over his shoulder while Emma ran to open the rarely used front door, only to find it locked. Stunned she turned to her mother. 'Why is the door locked – we never lock this door.'

'Your father locked up the other night after we heard about what happened,' said Jeannie.

Nick muttered unrepeatable comments under his breath about unnecessary bumps, fences, chickens and garden beds while he carried Bob around to the back door. Once he reached the bedroom, Nick gently laid Bob on his bed. He scrambled up and straddled the man so he could continue CPR.

'The ambulance is on its way; it shouldn't be much longer. We have one every fifty kilometres and the nearest one was available. How is he?' Jeannie frantically fussed around her husband, gently touching his face while holding his hand and murmuring loving words he was unable to hear. She twisted her head then lowered it towards his mouth. 'He's breathing,' she whispered.

'I think he's coming around. See if you can find a damp flannel to wipe off some of this grime.' Nick didn't pause while he spoke but continued pumping the chest, only ceasing long enough to check for a pulse. 'At last,' he huffed out as he flopped back onto his heels. 'He's breathing on his own but keep a close watch on him.'

Tears of relief spurted as Emma and her mother sponged the worst of the dirt from Bob's face and arms, fussing over him until they heard the siren of the ambulance nearing.

Emma only relaxed when the ambulance was on its way with her dad under more expert care than she could provide. Her mum followed in her car, leaving Emma and Nick to look after the farm.

Crashing into an armchair in the corner of the room, Nick closed his eyes. Emma knelt on the floor in front of him, resting her head on his knees. 'Thank you, Nick, I couldn't have even got Dad out of the cabin by myself.'

Lifting one hand, Nick ruffled her hair. 'You would have managed. It's amazing how you can find super strength in a crisis. You did well. My only complaint was the flowerbeds. I thought I asked you to not throw us off the back. My poor mother has only seen a black and blue version of me since she arrived home. All my bruises from my last adventure with you have only just faded. I hate to think what she's going to say when she sees me with more bruises. She was delighted when she found out with whom I had fallen in love. It seems you hold a special place in her heart. She might change her mind now. Come up here.'

Bending forward, he grasped Emma's hands and drew her up to sit on his lap. After bestowing a sensuous kiss on her mouth, he relaxed back with her head against his shoulder, his arms wrapped around her. His chest was still heaving, and Emma could feel the rapid beat of his heart, which gradually slowed to a more normal rate as he rested.

It wasn't until the house phone rang that either stirred. Jeannie was on the other end of the line to let them know they had arrived at the regional hospital and gave details of Bob's major heart attack, explaining how well he was now doing thanks to Nick.

After refreshing showers, Nick suggested they return to the paddock to see if they could retrieve the harvester and get it going again. Exhaustion made her reluctant until she pictured the crazy path cut through the unharvested wheat. There was no reason for such a thing to happen.

Once they reached the skewed behemoth, Emma stood to the side and studied it.

'Nick, this machine has a panic control. It's an inbuilt safety mechanism for such a reason. The engine should have cut out way over the other side of the hill as soon as Dad released the controls. I think something else caused the machine to do what it did. When we get it backed out of here, I need to check it over.'

After showing Nick how to unhitch the cutters, they were able to remove them by dragging them out of the way using one of the utilities and a tow rope made from the ever-present tool box of necessary supplies kept in every farm vehicle for any emergency and there was always something going wrong when you were in the far reaches of a 10,000 acre property. With the angle the machine was on, movement was slow at first but gradually they were able to ease the cutters out of the way. The sudden release of tension caused the machine to right itself with an echoing thud resulting in rising dust which seemed to find its way to cling to every bead of sweat on her dripping skin. She swiped the grime from her eyes, spat out a mouthful of gritty dust, then climbed into the cabin to start the engine. With care and direction from Nick, she was able to reverse the huge machine, change gears and slowly drive it onto level ground although steering was difficult with the wheels determined to go in any direction but the way she steered.

After hauling up the engine covers with Nick's strength again being used, she went over the engine with precision, searching for any faults. As she worked, she explained how they had all learnt to undertake basic repairs to machinery while still in primary school. It was a necessity on a farm. She knew exactly what each component was and how they linked together.

When she found broken steering linkage, Emma pointed to what appeared to be fresh hacksaw marks. A whistle echoed when Nick inspected the links carefully.

'I think we need to call Steve. This has been deliberately cut. Have you got any spare parts? We can replace these so you can get the harvest finished, but I'll keep this part to show Steve. I think Greg has found you and has been watching. He expected you to be on the machine this morning.' Nick eyed her. 'Maybe your dad had his heart attack through the stress of not being able to control the machine. Come on, let's lock this thing up and get back to the house. Have you got those rifles handy? If Greg is around, we might need them. And you go nowhere by yourself. Do you understand?'

Emma didn't need Nick to give her any more warnings – she wasn't about to go anywhere without Nick clinging like a limpet to her side, along with a loaded rifle. Make that two loaded rifles, she thought, and maybe even the bathroom was going to need an armed guard – and the toilet.

After the harvester cabin was secured, the short walk to the two vehicles was made at a rapid rate, two sets of eyes darting in all directions for any sign of an obsessed maniac. Emma drove her father's utility ahead of Nick, who followed in the other car. All the while she scanned the horizon for any sign of any other person or vehicle. A loaded rifle lay along the seat, the butt snug against her thigh within easy reach.

Arriving at the house, they parked the cars close to the house, using Emma's new tract through the front garden as the main thoroughfare, but avoiding the now flattened flowerbeds. Emma managed a grin at the sound of Nick's muttered uncouth words as they passed the crumpled rose bushes, interspersed with broken gerberas and wilting pink and yellow daisies, which had parted company from the roots. Maybe Mum would forgive her given the reason.

They took utmost care in locking all the vehicles and machinery before checking the livestock near the house by sidling back-to-back, both with a rifle in hand, much to Nick's disgust since he had informed her he didn't have a clue how to handle a fire-arm.

'Greg won't know whether or not you can handle a gun,' said Emma. 'Hold it across your stomach as though you are ready to aim. The safety catch is on.' Even though she was armed, her nerves were strung tighter than a piano wire for there were so many places around the sheds and house which would be perfect hiding spots for a surprise attack.

Once the stock and yards were checked, they ventured inside with Emma having the rifle ready to fire while they checked through the house, searching every possible crevice for trespassers and even places no human could fit, locking each door and window as they went. Nick spent half an hour talking on the phone with Steve, who, he informed her, was sending the local police to the farm and more personnel from other nearby areas, although being fifty kilometres from the nearest town, nothing was nearby.

Before darkness fell, Nick drew the curtains across every window before switching the lights on in each room so anyone watching from outside, wouldn't know which room they were in. The evening was eerily quiet. After eating one of her mother's re-heated frozen meals in the kitchen, Nick worked on his laptop computer while Emma attempted to read a book but having been up since the crack of dawn and with the stresses of the day taking their toll, she retired to the comfort of her welcome bed early, sleeping in her sister's room in case Greg had been watching and knew which bedroom she normally slept in. The thought of him spying through her window sent a shudder of disgust through her. The last thing she remembered was hearing Nick switch off all the lights. She followed the sound of his footsteps into the bedroom opposite where she was. Knowing he was close by eased her tension enough she could relax enough to sleep but first she checked her two companions, a rifle on the floor at the side of her bed and another on the pillow next to her. Both were loaded with the safety catch in place: she wasn't about to shoot herself in her sleep.

Chapter Twelve

At a strange sound, Emma's heart thundered and her eyes shot open to see Nick standing in the doorway holding a mug of coffee. Her held breath whooshed out in in relief. His teasing smile as he walked across to her bed, caused her heart to lurch against her ribs; his warm breath and the aroma of his aftershave when he bent to brush his lips across her mouth turned that lurch into a bucking bronco. Her eyes closed as she absorbed the sweetness of his kiss, which was broken by the ringing of the phone.

Silently cursing the caller for interrupting, Emma flew out of bed to answer it. The moment she heard her mother's voice, she took back her malicious thoughts as the reality of their situation came flooding back. The message from the hospital wasn't encouraging. Dad's condition hadn't worsened but he wasn't a whole lot better either. The doctors were transferring him to a city hospital, she was told, where he would receive more specialised care. Fighting down waves of anxiety, Emma chose not to inform her mother about what they had found with the harvester; there would be time for that when things were better. Her parents didn't need any more worries.

Petrified was the word Emma used to describe how she felt when they did the rounds of the animals. While she scooped out muck from the bottom of the water trough with an old plastic bucket, Emma thanked the heavens that most of the sheep had gone and the remaining flock was in the home paddocks and not in the far reaches of the farm where they would normally be grazing. Having to drive around ten thousand acres with a crazed maniac ready to pounce, wasn't her idea of a brilliant day on the farm she loved. But having to tend two hundred sheep close to the house and sheds with that same crazed maniac nearby wasn't much better. She felt kind of safe with Nick standing guard behind her, a rifle held in one hand within easy reach for her. Everywhere they went, Nick drove while Emma sat in the passenger seat with a loaded rifle cradled in her arms, one hand on the barrel and the other hovering close to the trigger – safety catch off.

A metre behind her, Nick stood guard while Emma searched the machinery shed for spare parts for the harvester. Her father always had bits and pieces for emergencies; all she had to do was find the correct part. Giving up her search of all the benches and trays for what she needed, she moved to the old machine they had stored in the shed; a machine which was kept well-maintained to take over if the newer, bigger machine ever had a major breakdown – like now. Maybe she should save herself hours of repairs and fuel this machine up and drive it out to the paddock. But the smaller length of cutters would take three times as long to harvest. It was almost an hour before she held up the part she wanted in triumph. Nick grinned then searched around and found an old rag on the bench. He reached out to wipe the worst of the black, oily splotches from her face and hands before they clambered into the old ute and headed for the harvester.

Most of the morning was spent repairing the harvester and removing damaged cutters, most of which came from the side where they ran into the dam bank. She ended up with a reduced width with each round, which in turn meant more rounds and a longer time to harvest, but at least they had a working machine. Work was interrupted when Steve rang from the city to inform them two police officers were waiting at the house. Being reluctant to leave the newly repaired machine unattended, Emma insisted on locking herself inside the cabin to continue work while Nick returned to the house to bring the officers back to her. They would want to see the machine in any case, argued Emma which finally swayed Nick to agree although he certainly didn't sound happy leaving her alone.

Emma was emptying grain at the silos parked on the fire-break near the open gate when Nick returned, the police car tailing him, leaving the ever-present trail of rising dust behind them. He drew to a halt alongside the header. After a lengthy discussion with the junior officer detailing their conversation in his trusty notebook, between bouts of hand-swishing to rid himself of sticky and persistent bush flies, Emma turned the header engine off. The sudden silence was profound, causing everyone to cease chatting for a moment. After the obligatory inspection of the damage, where four heads peered into the simmering hot engine casing, and Emma was rebuked for wiping away any suspect prints, the group traipsed over stiff honey-coloured stubble to where the machine had been parked two nights previous. Emma left the men searching the hard, dusty ground for unusual tracks or footprints while she returned to the mind-numbing task of steering the massive machine in ever decreasing circles.

Noticing a sole car driving off, Emma searched the paddock for Nick; finally spotting him perched on the bonnet of the old ute. She didn't have to be told his eyes would be forever scanning the horizon for the slightest movement; he'd been standing like a lonely sentinel on guard duty for the past couple of days. The thought of his concerned vigilance sent a warm fuzzy feeling snaking through her body. He was a good man – far better than creepy Greg. Her head shook in disgust at herself for ever going out with Greg. Dumb move, Emma Nicholls, plain dumb.

Late in the afternoon a large truck arrived, causing Emma to send another message of thanks to the heavens. Her father's regular wheat carter had turned up on the off chance he was needed after not hearing from Bob for a couple of days. In the furore, she had forgotten all about emptying the almost full silos, but now it meant she would be able to get a full day's work in the following day. She packed it in when the truck left. Even though there were still a couple of hours of daylight, she wanted to complete all the other farm chores before dusk; the very thought of traipsing around in the dark with an obsessive maniac lurking around sent a shiver down her spine.

Checking the windmills for the stock water, Emma wondered about the wisdom of her brother and sister coming home. Would it endanger their lives as well? But she sure needed their help. Both were experienced in harvesting and carrying out necessary chores, and it would help if she had someone to prepare meals. Plus, the house and sheds needed packing up and cleaning out. Even though the machinery and farm vehicles were staying with the property there were heaps of personal possessions needing to be sorted. With Nick due to leave at the end of the week things would be more difficult. The thought of not having him there to protect them was scary and she wondered if she could beg him to stay longer. Deciding she really needed her siblings, she ceased her contemplation and turned on the tap into the trough she had automatically cleaned out while deep in thought.

Without any untoward incidents over the next two days Emma was able to get most of the crop off, leaving only one last paddock to harvest. With the carting truck arriving each day, Emma worked from sun-up until dusk in the field. They ate breakfast in the dim light of dawn; Emma preparing a packed lunch while Nick washed the dishes. Animals and the water troughs were checked, both on their way out to the paddock and on the way back in, the pair returning each night, dusty and exhausted.

A ready supply of frozen meals Jeannie always had on hand for those emergency situations were more than welcome. The casseroles thawed on the sink during the day and heated in the oven while Emma showered. Any kind of romance, apart from a brief cuddle and a few stolen kisses, was put on hold.

A pleasant surprise awaited them when they arrived home at sundown on Wednesday. Mum was busy preparing a meal in the kitchen with delicious aroma of roasting meat wafting through the house as they walked in the door. A mixed sense of relief and elation washed over her as Emma ran into the kitchen to give her mother a hug. She plonked her tired body in the nearest chair with a sigh of relief which turned to one of alarm when she noticed all the curtains had been opened wide.

There was no choice but to relate the latest happenings while Nick went from room to room drawing the curtains closed and switching on all the lights. Expecting a gentle chastisement for keeping the details from her parents, Emma was delighted when she found her mother's arms wrapped around her shoulders.

'Em, honey, you should have told us, but I understand. Dad doesn't need the extra worry and I would have told him for we don't ever keep things from each other. I'm proud of you, honey.' Jeannie turned to Nick. 'Nick, you have no idea how glad I am you were here to look after Em. Thank you, from both Bob and me. We will get through this. Now you two have your showers while I serve up.'

The three lingered over the meal, talking about anything and everything until Emma begged exhaustion when she couldn't keep her eyes from drifting shut.

Knowing her mum left not long after lunch the following day to pick up Sally and Brian from the nearest bus stop, Emma sent Nick back to the house to meet her siblings, assuring him she was as safe as houses. She held up the fully loaded gun she had by her side.

'You'll only be gone for an hour and since there's been no sign of Greg, I'll be fine. I can see everything from the cabin so he can't sneak up on me. Go.'

Emma watched him drive off, leaving a trail of grey dust rising behind before climbing back into the header. After the engine rumbled to life she steered to the beginning of the next swathe. Even though their machine wasn't ancient, it wasn't one of those new-fangled headers which operated via electronics, computers and satellites. How easy it was for those lucky farmers where they pressed a few buttons and the machine virtually drove itself with unbelievable precision. She still had to steer and concentrate so she set her mind back to the task and made almost two rounds of the two hundred-acre paddock. She reached the low dip near the dam which had two rows of mature shady bushes growing behind the bank, giving shade to stock when they came in to drink. She passed the dam, doing a little curve outward to miss the run-off channel and approached the edge of the dense shrubbery. A man shot out, waving his arms in the air as he trampled a way through the un-harvested grain.

'What the…?' she muttered as she moved her hands to bring the machine to a standstill. A string of expletives followed when she recognised the man dressed in ragged trousers and torn shirt. She didn't realise her hand went to the horn until she jumped at the first long blast. Greg jumped as well and looked to be muttering something as he began approaching but Emma couldn't make out his words over the thrum of the engine. Petrified, she planted her fist twice more on the horn, praying Mum had arrived home. She wasn't sure whether Nick would hear over the rattles and engine noise of the old ute but sure hoped so and even if he did, would he realise what it meant.

Unsure what to do, she kept going straight. If the bastard wanted to stand in her way, then he deserved everything he got. She was within twenty metres before Greg turned away and ran on a diagonal, to the side and ahead, his actions giving her an idea. 'Time for payback, you bastard,' she muttered under her breath.

She aimed for the fleeing man, keeping the speed at a pace she could control if he stumbled and fell. No way did she want to kill him… well it was only half true, but he wasn't worth going to jail for.

After glancing towards the house, she realised her first round of blasts hadn't been heard so she sounded three more long blasts, enjoying the way Greg jerked at the first. Her brief joy turned to anger when he flicked a finger at her on the second blast. But a laugh broke out when she figured he thought she was doing it to scare him – well, good. When he made a sudden dart to the left, she followed. He glanced over his shoulder and Emma laughed again at the look of sheer terror on his face. 'Payback is sweet,' she yelled, despite knowing he couldn't hear her, but it sure felt good.

Greg raced forwards but made a quick dash to the right. Emma swung the wheel and followed, ensuring he couldn't escape from the reaches of the cutters. As she turned yet again to follow Greg's track, she noticed a cloud of nearing dust rising from behind the top of the hill.

The cavalry had arrived. Knowing help was nearby, she concentrated on her speed and maintaining what she figured was a safe distance. Every way he ran, she swerved, rounding him up like a lagging steer on a cattle muster. Greg looked terrified and exhausted, but Emma couldn't wipe the grin from her face.

'It couldn't happen to a more deserving character,' she muttered then glanced up at the sound of a car horn. At the sight of the utility, Emma brought the big machine to a halt, grabbed her rifle and opened the cabin door. She climbed out and braced her legs on the running board, her rifle aimed, ready to fire. Flicking off the safety catch was deliberate.

Greg stilled, leant over, his outstretched arms anchored to his knees. His laboured breath came out in rasping gasps while sweat from his bright red face dripped onto the stubble. In a slow jerky movement, he straightened, turned towards the row of low trees and stared at them. Suddenly, he turned and ran. Small puffs of dust rose at each footfall, the dark particles clinging to his dripping skin. Progress was slow but he reached the end of the cutters only to meet up with a wall of muscle standing in front of him, arms akimbo. Twisting around, he ran in the opposite direction, but Nick tackled him, throwing him in a vicious toss, leaving Greg winded, flat on his stomach.

Emma laughed, enjoying the spectacle from her viewpoint on the side of the harvester where she had a height advantage. 'Take a few steps back, Nick,' she yelled. 'I want this bastard to know what it feels like to look death in the face and I would hate it if I shot you by mistake.'

After Nick made a rapid retreat, Emma took aim. 'Stand up you slime bag.'

Greg didn't move so she fired. The bullet whistled about five metres past his head, but she knew it would feel and sound a lot closer, especially if he'd never been near gunfire before. He obeyed in an instant, pushing to his feet in a matter of seconds. He raised his eyes, staring at her with what Emma could only describe as pure hatred.

'You see the small white stone to the side of your right foot?' Emma called.

The moment he glanced down, Emma fired, sending the fist-sized piece of white quartz flying. He jerked backwards, his eyes remaining fixated on the stone as it spun around in the air. When the stone finally fell he turned his head and glared at her.

'That's to show you how accurate a shot I am. The gun is now aimed at the part of your body you were going to use to rape me. If you so much as move an inch, I will pull the trigger. It won't kill you, but you will never be able to rape anyone else.'

Greg's hands shot down to cover said region of his body. Emma's words about not moving registering in his brain too late, causing him to jerk as he looked up with terror fixated on his face.

It amused Emma to see Nick's hands move the same way in an automatic response.

'I wasn't talking to you, Nick.' she said in a much gentler tone, tempering her words with a smile. Nick looked sheepish as he moved his hands away.

Another movement caught Emma's eyes. She swung her head to see her mother was also there, standing a few metres back with a barely suppressed smile. Mum was mad at her. But who cared? Mum hadn't gone through what she had.

Emma turned her attention back to Greg. 'The bullet will go straight through your hands and make an even bigger mess, so take them away and stretch your arms out wide.'

He must have realised she meant what she said for Greg's arms moved away, out and up, his eyes following their tract before lifting further, seeking out Emma.

'For your information, the following bullet will enter to the left of your breastbone. You won't feel a thing.'

Greg stood unmoving except for his still heaving chest, arms outstretched, staring at Emma. She couldn't make out his look but hoped he was feeling the same sort of dread he had inflicted on her.

'Nick, could you ring the number we were given the other day by the police, and Mum, could you bring me the other loaded rifle, I feel like a bit of target practice. It's been a while and I might be a bit rusty. Also Greg needs any empty cans Dad has left lying around in the car. Would you toss them at his feet?'

Emma waited for her mother to climb up the steps on the side of the harvester to hand over the second rifle. She listened as Jeannie muttered quiet words of concern.

'It's okay, Mum, I'm not going to hurt him, but he will suffer for what he put us through.' Before her mother had reached the ground again, Emma turned back to Greg.

'Right, you creep, you have my permission to move. Bend down, pick up one of those cans then throw it as high as you can. The lower you throw it, the more chance you have of being shot.'

He remained like a statue.

'Now!' Emma yelled when he looked as though he was going to do nothing.

This time Greg obeyed, bending ever so slowly, then equally as slow he reached out and lifted one can. As he straightened, he tossed the can as high as his exhausted muscles would allow but he instantly hit the ground. Emma fired another bullet, sending the flying can spinning.

Greg lifted his head out of the dirt, spitting red soil out of his mouth. He pulled his body from the prostrate position and sat, knees bent, arms clung limply around them, eyes staring at Emma with pure venom.

'I didn't ask you to sit. Stand up!'

Again, he obeyed but a streak of defiance was obvious in the way he made slow work of rising to his feet, staggering to find his balance. She figured, with his poor level of fitness, he was probably exhausted but she didn't give a damn. He set the goal posts with his disgusting behaviour so he could suffer the consequences.

'This time, throw both cans up high at the same time.'

Taking his time, Greg picked up both cans, tossing them with renewed vigour then wincing when Emma fired off two rapid rounds, hitting both cans.

'Maybe now you have figured I can shoot well enough to turn your testicles into mincemeat with the first bullet. The second bullet will follow in a split second.' She turned to Nick who, it appeared, was finding it difficult to keep his amusement at bay. 'Nick how long have I got to play with my new toy?'

'They'll be here in about an hour,' Nick said with a wide grin spreading across his face.

'Terrific, I wonder if scumbag here has regained enough breath for me to play *chasey* with the harvester again. It was such fun.'

Greg sent Emma a look which seemed to be something like a plea.

'You're not begging me, are you? You thought it was fun to run me down, so why shouldn't I repay you the compliment. You didn't seem to care how I was feeling. I never did anything to hurt you and yet you treated me with utmost contempt and complete lack of respect. Explain to me why you don't deserve the same treatment.' Emma paused. 'Come on talk.'

Greg's continued silence was repaid by another bullet whistling past him. The sound of the crack made it appear to be a lot closer than it was, but it had the reaction she hoped for when he jumped. It was a bonus when she spied the wet patch spreading from his crotch down.

'Oh, poor baby, can't control himself,' scoffed Emma.

'Bitch, you'll pay for this,' Greg yelled.

'I've already paid. Now it's your turn to feel what it is like to be bullied.' She turned to Nick. 'The length of rope we used to tow the cutters: maybe you would enjoy putting it to good use? Maybe we should put him on the back of the ute, spreadeagled, so I can still get a good shot of his family jewels if he attempts to escape.'

Emma lowered her rifle to watch while Nick shoved Greg towards the ute, tied his hands behind his back and assisted him onto the tray with little resistance. The rope was long enough to loop between the tie bars against the cab then around Greg's ankles. Jumping down from the harvester with both rifles, she strode over to the car without bothering to glance at Greg – the sight of him causing bile to rise in her throat. Nick, Emma and her mum squeezed into the front of the utility while they drove back to the house. Every now and again Nick glanced in the rear vision mirror, but Emma kept her eyes straight ahead. She knew she had gone overboard in her treatment of the scumbag, but it was really nothing compared to what he had done to them. While he had intended physical harm she would never deliberately harm him, but she sure enjoyed having power over him for a change.

Nick reversed the car so it could be seen from the kitchen window, leaving it parked under the shade of a tree. Greg wouldn't die of hunger or thirst in the short time he would have to stay there, and Emma was darn sure she didn't want him contaminating her home.

Sally and Brian were agog when they saw the trussed-up man, sniggering at the damp trousers while listening to every word as Emma gave them a brief account of what had happened, sparing her siblings the worst of the details, not wanting to frighten them any more than they already were.

After the police arrived it took almost two hours for Nick to take them out to the crime scene, statements to be given and finally they took their handcuffed prisoner away. Emma wondered if Greg would complain about her firing shots at him, but he hadn't by the time he left. Only if the problem rose would she have to figure out a way to face it. She could always play the absolute denial game and she was almost certain Nick would back her up, but she wasn't so sure about Mum, who was one of the most honest people she'd ever met.

As they all trekked inside, Nick slung his arm around Emma's waist. 'Remind me to never pick a fight with you, Sweetness,' he said loud enough for everyone to hear.

Emma and Jeannie burst out laughing and it felt good to break the tension.

After a lively evening meal with all the family, Nick took Emma for a quiet stroll. Entwining his long fingers in her smaller ones, they sauntered under the mature Mallee trees surrounding the house, the sounds of the night creatures filling the air: soft bleats from the nearby sheep, cicadas rubbing their wings to emit their distinctive chirping and a mopoke owl hooting from somewhere over their heads. Emma led Nick to a pleasant oasis behind the main machinery shed where a small dam had been constructed to supply water to any young lambs or weak animals needing special care. Over the years, Jeannie had planted a variety of trees and bushes around the edge, creating a safe, sheltered haven for the sick or weak animals.

When they came to a standstill, Nick released her hand. His hands moved upwards, grasping her shoulders in a tender and gentle hold. He eased her closer until he was able to slide his arms around her back and hold her nestled against his body. His capacious chest had plenty of room to fit her shoulders snugly in a warm embrace. One hand slid up to cradle her head into his shoulder, holding her tight. She revelled in the sensation of warmth and utter contentment of having him so close.

Emma closed her eyes. It felt so right. She sighed as Nick settled a feathery caress on the top of her head. She smelt the spicy aroma of his aftershave; a scent she had learned to love.

'This feels unbelievably ...' Nick began, but Emma interrupted.

'Peaceful, wonderful, fantastic, right, delicious?' she queried.

'All of those, except the last one. This is what I regard as delicious.' Releasing his arms, he cupped Emma's cheeks then spent a few moments taking in the features of her face before settling his eyes, followed by his lips, onto her mouth. There was an unmistakable hunger in the way Nick explored her mouth. Everything quivered as the kiss fired every nerve in her body. It was followed by a rain of soft kisses falling around her face before she was enveloped in his arms again.

'Delicious is the taste of your soft, warm lips and the way you kiss me back,' Nick murmured. 'I think I had better get you back inside before you completely sweep me off my feet.'

Emma's mother was waiting for them when they entered the kitchen. She smiled but quickly turned serious before asking them to sit at the table. 'I've been thinking since I arrived home. When are you returning home, Nick?'

'Saturday morning.'

'I want you to take Emma with you. Sally and Brian can finish harvesting the last paddock and help me clean up.' She turned to Emma. 'Honey, I want you to keep an eye on Dad for me. He needs someone there with him. We will all be in the city for Christmas so we can be together. I want you to open the house we've bought, give it a good airing, and see it's clean. I'm going to get the removalist to do all the packing for me, and they can unpack at the other end. If you don't mind, I'd like to put your unit on the market; you can live with us until you go away. We won't need it for Sally and Brian now. I've rung the new owners of this place and they don't mind if we don't clear out the sheds until Dad is better. They were very understanding.' Jeannie sat looking at the pair of them. 'What do you think?' she asked.

'Mum, I don't mind staying. You need the help,' Emma argued.

'We can manage, and Dad needs you more. He'll be feeling lonely right now. I've got plenty of friends I can call on if I need them. Nick, do you mind?'

'Do I mind spending six hours with Emma sitting next to me? Not in the least – it will be my very great pleasure.'

Chapter Thirteen

The morning sun was sending its first salmon and gold rays over the distant horizon, when Emma and Nick drove down the dusty gravel driveway. A deep sigh whistled from her lips as Emma settled back in the passenger seat. The previous twenty-four hours had been hectic, leaving her bone-weary tired.

While her brother and sister spent the daylight hours harvesting, Emma had sorted through the belongings she still had at the farm, packed what she wanted to keep, stacking them in cartons for the removalists. Once her old room was emptied, she scrubbed and polished until every surface gleamed. When finished, she stood in the doorway, casting her eyes over what had been her sanctuary all her life. The only things left were her dismantled bed, antique white dressing table and matching wardrobe, all devoid of any bedding, clothes or knickknacks, waiting for the removal van. The room looked soul-less. Never again would she sleep in her warm, cosy haven. Her breath caught as a lump lodged in her throat and she fought back tears of sadness. Murmuring a silent farewell, she shut the door, hefted her shoulders on a sigh and straightened.

Nick had been an amazing help, working on the outside of the house, ridding it of cobwebs and hosing down dusty windows and verandas. In between those tasks he carted an ever-increasing pile of unwanted junk to the bonfire to be burnt. The flames had little opportunity to die down from the constant feeding and at times she had been afraid the soaring red cinders would escape his watchful eye even though they had the farm fire-fighting unit on stand-by. The clean-up continued late into the evening and it had been almost midnight before they doused the hot coals with water.

As Nick drove out of the gate, Emma turned around to have a last lingering look at what had been her home for all twenty-one years of her life. Nick caught her glance, pulled over onto the verge, reached over to open her door and climbed out of the car. He stood with her in his arms while she sent a silent farewell to the farm, knowing it was unlikely she would ever be back. Retrieving the camera from the back seat, Nick urged Emma to stand by the gate. He snapped two photographs to add to the ones she had taken earlier in the week.

'Are you all right?' he asked as they folded themselves back into the car.

'Yes,' she sighed, 'it's a bit hard saying goodbye. Every time I have gone away, it was with the knowledge I would always come home. Now I don't really have a home. My unit is to be sold, I'll be staying in Mum's new house for a few months and then I'm leaving to go overseas.' Her words about leaving sent a tremor through her. It had been a dream for years to travel for a year after uni. Now she wasn't so sure. She'd just found Nick and it was going to be hard to leave him.

Every now and again, Emma wanted to take another photo for her memory album, so Nick obliged, ensuring she featured in each frame. They pulled into a roadhouse for morning tea where Nick was able to stretch his legs and rest from the constant concentration of driving. He refused Emma's offer to drive, referring with a deep chuckle, to her navigation skills through fences and garden beds–a comment for which he received a not too gentle nudge to his ribcage. There were no other stops on the journey until they arrived at Nick's home in the early afternoon. It was difficult alighting from the car with stiff muscles protesting as Emma took the time straightening to stretch out the kinks.

'We'll leave everything while we see if we can find a late lunch and a coffee,' said Nick as he slid his fingers around Emma's hand to lead her inside where his parents welcomed them with a fervour Emma wasn't used to. She was hugged and kissed before being hugged again.

'Have you two had lunch?' asked Nick's mother. 'We are about to eat; give me a few minutes and you can join us.'

Emma assisted Mrs Hamilton while Nick sat next to his father outlining their traumatic week, sending waves of embarrassment through her. Everything had been her fault and she wondered if she would ever forgive herself for saying yes the first time Greg had asked her out. If only she'd known.

After a delicious and refreshing lunch of cold meats, salad and fresh fruit, Nick unpacked his own belongings before driving Emma to her unit. She stood staring at it for a few moments before walking up the path and opening the door, recalling with an unbidden shudder the reason she had moved out. The first thing she noticed was the flashing red light on her answering machine and she wondered how many ghastly messages Greg had left. Nick noticed her glance, strode past her without saying a word, switched off the offending machine and removed the tape, slipping it into his pocket.

'I'll give the tape to Steve. There's no point in listening to those foul words. I'll ask Steve to pass on any other messages to you.'

No further comment was made while Nick assisted Emma to carry in her belongings. Mission completed, he asked what her dinner plans were.

'First, I'm going to have a long, steaming hot shower. Next, I'm going to the hospital to see Dad. I might stay and eat with him, depending on how he feels. When I get home I would like an early night. I feel exhausted and I guess you must be as well. It's been a very long week.'

'Can I call you in the morning? I think I might be in bed quite early as well.' Lowering his head, he brushed her lips with his. 'Rest well, Sweetness,' he said as he left.

Emma stood a long time under the gushing warm water, relishing in the soothing spray before dressing. The drive to the hospital didn't take long for it was thankfully close. Not knowing what to expect, she was shocked when she saw the machinery her father was hooked up to, a sudden thought flashing through her mind that her father's condition was a lot worse than she'd been told. There seemed to be more tubes, cords, patches and machinery than person. His eyes were closed, so Emma approached slowly.

'Dad?' she whispered then jumped when his eyes flew open; a broad smile instantly spreading across his face.

'Em, it's so good to see you. Come and give me a hug.'

Overcome, Emma ran the final steps, paused and took care to weave her way amongst all the wires and tubes to place her head on her father's chest, hugging him as hard as she dared. She felt tears come to her eyes, tears she had no control over.

'Honey don't cry. I'm fine and getting stronger every day. This jungle of wires and tubes measure everything which needs to be measured, and those machines will beep very loud if my heart plays up again. I'll have a room full of experts crowding in here within seconds. Your mother rang me and told me what happened. I'm proud of you, Emma. You were a bit naughty with the rifles, although I must agree with your mother how this lowlife deserved it. How's Nick? You must bring him in so I can thank him for saving my life. I believe he has been a great help to you all. He's a great chap; don't let him get away.' He paused as he eyed her. 'I can see it in your eyes how much you love the man.'

Emma stood up straight, staring at her father, a raft of emotions passing through her body. She kept hold of his hand as she searched for a chair, dragged it over with her foot, wincing at the strident screech. She sank down, giving a shiver when the cold vinyl touched her warm skin.

'Daddy, I hardly know him, we've only met a couple of weeks ago.'

'You only meet your life partner once and it only takes a second or two. I knew your mother was the right person for me the instant I set eyes on her. Trust your heart. Take your time to get to know each other better but your heart will tell you all you need to know. Don't let your brain dictate what your heart feels. Even if you are the poorest people in the world, if you have the right partner, life will always be worthwhile.'

'Dad, can I ask about the harvester and what happened? I knew something was amiss because the harvester should have stopped if you had collapsed and released the controls. We found where the steering linkage had been cut through.'

'The policeman friend of Nick's, Steve, came to talk to me. I didn't have the heart attack first. The machine had a mind of its own and I couldn't control it. I fought to get it back on track. I guess it was the tension and fear of having an accident which sent my heart into overdrive. What really frightened me was knowing you would have been driving it if Nick hadn't arrived. Steve told me what they found. I would never have been able to live with myself if you had been hurt, Em.'

'Oh, Daddy, if I hadn't gone out with the creep, none of this would have happened. I love you, Dad. I'm so sorry.' Her head dropped onto her father's chest again.

He reached up with one hand to hold her close. 'Em, I certainly don't blame you for the actions of others. Saunders is in jail now and you have a great man who loves you. What more could a father ever want for his daughter?'

Feeling content, Emma stayed with her father until the early evening when, seeing he was tiring, she gave him a warm embrace and left so he could get the rest he needed.

The next few days were busy while Emma packed up her own unit, aired and cleaned her parents' new home, while ensuring she spent a couple of hours each day with her father. Nick helped her find an Estate Agent to put the unit on the market and a large 'For Sale' sign was planted in the front lawn. It was an opportune time to sell because the next batch of university students would be looking for places like it since it was so close to the university.

Resting before going out for the evening, Emma was browsing through a couple of magazines with her legs flung over the arms of the chair in the corner of the room while Nick was processing Emma's digital photographs on a bank of computer gear in his father's study.

'I've done a cursory run through of your photographs and would like you to pick out which ones you want printed for your album. Come over and have a look. A couple of photos warrant special consideration. I think you may be surprised at what you have captured.'

As Emma had taken several shots at each location, they spent almost an hour comparing each view to cull those photos not quite making the mark. When Nick reached the section he was referring to, he slowed so Emma had time to take in the whole image. The earlier photos had been taken not long after Emma had been told the farm was sold. When at first, she didn't see to what he was referring, Nick paused, urging her to take a closer look. He enlarged one photograph. Emma concentrated on the main subject of the photo while Nick played with the mouse and a few keys, further enlarging a section of the background and eliminating the main subject from the vista.

'Take a close look, Emma, what do you see?' Emma studied the enlarged background trying to make things out. Her eyes widened.

'That looks like Greg's car. He was watching me all the time I was home?' A shudder snaked across her shoulders while she stared, unable to drag her eyes away from the unfolding scene.

Clicking onto the next photo, Nick went through the same process, bringing the car into sharper focus. 'I don't have the right equipment here, but I'm sure these images can be enlarged even further and enhanced to make them clearer. I could do it if I was in London. Look there.' He pointed to the screen with one stretched finger. 'You can see Greg in this shot and its possible to make out the number plate. Do you mind if I transfer these three shots to Steve's work computer? The photos are dated which proves he was there. I rang Steve to let him know what I found,' Nick sat back staring at her.

Stunned didn't describe how she felt – creepy was a far better word. 'Of course, anything to get him thrown in jail. I'd prefer for ever, but I know it will never happen. No-one these days goes to jail forever.'

Nick twiddled and typed before settling back. 'Done. Hopefully Steve's crew can do the rest.'

'You'll have to give me some lessons. I only use my computer to search for information and writing up my assignments. I've never bothered with anything else. I have an email address for research but don't bother with personal emails. If I want to talk to someone, I ring them.'

'Why don't you send emails?'

'There's no point, I have no-one to send messages to.'

'You could talk to me.' Nick smiled.

'I'd rather talk to you on the phone, or even better – in person.'

'Could get rather expensive if we are on opposite sides of the world.'

Nick's mentioning how they could soon be parted sent a hollow chill through her. All of a sudden, the thought of flying to the other side of the world to explore and find work wasn't such a wonderful idea. 'I won't have my computer with me when I go away, so there's still no point,' Emma argued.

'If you use either of my flats, and I sincerely hope you do, there's a computer in each one. You log on to your own address and you can send and receive your own emails. It's quite simple. Think about it. Now, how long do you need to get ready for tonight? How about I take you home and pick you up at around six? We're eating first to give you the energy to dance the night away.'

Despite her cajoling and begging Nick refused to give Emma any more details but shook his head with a grin at each question.

They had an early meal at a quiet little restaurant on the other side of the city. After a short drive Emma was being ushered into a large room, set up purely for dancing. 'I never knew this place existed,' she said as she surveyed the large hall-like room.

'I was told it hasn't been here very long. Since there has been a new surge in the popularity of ballroom dancing, apparently this place has become all the rage. I thought we might give it a try. It's supposed to be a ballroom night tonight, so I doubt I'll get the opportunity to be seduced by your evocative tango. A great pity from my point of view, but we could come back on a Latin American night.' With a seductive grin on his face, Nick found them a table, where they joined three other couples. Not giving her time to settle, Emma was whisked onto her feet and given little chance to rest in between brackets.

Halfway through the evening, Emma begged for a break. Nick melted into the crowd at the supper bar to find some refreshment. When he returned with a tray of drinks and snacks, he set them down in front of her. She only managed a few sips from her coffee when it was announced a special request had been made for tango music. Rising to his feet, Nick held out his hand in a silent invitation. The guilty grin on his face told her exactly who had made the request.

'What if I beg off from dancing with you?' asked Emma with a cheeky smile.

'If you dance with someone else, I would cut in on him. If you stay seated, I'd be disappointed and would do my best to prise you out of your chair. I might even throw you over my shoulder and carry you into the middle of the floor to embarrass you into dancing, but I hope you won't say no. Please tango with me, Sweetness?'

Getting straight into character, Emma sent a seductive glance towards her partner as she stood. Grasping Nick's proffered fingers, she sashayed past him, her body already swaying sinuously in time with the music, her eyes staring into his with a flirtatious look. Even though there were other dancers on the floor, Emma was unaware of anybody other than Nick while she gave the dance everything she could until it ended. The final moment of the music had Emma spinning around and ending up in his arms.

Nick didn't let go but tightened his grip as he continued to stare into her eyes.

She was surprised when he led her from the floor but bypassed their table and continued out the main doors, across the car park until they reached a clump of trees whereupon Emma found her lips ravished. His crotch pressing into her indicated things could get out of hand, so Emma surfaced before taking a step back, feeling overcome by raw emotion.

'I cannot believe you danced like that with other men at university functions and they weren't lining up begging you to go out with them. What's wrong with them all?' Nick rasped then sucked in a long breath. 'You have left me breathless. Where on earth did you learn that?' His voice sounded tortured as he moved further away and brushed a hand through his hair while spinning around in a full circle.

She was kind of glad he'd moved back but disappointed at the same time. She might never have slept with a man, but she wasn't naïve and knew he was fighting for control. But she wasn't keen on the separation, even though it was only a couple of metres.

'At boarding school. I took classes as an after-school option. Trouble is we never had boys to partner us – only the other girls, so we all used to really let go and had fun making it as sexy as we could.'

He glanced up. 'You certainly know how to make it sexy. My heart is pounding. I'm not sure it was the wisest thing I have ever done in requesting a tango. Are you game to come for a short walk with me? I think we might be safe from being run over and I need time to get my heart back to its normal rhythm.' Nick kept Emma away by restricting his touch to holding her hand while they wandered around the outer boundaries of the hall grounds.

'Where did you learn how to dance, Nick?'

'I was asked to partner a girl who was making her debut. I decided I didn't want to embarrass her or myself, so took a few lessons. I enjoyed the experience a great deal and am grateful I had the lessons because I've had to attend many business functions over the past few years where dancing featured. Ballroom type dancing is a lot more popular in Europe than here. Without the lessons, I would have been embarrassed quite a few times. However, the tango will never be quite the same—I will always envisage you being opposite me, and my blood will boil at the memory.' Nick led Emma inside, straight back onto the dance floor but moving to a far more sedate and safe quickstep.

Chapter Fourteen

S ince the removal truck arrived before the family, Emma was left to make the decisions on where furniture should be placed. When she saw the never-ending number of boxes wheeled down the ramp into the various rooms, she was thankful she didn't have to do the unpacking. After having to force her aching body to climb out of bed after the late night of continuous dancing she felt in desperate need of more rest. Seeking somewhere to sit for a few minutes, she unwrapped the covers from a chair, dragged it over into a corner, sighing as she sank into the cushion. She awoke to giggles and pokes and was stunned to see Brian and Sally standing in front of her. How long had she been asleep? What stunned her even more was how the furniture had been set up and uncovered and there wasn't a box in sight.

After a quick discussion about where everyone was going to sleep, Mum and her siblings left to visit Dad in hospital, leaving Emma to sort her own stuff. Deciding her siblings needed the larger rooms to study in, Emma chose the smallest bedroom. She was in the process of sorting out her personal belongings when Nick rang.

'Where are you, Sweetness, I need to see you? I have something important to tell you.'

'I'm at Mum's house. Tell me over the phone.'

'I'm leaving now, wait there for me.'

Completely mystified Emma was left staring at the silent phone. With full boxes from her unit still in her car, she spent the time waiting for Nick by carting them inside. Nick pulled up as she was loading up her arms.

'Perfect timing,' she said, nodding towards the open door.

'How much more have you got at your unit?' he asked, before bending to haul out a few small cartons.

'Another car load and my furniture, why?' She dropped her box of books onto the floor in her bedroom, groaning as her back straightened. There was something about Nick's face she didn't like. 'What's wrong?'

'I had a call from Steve. He was at Greg's hearing this morning. They're releasing Greg on bail.'

Her stomach lurched. 'How, why…? He almost killed us–and Dad. They must know he'll come looking for me again.' A hand of frustration swept down her face. 'Nick, I can't move in here. Not now. I can't put my family in danger, especially with Dad so ill.'

'Steve was stunned with the judge's decision, which was based on the fact he's only up on assault charges. Apparently,

Greg spun some story about you inviting him to your place and the farm. You didn't want your parents to know you were having a physical relationship. He claimed you snuck out every night at the farm and met with him behind the shed. Most nights the pair of you made love.'

'But what about us being run down? We weren't at the farm when he almost killed us.

'He convinced the judge it was an accident when he lost control of his car while looking for you. The judge believed him. Steve did get the judge to impose a condition of bail to stay away from you.'

'And what's this about a physical relationship? I've never…' Realising the admission she was about to make, Emma clamped her lips together, a blush riding up her cheeks. Her chagrin was short-lived as anger at the injustice rose to the surface. 'You think a piece of paper is going to keep him away? I doubt it. I don't believe this. Now I'm scared. What am I going to do?' Her trembling body seemed to automatically melt into his arms seeking protection. 'You don't believe any of those lies do you?' She murmured the words against his chest as her self-confidence zoomed down to zero so fast it made roadside white-posts look like a picket fence. Wriggling her way out of his arms, she fled from the room, down the passage, fighting back tears of anger and frustration she refused to allow free reign.

Chasing after her Nick caught her by the arm, spinning her around to face him. 'Emma, of course I don't believe any of it. I know none of it is true. I wish I'd known about the hearing. I would have gone and given evidence. But we do need to figure out how to keep you safe. It's imperative we empty your unit today. Greg doesn't know about this house, but I agree with you, you can't stay here and you probably can't stay at my place because it will be the second place he'll look for you. I need time to think. Let's collect the rest of your personal belongings. We'll worry about the furniture later. What were you going to do with it?'

'There's too much to come here. Mum suggested it should stay in the unit until it was sold because it looks more like a home and welcoming with furniture. Maybe the new owner might be interested otherwise we could sell it.'

'I figure you'll be safe enough for a few nights here, definitely tonight. It gives us a few days to come up with something. Let's go?'

Emma drove her car with Nick in the passenger seat. They managed to cram in the remainder of her personal belongings, returning to the new house where her mum greeted them. They had no choice but to relate all the details about the latest developments.

Emma was on the receiving end of a long hug. 'Honey, I do have one suggestion to ensure he couldn't find you until this man goes to court. Why don't you bring forward your plans to go overseas? Much as I hate to see you go, I'd prefer you were out of harm's way. I presume you would have to come back for any court hearings, but it gives us time to come up with some other plan. It takes months for these things to end up in court and if he's out on bail the entire time – you won't be safe here.'

'What an excellent idea,' said Nick. 'You can stay in either of my units, so you don't have to find somewhere to live and I can help you find employment; I know a couple of companies who would take you on. You might not be using your language skills but who knows? You will need a working visa though, which could take time, especially in France. I can make a few phone calls tonight. What do you think?'

'I'm not so sure, it's a bit sudden but… I want to keep all of you safe and I guess it might be the only way. Being here puts you all in danger. I feel so confused. Can I think about this overnight? First, though, I'm going to empty the car.' She stalked outside to do something positive. Working eased her churning thoughts to a level she could think straight.

What remained of the afternoon was spent with the entire family sorting things, making beds so they had somewhere to sleep then carting and emptying boxes, boxes and more boxes. Nick left towards evening, returning later with enough takeaway food to feed double the people. Handing the containers of aromatic food over, he left, saying he would ring her during the evening, but had important work to attend to.

His call later in the evening was so brief, Emma began to worry. He would be around early the next morning, were his only words.

Seven the next morning, Emma was washing breakfast dishes when a loud knock came from the front door. She dropped the dishcloth, dried her hands on a tea towel as she raced down the passage but paused at the door before opening it. Figuring it couldn't be Greg because he didn't know about the new house, she yanked the door open, and jolted at the sight of Nick. He'd said he was going to be early, but she hadn't expected this early.

'Good morning, Sweetness.'

'What are you doing here so early?'

'I thought I said I would be here first thing.' After stepping inside he shut the door and led the way along the passage to the kitchen. 'I'm disappointed you weren't expecting me,' he teased as his hands slid around her waist, tugging her closer. 'I have something for you–an early Christmas present.' He gently pushed her into a chair.

'You've already given me a Christmas present,' Emma protested, but was silenced once again with a kiss as Nick pressed a large envelope into her hands. It had red and green ribbons tied around it.

'This one is special, and you need it early because it requires some action from you as soon as possible. Go on, open it.'

Nick perched on a chair opposite Emma while her mother prepared coffee.

Emma felt her blush rising from the neck up as she took her time to remove the ribbons and slit open the end of the envelope. Pulling out some folded papers, she stared down to the floor when two keys bounced off the tiles with a metallic tinkle. Each had a different coloured ribbon tied through the end with a small name card attached.

Nick scooped them up and held them in one hand while the other hand pointed to the pages. With her heart lodged in her mouth she took her time opening them out. The top page was an electronic airline ticket in her name. It took a while for her to realise exactly what it was. She glanced at Nick, stunned.

'Keep going,' Nick urged.

Slipping the first page behind the others she read the address of Nick's London flat.

Nick handed over the key with the red ribbon. 'You'll have to stay there until you can get your French visa, which I'm still working on, but I need your passport details first, which I also have to confirm with the airline. Keep going.'

The third paper contained the details of Paris with a map showing where Nick's flat was situated. He handed over the second key. Emma's jaw had dropped, rendering her incapable of speech.

Nick removed the papers from her hand and showed her the fourth piece of paper. 'These are details of jobs you have been offered in London and this paper,' he indicated the final sheet, 'Has the Paris ones. Did you note the date you were leaving?' He shuffled the papers, searching for the ticket then ran his finger down the lines until he reached the correct entry, holding it out so Emma could read it.

Her eyes flew open. 'But that's only…' she paused as she counted, 'Five days.'

'Which is why I had to give it to you today. You need to pack and get organised. And let me tell you, it's freezing cold in London right now. You need layers and layers of clothes which you can peel off when you go inside. You need to find your passport this morning to show a few people to formalise everything. We need to do it this morning, I've made a couple of appointments – the first one is at nine, so scoot – find your passport.'

Jeannie had a smile on her face as she handed Nick a mug of coffee. 'That went better than I expected. I thought you would get a whole raft of excuses and reasons on why she couldn't go.'

Too stunned to say anything, Emma strode to her bedroom. Having only just packed, she knew exactly where her passport was. When she returned, passport in hand, she wasn't given any opportunity to comment. Nick had her out the door and into his car in an instant. Before returning her back home, he took her to visit her father, where he explained where Emma was going and why. Despite his illness he had to be told and Nick was tactful, thank goodness. She had been afraid the news would give Dad a setback, but he smiled and shook Nick's hand in appreciation.

'You have my deepest gratitude for everything, Nick. My family's safety is the most important thing in my life right now. If it means Emma needs to go away, I'm all for it. I entrust her care to you. Thank you from the bottom of my heart. It will be one thing I won't have to worry about. And you, young lady,' he jerked a pointed finger in her direction, 'Are to take no chances until you leave. Don't stay home alone and don't go out alone. Brian has a gun licence, ask him to place his loaded rifle under his bed. You can't go playing the same games in a built-up residential area like you did at home and you don't have a current licence.'

Nick excused himself to take a phone call while Emma said her goodbyes to her father. When she walked outside into the corridor, Nick was still talking, his face serious which sent a warning wave of worry through her. She waited until the call ended before moving up to Nick.

'What's wrong?'

Nick placed his arm around her waist and escorted her along the corridor, waiting until they were in the privacy of the lift before he spoke. 'Saunders has been released. He returned to his own home. Steve tells me it's not far away from where you lived. He was tailed and after settling in, drove straight to your unit and walked around outside trying to get a look in the windows. Thank goodness we thought to close all the blinds. This was despite him not being allowed anywhere near you but since you weren't there, and don't live there any more, they can't haul him in for breach of his restraining order. I need to get you home to your mother. More important, I need to keep away from you.'

'Why?'

'There's every chance he'll keep tabs on my place and follow me whenever I go out. The last thing I want to do is lead him to you. My guess is, he will keep an eye on your place for tonight because he doesn't know you have already moved out. Once he discovers you aren't there he'll probably watch my every movement. I feel so uncomfortable knowing he's not far away from any of our homes.'

'But he doesn't know we moved to the city,' said Emma. 'Surely he thinks I'm still at the farm. I mean, he could see we were still harvesting and he must have figured out Dad had been taken to hospital.'

'If only that was true, but Steve told me it had been revealed in court you had returned to the city. They needed to give details to convince the judge you needed a restraining order.'

Emma made no comment while they walked from the hospital. What could she say? Terrified Greg was watching, she searched in all directions once they were out in the open, seeking out any sign he may be nearby. She was no more at ease during the ten metres between car and house. After relaying her dad's message to Brian, Nick urged Emma to begin packing and only after ensuring she was safe inside and securing her promise not to venture out did he leave. As if she would have the gumption.

Sorting through clothes was a tedious task. Winter outfits piled on her bed while other clothes were folded in neat piles and placed in drawers or hung in the wardrobe. By the time Nick rang midway through the evening, she had one suitcase with an overflowing heap of clothes. They were never going to fit so she sat on the end of her bed sighing aloud as she opened out her new mobile phone.

'What was the big sigh for?' Nick asked with a chuckle.

'Trying to cull the huge pile of winter clothes so they will jam into my case. I'm about to give up and start again in the morning. They're going to let Dad out for Christmas. I'm so glad we can be together for Christmas dinner. They put two of those balloon things in two of his arteries to open them up. When am I going to see you?'

'It pleases me that you miss me, Sweetness. I'll figure something out. There's no way we won't be together for at least some of Christmas Day. I have an idea I'm working on. You take care and sweet dreams and Emma?'

'Yes?'

'I love you.'

Chapter Fifteen

Being cooped up in a house was not Emma's idea of a great way to spend an entire day. Enlisting her mother's help with the packing, she managed to reduce the amount of clothing to a level she wouldn't have to get someone to sit on top of her case every time she wanted to zip it shut. Her mother suggested she take a bare minimum and buy anything else she needed. When Emma heard about the wonderful post-Christmas sales in London, she agreed it would be a terrific idea and willingly threw most of her belongings back into her wardrobe. To make it even better she was informed her parents would be giving her a generous amount of money instead of a Christmas present. Packing complete, she spent the remainder of the day with her siblings, having fun.

There were no qualms or second thoughts when her family departed to enjoy their evening meal with Bob. To Emma, it meant she could have peace and quiet while she had a lingering phone conversation with Nick without being ever-conscious of being overheard. Emma settled herself onto the settee, legs tucked underneath her as she dialled Nick's mobile number on the cordless phone. The light-hearted banter, she knew, was to keep her mind off Greg, but it eased her tension a lot to be able to laugh.

When she spied a sudden movement of a shadow, Emma screamed like a tortured banshee. Dropping the phone on the lounge, she fled to the other end of the room and spun around to see what it was. A gasp blew from deep down at the sight of Greg standing in the doorway.

'How did you find me?' she stuttered as she sidled behind the settee which divided the lounge area from the dining section in the large open-plan space. She managed a quick glance into the kitchen, honing her eyes on the knife block, wondering if she could make it that far without being caught.

'Piece of cake but I'm not here to talk.'

'Then why…?'

'You're going to pay for your little games with your rifle. Try this for size.'

A scream wound its way up from the depths of her abdomen and flew from her mouth at the sight of the vicious looking carving knife. It was long; long enough to go right through her. It was narrow and glinted as though it was brand-spanking new. Oh, God! No way did they possess a knife anywhere near the length of the lethal weapon Greg was waving around and around as though to mesmerise her.

At the thought, she swung her eyes away in time to spy Greg stepping to his side. She followed suit, figuring whichever way she ran, he would catch her. He was too close to miss and he was beyond angry.

Emma didn't have a clue as to what she should do but prayed Nick had heard her scream and had the presence of mind to realise why. She dropped a quick glance onto the lounge. She hadn't hung up. The green light was still on. Maybe she should talk, let Nick know what was going on – if he was still listening. God, please let him still be listening.

'How did you find me?' she asked again as she sidled three steps to the right. Greg followed: three steps, swinging the knife through the air in a Z shape.

Emma sidled back to the centre.

He took a step closer to the less than a metre-wide piece of furniture separating them, thrusting the knife towards her. Her innards tied themselves into tight knots as she jumped back.

'How?' she demanded as a way of keeping him talking.

'I'll tell you later but first I've come for my Christmas present.' Greg jumped onto the settee.

Emma stepped back bumping into a dining chair, which banged against the table. She reached to her side, grabbed the backrest and hoisted the chair up and around, swinging wildly from side-to-side before thrusting it forwards. She missed Greg but managed to catch the end of the knife. It went flying across the room and hit the end wall before clattering to the tiled hearth in front of the fire.

Greg eyed it for a split second but immediately swung his eyes back to Emma. She guessed he was calculating whether he could reach the knife without giving her a head start to escape. She doubted it but prayed he would go after the darn thing.

'Come here you little bitch,' he screamed as he lunged forwards.

She was doing no such thing and flung her body sideways, catching the edge of another chair. She struggled to maintain her balance but fell when Greg's fist caught the side of her head.

'Got you,' he rasped out as his other hand came across her chest and he fell from the settee, landing on top of her and pinning her to the ground.

She bucked and squirmed, desperate to get away.

'There's no escape,' Greg spat into her face. 'You are going to suffer for humiliating me.'

A sob escaped her mouth, but she wasn't giving up. Emma forced one knee up but couldn't get enough leverage for a decent kick. Instead her foot caught the dining chair, sending it crashing to the floor.

'Stay still, you little hellcat,' Greg sputtered.

Emma's head reeled to the side a split second before the pain from the fierce punch registered. Things went blurry but she could make out the sound of tearing fabric before cool air from the air-conditioner hit her exposed skin across her chest. In a maniacal frenzy Greg tore her blouse and bra away and flung them across the room.

With her heart hammering she was beyond formulating words. All she could do was fight until she had no fight left. Sucking in a breath of courage, Emma tensed up every muscle in her body on a held breath. Huffing out she bucked as hard as she could, desperate to dislodge him.

Thwack, thwack.

Her head rocked from one side to the other as daylight faded into a fuzzy grey. When her vision cleared, she saw Greg standing at her feet with her shorts in one hand and shredded knickers in the other. He tossed them to the floor and slid down the zipper of his jeans.

'Oh, God, don't,' she whimpered, 'Please don't.'

'Don't what?' Greg sneered as he dropped on top of her. 'Don't take what's mine?'

'Emma!' bellowed a voice from outside.

Greg swore as he glanced up. When he looked at her again it was with pure hatred. 'You're dead, bitch,' he spat before lifting his hand. The punch rocked her before everything went black.

'We were talking on the phone when she dropped it. I heard everything. The line is still open. God, it was ghastly. I heard him hit her, I heard her clothes being ripped apart, I heard the silence, I heard her desperate screams and I heard her quiet sobbing as he …' Emma heard through the fog in her brain.

'I'll never forgive myself for not being here for her – she shouldn't have been alone. Why was she alone?' Nick wailed but Emma couldn't seem to get her eyes to open or her mouth to work.

But she did feel like she was floating. Was she dead? Is this what it felt like? Her arms were lifted and shoved before a soft warmth swept over her cold skin. Cold, why was she so cold? Oh, yes, she was dead. And now she was flying, maybe to heaven. But those loud sirens, surely they didn't have sirens in heaven. And why would the sound make her head pound? She tried to talk, but nothing worked, she couldn't make any sense of anything. Her mouth was covered, and a delicious sensation washed over her.

'I'm not leaving her,' she heard and knew it was Nick but still her eyes refused to open. 'I have to be with her. Dad, can you wait here until her mother gets home and maybe… well maybe you shouldn't tell her everything? She's had a rough trot lately. Maybe we should wait for the report. I don't know.'

The next time she was aware of anything, Emma somehow knew she was moving. One hand felt warm and she managed to grip it.

'Emma,' she heard and turned her head towards the voice but it was all she could manage before everything went black again.

At the feel of a warm hand on her wrist, her eyes opened to see a strange man dressed in a pale blue top looking at her.

'Ah, you've come back to us. I'm Dr James Carruthers. You're in hospital. Do you remember what happened?' He dropped her hand and placed it across her stomach.

'Greg Saunders, he attacked me, raped me. Oh, God.' Tears spurted and she turned her head away, wincing at the pain.

'You're going to have some nasty bruises on your face for a while. You were on the receiving end of at least three hefty blows. We will be keeping you in for observation overnight to check for concussion. More important, Miss Nicholls, you are still a virgin. There is no evidence to show there was any penetration. He didn't rape you. Your fiancé reached you in time. I'll show him in.' There were fading footsteps followed by silence.

'Sweetheart,' she heard but shame prevented her from turning over. She felt a hand brush hair from her eyes. 'Emma?'

'Go away.'

A knock sounded. She felt and heard Nick stand. His footsteps faded. Silence ensued. Emma was glad he was gone but missed him at the same time.

'Em,' she heard.

'Mum.'

It was a struggle to turn over because everything hurt but she managed and reached out her arms for the warmth and comfort only her mother could give. Mum flew across the room and hugged her until Emma's renewed bout of tears subsided. With her arms still around Emma's shoulders, Jeannie perched on the side of bed.

'Em, why won't you talk to Nick? He blames himself for not being there for you. His father said he heard everything on the phone and was absolutely distraught when he couldn't get to you.'

'Mum, I'm so ashamed. How could Nick ever want me now?'

'Honey, Nick loves you and you have done nothing to be ashamed of. Thank goodness he and his dad managed to reach you in time. They frightened the creep away. The police are searching for him. The doctor said you can go home first thing in the morning but I'm sending you to Nick's place. Dad is also coming home tomorrow and when I mentioned this to John Hamilton, he suggested maybe you would be safer locked up in their house with two men watching over you. Dad is not quite up to fighting off marauders yet. I have a sneaking suspicion Nick won't leave your side tonight. Don't turn your back on him, Em.

I know you love him as much as he loves you. I must get home to Brian and Sally but I'm going to send Nick back in. Talk to him. I'll see you tomorrow. I love you, honey.'

Emma was on the receiving end of another gentle but long and warm hug, giving her the sensation of being safe. Then her mum left, leaving the door open for Nick.

'Emma Nicholls, you could never do anything to make me not want you,' he called out while he strode towards her. Reaching her side, he bent down and pulled back the covers of her bed, scooped her up in his arms then sat with her cradled in his lap as he sank into the bedside seat.

'I love you, Sweetness, so much, I told the doctor you were my future wife. I wasn't lying; it's something I've been seriously thinking about.'

'You have?' Emma squeaked against Nick's bare shoulder. 'Why aren't you wearing a shirt?'

'Because you're wearing it.'

'Oh, why?'

'I... uh... it was the first thing I could lay my hands on when I found you. You were...'

'I know, I'm so ashamed.'

'No, Emma. You have nothing to be ashamed about. The shame lives with the bastard who caused this. Not you. Now tell me something.'

'What?'

'If I asked you to marry me what would you answer?'

'I'd probably say yes,' whispered Emma, loving the feel of her cheek against bare chest, his coarse chest hairs rubbing against her sensitive nerve endings, which in turn were sending electrical pulsing down through her body. For some reason she didn't understand, she felt safe.

'What would it take to turn the probably into definitely?' Nick murmured against her hair.

'Time. Don't ask me yet. Give me more time. Wait until we get rid of all these bad things which are happening.' Emma paused, wriggling in his arms so she could glance up at him before planting a kiss on his warm lips.

'And what do I have to do to get my shirt back?' he asked, his smile cheeky. 'Mind you, it looks better on you than on me. I'm surprised they didn't give you a hospital gown.'

'They tried to,' Emma whispered. 'But I liked the smell of you on the shirt, I felt closer to you and safer. Nick, I love you. I know for sure now.'

At her words, his breath hitched but suddenly, he began shaking with suppressed laughter.

'What are you laughing at?'

'Sweetness, I truly appreciate your words. I'm over the moon that you feel the same about me as I do you, but you picked a devil of a time to say them. Here I am holding you in my arms against my naked chest; feeling the warmth and softness of your gorgeous body while we are both declaring our love for each other. I'm on the verge of proposing to you, we're sitting in a hospital ward and between us we share three items of clothing and I'm wearing two of them. All we need now is for someone to start playing a tango and I'll be a quivering jellified mess. Sweetheart and love of my life, I'm going to put you back into bed so the sight of nearly every inch of your delectable legs doesn't turn me on any more than you already have. I'm going to leave so I can go home to shower – make it a very long, freezing cold one. When I dress, it will be several layers but first, I need to find a taxi driver who will agree to take a half naked man in his cab. I might have to send him up here to see where my shirt is. But I'll be back. I'm not going to risk leaving you by yourself tonight. First thing tomorrow morning I'm taking you home and you will not be out of my sight until you get on your plane, even if I need to resort to camping on the floor by your bed. I'm going to get a nurse to guard you with her life while I'm away.'

Nick did temper his actions and words while he settled Emma back into her bed with a few sensuous kisses which left her as weak as when she'd been semi-conscious. Grinning, he pulled the blanket up and tucked it around her neck. 'I don't think I'll ever be able to wear that shirt again without the vision of you in it'

'Perhaps I should keep it.'

'It's yours.' His stare was intense as he studied her for a moment. He reached down with the tip of two fingers, barely touching her. 'How does it feel, Sweetness? I feel your pain in my heart for not being there to protect you and I would give anything to be able to rewind the clock, or for it to have been me.'

'It aches but is not too bad. They gave me a couple of strong painkillers. Nick…' she paused before finding the nerve to continue. 'He had a knife,' her voice cracked. 'I was so scared.'

He reached out and slid one finger on a slow tract down her swollen cheek. He moved his finger to mop up a sole tear she'd felt roll down. Then he knelt and replaced his finger with a very soft, fleeting kiss. His mouth moved lower and found Emma's quivering lips as she tried to fight for control over her tears. His warm kiss stilled her trembling.

'Are you sure you'll be okay while I'm away? I can stay if you like.' He grasped her hand and she felt his thumb moving in calming circles around her palm.

'Whether you are here or not, I'll still feel the same, but I'll be fine as long as someone is in the room.' She squeezed his hand tight.

'I'll be back as soon as I can. I love you, Emma.'

Nick was back in less than an hour, carrying his laptop computer and another bag, which he dropped down by his side. Emma had managed to get upright and was sitting up against a pile of plumped up pillows. She'd sent her tears to purgatory. Curious, she asked what was in the bag.

'You'll find out in the morning if you behave yourself,' he teased. For the next half hour he talked about anything and everything but mostly discussing her life in London and what she could expect. She knew it was an attempt to keep her mind away from the day's ordeal and appreciated it.

Emma woke to the sensation of something hard and warm curled against her back. Something heavy was draped over her waist. The scent told her who it was.

'Nick?'

Silence.

She wriggled around and smiled at the sleeping man. Desperate to relieve a bursting bladder, she took care to not awaken Nick as she edged out of the bed. She was halfway across the room when she caught sight of the bag Nick had brought with him. Devilment made her peek. She grinned. Clothes–her clothes. She lifted the bag and took it with her to the attached bathroom where she showered and dressed. She peeked around the door to see Nick sitting on the side of the bed.

'You snooped, Emma. How long have you been up?'

'Long enough to have a shower and get dressed. I'm looking forward to seeing the doctor's face when he does his rounds.' Her attempted smile turned to a grimace when sore face muscles protested.

Flinging back the covers Nick headed for the bathroom. 'You were having bad dreams again' A few minutes later he emerged wiping his face with the towel Emma had used. 'I should have thought to bring you in a few basic toiletries.'

'Good morning.' A nurse entering the room, wheeling her blood pressure monitor in front of her, interrupted Nick. 'The doctor says you can go after I've checked you. We kept you in for observation because you had mild concussion.' The nurse busied herself checking Emma's pulse, blood pressure and pupil dilation. She smiled at Nick as she spoke over her shoulder. 'We had difficulty finding Emma's arm during the night, we almost had to take your blood pressure.'

Even though there was a wry grin on Nick's face, Emma could see he was a little embarrassed at being caught in a compromising situation.

'Emma was calling out in her sleep. It was the only way I was able to calm her.'

'That doesn't surprise me. She went through a nasty ordeal. Now Emma, you are free to go, but you must take it easy for a few days. Here is a packet of prescribed painkillers you can take if needed. The instructions are on the side.'

Emma thanked the nurse as she was handed the small cardboard package. She picked up the only other item she had with her, Nick's T-shirt and headed for the door, not waiting for Nick. He spoke with the nurse for a moment, grabbed his laptop and chased after Emma, thrusting his hand under her elbow as he caught up with her at the lift.

Emma insisted on visiting her family on the way home where her mum coerced them to have breakfast. After the light meal, her mum spent time helping Emma pack clothes for the few days she would be staying with Nick's family before leaving for London. Sally joined in the women's session while Nick chatted with Brian as they cleaned up the breakfast dishes. Ready, Emma searched out the boys. Nick suggested he also take Emma's bags for London. With the cases stowed in the boot of Nick's car, Emma hugged each member of her family, promising to see them every day before she went away. Somehow, she would carry out her promise even if it had to be under police escort.

It amused Emma how she was barely left alone for the rest of the day. If Nick wasn't pandering to her every need, Caroline was by her side. Nick's parents also seemed to appear every now and again to sit beside her to chat. The only time she was without one of the Hamilton clan was when she visited the bathroom and when a police officer was interviewing her to give them all the details of her attack.

Having to talk about the attack was like reliving it. The tears she'd sent away came back with a vengeance. The officer left her for a moment only to be replaced by Nick, who sat next to her, drew her into his lap and soothed her while she wept on his shoulder. The officer returned with coffee for all three. The silence while they drank seemed to renew her energy until the officer asked the next question.

'Can Nick stay?' Emma asked and was relieved when the officer agreed. It felt awkward answering intimate questions with Nick there, but it would have been harder without him. He seemed to give her strength. She wasn't sure if Nick believed her when she revealed she had never invited Greg into her home. She always met him or was waiting outside her door when they went out. He had never been inside her flat before, or since, the night Nick had gotten rid of him.

It was a shock when she was told how Greg discovered where she was living. One of his brothers was in Real Estate. The moment Greg realised Emma had moved from her unit they had searched records for any house purchased or owned by anyone by the name of Nicholls. Her car parked in the driveway had confirmed her whereabouts. The police were still looking to arrest Greg for breach of bail conditions, but he hadn't been spotted at either his own home or at any home belonging to other family members. Hearing these words, Emma insisted she wasn't returning home from overseas until she could be assured Greg was in jail.

'I will only return home if you can guarantee my safety. If he's not locked away, I'm not coming. I'll do a video conference even if I must do it in the middle of the night.

Chapter Sixteen

Being Christmas morning made little difference to Emma except she was up earlier than usual. The forecast last night had predicted a very hot day, so she dressed in a pair of white shorts and a bright red close-fitting T-shirt with sparkling Christmas emblems emblazoned all over it. Hating being up by herself on such a special morning she made two mugs of coffee then tried to figure out the best way to wake Nick. Pushing open his door with her foot, she peeked in, carried his coffee across the carpet and set it down on the bedside table before twiddling with the dials on the radio. She turned it on, waking Nick the instant his eardrums were blasted with an extremely loud version of *The Twelve Days of Christmas*.

A loud groan and curse emanated from Nick's mouth as Emma turned the volume down to an acceptable level.

'That's not a very nice way to say Happy Christmas,' laughed Emma, blushing at his uncouth words. 'Come on, get up, you can't sleep in on Christmas Day.' Bending at the waist she planted a kiss on his mouth. 'Happy Christmas, Nick, here's your coffee. I'll give you ten minutes and then I'm resorting to ice blocks.'

Nick lifted his head a fraction to peek at the bedside clock, emitting a loud groan as his head fell back onto the pillow. 'It's not even six o'clock. Don't you ever sleep after sun-up?' He paused as his bleary eyes absorbed what she was wearing. 'You're testing my willpower coming in to my bedroom dressed in so little, Sweetness. Did I ever tell you how beautiful you are?' He reached out to grab Emma's hand, but she moved away and left the room, laughing.

'Ten minutes, Nick,' she repeated before shutting the door behind her. With her mobile phone and coffee in hand she moved to the patio by the pool where she knew she wouldn't disturb the rest of the household while speaking with her family who she knew would be up. None of them ever slept beyond daybreak unless they were in the throes of some dastardly illness. She was still on the phone when Nick joined her, also dressed in shorts and smart T-shirt, but not quite as revealing as Emma's outfit. He sank down into a patio chair next to her, waiting for her to complete her call.

'Only your family would be awake at this ridiculous early hour,' he commented as she hung up. 'What other subtle ways do you have to wake a person? I'd like to be warned beforehand. The kiss and coffee would have sufficed, my love. Mind you, the sight of your legs disappearing into those skimpy shorts did wonders to get my brain functioning. Happy Christmas, Sweetness.' Leaning towards her, his kiss held much more than friendly warmth before lounging back in his chair.

'Now, why are we up so early? Was there any particular reason?'

'I was thinking of going for a walk about half an hour ago but figured it might not be such a good idea.' She felt a tremor snake down her spine. 'I feel like a caged tiger, not being free to do anything I want. If someone else had been up I would have let you sleep, but I guess I needed company and it's Christmas.'

'I'm so pleased common sense prevailed about the walk and I wish there was some way we could go somewhere alone, but it's only for another couple of days. By the way, we're having guests around for lunch.' Nick eyed Emma's legs and she didn't need him to tell her what he was thinking.

'You don't have to worry. I'll change into something more appropriate. I won't embarrass you.' Emma retorted.

'You could never embarrass me because of the way you look. My problem is I won't be able to keep my eyes off your legs and your cute little butt. Let's get some breakfast going. If I'm up, I can't see why everyone else doesn't have to suffer the same fate.'

To ensure the rest of the household roused they made as much noise as possible while preparing ham and cheese omelettes to be delivered in bed for the rest of the family. Emma grinned when Nick woke his sister and received the same mouthful of abuse he had emitted earlier. His parents were far more appreciative of their efforts, especially since it was such a rare occurrence they were treated to such a luxury as breakfast in bed. Emma and Nick enjoyed their own food outside under the patio where it was still cool, but the atmosphere already indicated the promised heat with cicadas in full voice and a couple of black crows cawing. Food finished, Nick put on a Christmas CD and turned it up. The whole house could hear it – clearly. Only Caroline complained about the noise, yelling out how she would pay Emma back.

After a fun-filled round of personal gift giving the women settled into the kitchen to prepare a traditional baked lunch of turkey and vegetables while the men readied the dining room and cleaned the pool. Apparently, according to Nick, all their guests were bringing bathers to cool off in the pool, since the temperature was to soar. At one stage, Emma quietly begged Nick to take her to see her family.

'Everything is planned. You'll get to see and spend time with them, but now, since everything is ready, how about you have first shower and dress?'

When the doorbell rang an hour later, Nick sent Emma to open the door. She couldn't hold back her grin when she saw their lunch guests were her family. Lunch and the rest of the afternoon, for Emma, was perfect. She was able to enjoy the very best from both her worlds, her family and the very special man in her life. Brian and Sally spent most of the afternoon in the pool, an absolute luxury they had only ever dreamed about. Swimming for them was in one of the farm dams where they were used to chasing off the sheep, swimming in the freezing cold water and not daring to put their feet down in the accumulation of mud, slime and unmentionables.

The adults chatted companionably in the air-conditioned lounge after Caroline had left after lunch to spend time with Justin and his family while Emma and Nick alternated between the pool and the lounge. By late afternoon, when her dad hinted he was tired, the rest of her family left so he could get the rest he needed. Nick's parents went to visit nearby friends for dinner while Emma and Nick settled down to watch a DVD and picked at leftovers for their evening meal, neither being particularly hungry.

Halfway through the movie, Nick switched it off.

'Hey, I was enjoying that,' Emma grumbled.

'Why don't we risk going for a drive. We've been locked up in here all day.'

Emma shot to her feet, more than eager to escape the confines of the house. 'If I lie across the back seat until we get well away from here, it will appear I'm not in the car. Please Nick, let's try it?'

While driving, Nick chatted while keeping a watchful eye out for trailing vehicles, driving in heavy traffic and weaving through back streets. Once satisfied they weren't being followed, he headed south, following the coastline. After climbing over to the front passenger seat, Emma wound down her window to allow the cooler coastal breeze to blow through her hair. The smell of salt and the freshness of the air after the hot, sultry day reinvigorated her.

They reached Rockingham, a large coastal town where a mass of people was making the most of the cool seaside beaches, having picnic meals on the lawns and sand. Confident they would be safe in the large gathering of people Nick parked the car where he could keep an eye on it. They walked hand-in-hand among the crowd until they found a large enough vacant spot where they sank down onto the cool damp sand. Emma settled between his bent legs and leant against his chest, her eyes closed while she lapped up the cool evening air and the sounds of happy families. To her, this was what Christmas should be about.

'Thank you for today, it was perfect.' Twisting around, she placed her arms around his neck and drew his head down so she could kiss him. When she turned back to watch the tiny wavelets rush up the sand with a smooth whishing sound, her mind focussed on how much she was going to miss having Nick with her. She crossed her arms over her body, placing her hands along Nick's arms, allowing her fingers to skim along his warm, smooth skin, the hairs on his arms having an erotic affect on the nerve endings in her fingertips. Drawing her legs up, she wrapped her arms around her shins, her head resting on her knees.

Releasing his hold, Nick ran two fingertips down her spine. Her skin quivered in response. 'What's wrong? You've suddenly gone very quiet. What are you thinking about?'

'I'm thinking about you,' she whispered.

'Now I'm worried. Why do thoughts of me make you so sad?' He swung his legs from around her and moved so he was kneeling in front of her hunched body. Reaching out with one hand, he gently grasped her chin, turning her face to look up.

'After tomorrow, I don't know when I'm going to see you again and the thought of not having you with me makes me not want to go.'

Sitting back on his heels he eyed her. 'What if I told you I was going with you?'

Her eyes flew open when the words registered. She stared at him before dropping her eyes again. 'Don't tease me. I'm going to miss you so much. I can't believe how strong my feelings are for you. We've only known each other a few weeks but when we're together I feel… I don't know how to explain it, but I feel… complete.'

He leant forwards and pecked her mouth. 'I feel the same and often lay awake at night questioning whether or not this is real enduring love. But deep in here,' he thumped a clenched fist against the left side of his chest. 'I know the answer. I've had girlfriends before but have never felt this unique intensity of emotion before. I feel as though you are a part of me – you belong… we belong together.'

'Dad says it only takes a few seconds to meet your life's partner and he knew Mum was right the moment he set eyes on her. I never really believed it could happen so quick but, the very thought of climbing those steps onto the plane tells me I don't want to go.'

Grasping the side of her face with his hands he stared into her eyes. 'Emma, look at me.' He waited until she caught his stare. 'It was going to be a surprise, but I will be on the plane with you. I'm staying with you for a couple of weeks until you get settled.'

It took a few moments to register, but when it did, Nick found himself flat on his back with a delighted, excited Emma on top of him, her sudden tears of joy blending with the desperate kisses all over his face. He laughed at her unrestrained elation before disentangling himself from her body, but he finally managed to clamber upright, pulling her up after him.

'Come on, Let's go home so I can show you my ticket to prove it to you.' They ran back to the car with him tugging her along but she giggled so much she could barely keep in a straight line, but she was elated. The day was getting better and better, in fact it was one of the best. She was on such a high she turned on the radio, increased the volume and sang at the top of her voice to all the carols being played. Several suburbs before they reached home, she clambered into the back seat and hid, but if anyone had been listening in, they would have noted the uncontrolled giggle emanating from the back seat. Emma almost bounced back into the house, arousing the interest of the three sets of eyes as Nick's family watched them wander in.

'What are you so happy about, Mouse?' asked Caroline.

Embarrassed at becoming the centre of attention, Emma came to a sudden standstill. She looked to Nick for support, but he shrugged his shoulders and left her standing in the middle of the room, returning a few moments later with the all-important piece of paper, which he held it in front of her eyes so she could read it.

'Emma has discovered I'm flying to London with her. She wangled it out of me, but take a closer look, mine is a return flight. I'm only staying for two weeks. After that you are on your own in the big wide world. Compared to your farm, you're going to find it so crowded, but I'm pretty sure you will love the atmosphere.'

Emma didn't miss the way his parents sent a secretive smile to each other and wondered if they thought he wouldn't return, but she understood why he wanted to spend time with them so was sure he would come home.

'Well, now you know Nick is going with you, you won't mind spending some time with me. Sandy is coming around in the morning so we can have a girl's session.' Caroline swung her arm around Emma's waist. 'Sorry, Nick, but this is ladies only. Sandy and I are stealing Mouse from you for a few hours.'

'If you stay here, I'll leave you alone, but if you go out, I'm afraid I'll be spoiling your party and joining you. I promised her parents I'd keep Emma out of harm's way.' Nick's determination showed on his face as well as in his voice.

'We're staying in. I don't want that crank coming anywhere near any of us. But you had better put in some ear plugs.' Nick raised his eyebrows at his sister's wide grin.

The next morning the three girls locked themselves in Caroline's room. Wild peals of laughter were interspersed with relative silences while they talked – most nonsensical chitchat with some serious boy-talk although Emma glossed over her experiences with Nick. Some things she never wanted to share – especially how deep her feelings were for him. She made out they were two people finding their way and enjoying each other's company along the journey. Mid-morning, they emerged for the first time, dressed in bathers and the raucous jollity transferred out to the pool area. Nick offered to make morning coffee.

Emma felt his eyes on her through the kitchen window, but it didn't stop her from being the instigator of most of the laughter. This was the last time they would be together for ages and ages. The girls would think it odd if she changed the way they always were together, but she was super-sensitive to Nick's presence.

Chapter Seventeen

As with most nights since ridding herself of Greg, Emma had a disturbed sleep. A couple of times she woke to find Nick kneeling at the side of her bed, whispering calming words. Almost as soon as she awoke, darkness claimed her again.

She woke again and grabbed Greg around his neck. 'No, no, no! Please don't?' she screamed.

'Emma, wake up, it's okay, you're safe. You were only dreaming,' she heard whispered against her ear.

Her eyes shot open. 'Oh, Nick, he was chasing me with that knife, trying to stab me. I kept seeing the knife coming down towards my neck.' Her voice wavered and cracked in rhythm with shudders of her body.

'Tomorrow night we'll be up in the air, flying away from here. He will never know where you are. You will be safe, and I will be with you. Hush now – go back to sleep.'

Despite her broken, restless night, Emma was up at the crack of dawn feeling on top of the world until she recalled the dreams she'd had. In an instant her mood dropped until she forced the memories away and concentrated on what she needed to do. She was going away – far, far away from Greg. After making a cup of black tea she stripped her bed of the sheets, shoved them in the washer, tidied the room and packed her summer clothes in a bag to be returned to her parent's place. It was still only a few minutes past six when she made Nick his coffee, this time using his suggestion at waking him. Kneeling by his bed, she slanted her mouth over his none too gently; to ensure she woke him. She felt his response as he kissed her back. Suddenly, she found herself trapped when his arms crushed her to his body. Struggling frantically, she attempted to free herself, but Nick didn't ease his grip until her lips softened under his.

'Now this is what I call a perfect way to be woken up. You can do this anytime you like.' He eyed the blush Emma could feel heating her face as she crawled away on her knees until she was far enough away, he couldn't reach her. When she rose, her legs were shaking and she rocked to and fro before finding her balance. One glance at Nick told her he was amused.

'I presume it is still some ungodly hour and if I don't get up, I'll suffer some dastardly consequence. It'll be interesting to see what happens in London. The sun doesn't rise until quite late in the morning this time of the year. If you rely on the sun – you'll be late for work every single day. I look forward to seeing how you handle it. Maybe it will be me who will have to wake you each morning.' He laughed. 'I'll enjoy kissing you awake, immensely.' Nick laughed again as she turned and hurrumphed with her hands on her hips.

Even though their plane wasn't leaving until early afternoon Emma was ready to go by breakfast time. Nick had little to take with him, fitting all he needed in a small backpack since he had a full wardrobe of clothes in London. He added a large thick jacket to his tiny bag. They had time to visit her family for a couple of hours before leaving for the airport. Once they had checked in, they sat in a coffee lounge with all members of both families along with Sandy, who claimed she wasn't missing out on seeing her friend off. Emma felt her excitement mounting as it drew closer and closer to embarkation time, but her elation turned to sadness when she said her final farewells and there were some unshed tears making everything blurry when she gave a final wave before the doors closed behind them as they walked through customs.

Nick must have noticed for he slung his arm around her shoulders. 'Are you okay?'

'I'm fine. It's so hard saying goodbye, not knowing when I'll be back.'

Emma enjoyed the flight to Singapore, especially since they had the comfort of business class seats. The three-hour stopover, however, was boring. There were only so many times you could walk through the same shops when you didn't want to buy anything, and the seats weren't the most comfortable, they certainly didn't accommodate reclining bodies seeking sleep. But walking gave her exercise which was needed since the next leg was going to be long and cramped.

She was able to sleep, sort of, on the next leg of their journey but it was not peaceful with visions of the hateful knife waving around. Nick's wry comment to her, when they were having breakfast, about her scaring the entire planeload of people had her blushing. He also complained, with a grin, how passengers were looking at him as though he was to blame for all the rainbow colours on her face.

After landing at Heathrow Airport, she was thankful Nick knew what to do as he guided her through British customs, onto the Underground and through changes onto three different train lines. If she'd had to do it alone, she would probably still be standing in the middle of the hordes of people at the airport. It amazed her at the number of people moving around at such an early hour of the morning, especially since it was still so dark. It wasn't until they came up to the surface out into the roadway, the freezing chill of the air hit. Nick laughed as her warm breath turned to white mist, every time she opened her mouth or even breathed out. He stopped to assist her to put on the long, warm parka he had insisted she purchase. Zipping the parka up for her, he pulled the hood over her hair before shrugging into his own warm jacket, the only item of clothing he'd packed. Managing to hail down a taxi, he loaded their luggage into the boot for the short trip to his flat. Nick unlocked the door and ushered Emma inside before returning to the roadside to gather up their luggage.

While Nick turned on the central heating to warm up the freezing flat, Emma wandered around. The flat was much more luxurious than she had imagined. She'd heard about the tiny bed-sits which were common and very expensive in London. Nick's place was large, encompassing the entire first floor of a four-storey terrace building and was beautifully decorated. The only part which didn't belong to him alone was the communal entry lobby and impressive staircase. She was glad she didn't have to climb four storeys of steps. Nick showed her the three bedrooms, placing her suitcases in the largest guest room. One room was set up with a vast array of computer equipment while a spacious lounge had a dining table at the end nearest the kitchen. Emma was surprised to see a washing machine and drier in one wall of the roomy kitchen, but Nick explained it was the norm in central London because most flats and houses didn't have an actual laundry or a yard to hang out washing but in this weather the washing would never dry. The modernised bathroom overlooking the main street was enormous, containing a new shower recess as well as a large bathtub. Emma eyed the enormous tub, eager to fill it to the brim to have a long, long soak.

Pulling sheets from a cupboard, Nick assisted Emma to make up her bed. 'How do you feel? Jet lag will hit before the end of the day, but I need to buy a few supplies, so if you feel up to it, would you like to join me, and I'll show you around the local area.'

Emma was eager to go with him, but he ensured she was rugged up well, insisting on her wearing warm gloves. She had never worn gloves before but certainly appreciated them when her fingers froze, even with them on. It didn't take long for her gloved hands to be tucked into the large pockets of her parka seeking the extra warmth.

Within easy walking distance from the flat, was a largish shopping centre where Emma welcomed the warmth the moment they were inside. She understood Nick's words about being able to take off layers as they peeled off the gloves and parkas when they entered a small café for a bite to eat. After the meal, Nick showed Emma the shops in the centre before purchasing the fresh groceries they needed to fill the refrigerator Nick had turned on before leaving the house. Emma was intrigued by the variety of fresh fruit, vegetables and meat and thoroughly enjoyed the experience of shopping with Nick. She was overawed by the beauty and extent of all the Christmas decorations everywhere and eyed all the 'sale' signs in every window. She was anxious to spend a few days shopping for new winter clothes.

Rain had started falling when they stepped outside the centre—a cold sleety rain making the footpaths slippery and Emma's nose red and stinging with cold. When they arrived home, the central heating had warmed the flat enough so Emma could thaw out. Nick kept her awake by chatting and turning on the television but by late afternoon she begged to lie down because she was having difficulty in keeping her eyes open.

She presumed it was morning before she stirred to the aroma of coffee, but it was hard to tell with the dull greyness outside the window. Where was the sun? Nick set the large mug with steam rising on her bedside table before kneeling next to her. Taking her in his arms, he captured her mouth with a searing kiss. A moan escaped when he broke the kiss, rose and left, closing the door behind him. She knew she wouldn't be able to go back to sleep, rarely did once she was awake, so she sipped the coffee and climbed from the snuggly warm bed. When the cold hit she raced to her suitcase, yanked out a set of clothes and ran to the bathroom where she turned on the hot water before daring to strip off the fleecy pyjamas her mother had insisted she pack. They might not be the sexiest looking night-wear but she appreciated the soft warmth.

Emma emerged from the still steaming bathroom, tossed her pyjamas on the bed and followed her nose towards the kitchen. She could smell bacon. Yum.

'Breakfast is ready.' Nick placed a plate covered in two eggs surrounded by a nest of crispy bacon – exactly how she liked it. Toast was popping out of the top of a large toaster.

'How would you like to see some of the sights of London today?'

Emma paused before answering. It had taken her the entire time in the shower to dampen down the strong feelings of desire Nick had aroused in her. Feelings which were strange to her and yet ones she thoroughly enjoyed. She eyed him as he moved closer and closer, finally claiming her mouth again, this time with much more gentleness and less impassioned, but Emma's senses became inflamed in an instant and she was unable to resist yielding to his embrace.

'I love you, Nick,' she whispered.

'I know, and I shouldn't have kissed you to wake you up. I promise I'll try the ice blocks next time. Much as I want to have you by my side on a permanent basis, I believe you're not ready. Maybe we both need time.' After another brief kiss, which he kept chaste, he released his arms. 'Now, how about breakfast?'

Despite the icy cold weather, they spent the day wandering the streets of London. They explored a lot of the well-known spots, Covent Garden, The West End, Piccadilly Circus, Trafalgar Square, Parliament House and Big Ben. Nick stood back with a wry grin on his face while Emma gave in to the temptation of some of the sales as they passed various stores. He nodded his approval at some of the clothes she tried on or shook his head if he didn't think they suited her.

They lunched at Waxy O'Connor's Irish Pub. Emma was amazed how such a small non-descript entrance opened into such a fascinating place, which went down two flights of winding stairs, underground. Built to resemble an underground cavern with artificial tree roots, little nooks and crannies with tables and chairs all over the place it was a delightful place she hoped they would visit again.

They arrived home, footsore, exhausted, but content, in time to cook a stir-fry for dinner before falling into bed. Emma's sleep was so deep her night went undisturbed by those ghastly nightmares.

The following day, they explored Oxford Street where Emma was able to purchase more clothes and shoes. She couldn't believe the extensive range, the quality and the prices at the sales. Harrods and the surrounding area of Knightsbridge was the target the following day. Emma fell in love with the food hall section of Harrods and Fortnum and Masons. The smells were glorious. She especially liked the cheese section where she begged a few tastes before buying a selection of small pieces. Nick picked out a bunch of deep red, long-stemmed roses and presented them to her when they sat at a coffee bar, the aroma of the freshly ground coffee beans invading her nostrils, the smell intoxicating.

Emma found a few gifts to send home to each member of her family, Caroline and Sandy, to say, *I've been here, here's a little part of Harrods for you.* She posted them from the mail section down in the basement so they would have the Harrods' postmark on them. Dinner that night was a mixture of all the samples of goodies they had purchased. Another exhausting but wonderful day was followed by another night without the tormenting nightmares.

Nick called a halt to the shopping and sightseeing by declaring Sunday, New Year's Eve, a rest day. She soon discovered it was because he had plans to take her into central London to see in the New Year and they would be up late, very late. To fill in the morning he insisted she read the details on the jobs waiting for her, to see which one took her fancy the most because Tuesday would be spent visiting the firms who had offered her a position. Nick spent the day catching up on work while Emma completed her unpacking, placing her belongings in the wardrobe and chest of drawers in her room.

She studied her list of job offers assiduously, numbering them in order of preference, setting the list down in front of Nick when she handed him the light lunch she had prepared.

At Nick's insistence, Emma was rugged up well when they ventured forth for an evening in central London. They found a table at a popular eatery to have dinner after which they roamed around calling in at various pubs, for the atmosphere. In one place, they joined in the dancing, the steady rhythm drawing them onto the floor, and into each other's arms. Nick led her to Trafalgar Square with what seemed to be the entire population of England. The place was packed, the atmosphere electric. While they waited for the countdown to midnight, they watched the fascinating crowd, being drawn into the hyped-up emotions of the masses. The countdown was deafening as the crowd joined in. The loud cries of 'Happy New Year' echoed around the buildings as Nick drew Emma into his arms for a kiss. She didn't want him to let her go and stood for a long while wrapped in his arms, her head resting on his shoulder, absorbing the electrically charged atmosphere and the warmth and intimacy of being held so close.

She heard Nick whisper in her ear, 'I love you so much, Sweetness,' before releasing her, grabbing her hand and joining the very long queues for the late-night underground rail services to deliver the thousands of people back to their homes.

Chapter Eighteen

New Year's Day, being a public holiday was a lazy day, catching up on chores, unpacking and sleeping. Next morning was busy, visiting the three companies with job opportunities in descending order of preference. Nick introduced Emma to work colleagues and friends then waited outside while she was interviewed at each place. She was able to show the work visa Steve McDonald had been able to secure at short notice. Having a British born grandparent had made it a lot easier. She couldn't present her final exam results as they hadn't yet been issued but on the results from all her previous years, prospective bosses could see she didn't mind hard work and had achieved high marks which embarrassed her for she hated trying to sell herself.

It was the last firm Emma really took a liking to. The job entailed exactly what she had studied for–there would be a lot of translation work. Emma was given a few passages to translate from English and some to English both in written and oral forms. The fluency and speed with which she was able to achieve this seemed to impress the three interviewers, resulting in her being offered a position on the spot. Stunned with the offer, Emma accepted without even thinking about it. Anything would do to start off. If she proved her capabilities, she could aim higher. Overjoyed, she bounced out of the interview room.

'I got the job,' she said before she'd even reached Nick.

'Congratulations, let's go and celebrate.' He wrapped one arm around her shoulder and headed along the passage.

'Nick, darling, what are you doing back so soon?'

Emma heard Nick groan as he stopped dead in his tracks. Taking his time he turned to face the owner of the plummy English voice, keeping his arm in a tight embrace, his fingers gripping into Emma's upper arm.

'Jacqui, I've brought Emma in for an interview. Emma, this is Jacqui Hartford-Jones. Jacqui – Emma Nicholls.'

Stunned, Emma watched as Jacqui edged her way between Nick and herself, forcing them apart, giving Emma a bit of a shove with her hip as she wrapped her arms around Nick's neck and kissed him seductively on the lips. A stab of something uncomfortable hit her insides as she watched Nick frown before grabbing Jacqui's hands and yanking them down while stepping backwards.

'Darling, I'm so glad you saw the light and have returned so soon from your colonial backwater. I knew you couldn't stay away for long. I've missed you, Nick.'

'I hate to disappoint you, Jacqui, but I'm only here for a short time then I'm returning home. Emma will be a work colleague of yours. She starts next week, so I trust you will look after her.'

Emma didn't like the way Jacqui looked her up and down with a supercilious smirk; one she felt sure Nick didn't see since he was standing back. After sweeping Emma's body with a look of disdain, Jacqui turned her attention back to Nick.

'Of course, darling, I'll make sure she learns about everything.' Standing on tip-toes she pressed her mouth against his lips in what appeared to be a provocative and too ardent a kiss for Emma's liking.

Feeling a sudden searing stab of jealously Emma turned away from the scene, forcing her body up tall as she continued along the passage alone, fighting back threatening tears. She heard running footsteps before Nick's arm swept around her waist. For the first time since meeting him, his touch didn't feel so good. She so wanted to say something but didn't have a clue how one was supposed handle something like this. What was his relationship with the woman? Had they been an item? Jacqui sure gave the impression they had. And Nick had looked miffed. Why? Because he'd been caught catching up with an old flame? Or maybe not so old?

For the rest of the afternoon, Emma insinuated she needed to sort clothes and study the papers she'd been handed which detailed her job requirements. With her mind churning she absorbed little from the pages but instead decided to dismiss her unease and see how things panned out. By the time the evening meal was ready things were back to normal.

The next few days were relaxing while Nick showed Emma a few other places of interest while teaching her the different ways she could get to work, making her lead him to and from work until she understood the Underground system and bus routes well. Nick set up an email address for her on his main computer then showed her how to use this super-dooper piece of the very latest and best in computer technology. She figured she would never have the need for most of the icons so concentrated on learning only about the things she would need: her email and the internet for research.

Early Saturday morning when there was a knock at the door, Nick called from the kitchen for her to open it. Petrified it was snobby Jacqui, she dawdled with reluctance and opened the door a few centimetres, ready to slam it shut again. Shock hit when she spied the large arrangement of flowers thrust into her arms and a hidden voice said her name. Balancing the arrangement on her hip, she reached for the card. *My Darling Emma, Happy twenty-second birthday. All my love, Nick.*

'Oh, my,' slipped from her lips as she slid the door shut with the side of her foot. When she turned it was to see Nick standing in front of her with an inane grin spread across his face.

'How did you know?' she asked, her voice coming out husky as she buried her nose in the blooms to hide how close she was to tears.

'Your mother had a few words with me before we left. I'm to give you these.' He drew out a small pile of gifts from behind a chair, placing them in Emma's arms after he removed the flowers and set them on the table. With Emma settled into the sofa he watched while she opened each gift from various members of her family. As the last present was opened, he picked up his phone and dialled, waiting for his call to be answered before handing Emma the phone.

A range of mixed emotions tumbled through her innards while she spoke with each member of her family. She grinned, she laughed, she listened but frowned at the news about her father's health. She sat in contemplative silence for a few moments after she hung up, feelings of homesickness engulfing her. Nick must have realised how she was feeling for he rose, drew her up into his arms and held her close until her sad thoughts eased.

'Today is a happy day, Sweetness. It's your day, so what would you like to do? But tonight we are going out for dinner.' When he released her, his hands moved to each side of her face as he caught her eyes.

'Where are we going tonight?' she asked.

'That's to be a surprise, why?'

'Because if I don't have a suitable outfit, I'd like to purchase something appropriate. I didn't bring many dressy clothes with me.'

'Shopping it is because the only clue I'm going to give you is I'm wearing a dinner suit. How about we head back to Oxford St?'

Within minutes they were rugged up against the bitter cold of the morning and were trudging through a fresh layer of snow which must have fallen overnight. She was miffed at having missed the sight, but the crisp whiteness looked so pretty. It didn't take long for her toes to lose feeling, so she was glad when they boarded a train.

Emma was glad Nick was with her because she found so many outfits to choose from, far more than in the entire city of Perth in only a couple of shops. As she held each against her body, Nick would stand back to assess it. He was determined when he said no or maybe but, in the end he rejected them all.

The third shop they entered was a more upmarket place where she was immediately drawn to an electric blue, long, sheath dress, with beading along the bodice and flowing down parts of the skirt. Pulling the hanger from the rack, she held it up for a closer look. It was far more sophisticated than anything she had ever worn before and looked way too expensive.

'Go and try it on. For me,' Nick said as she thrust the hanger back on the rail.

After asking an assistant to help her he sat on a padded chair to wait. The assistant kept leaving the dressing room for minutes at a time and returning with bits and pieces to add to the outfit so Emma could see the whole picture.

When she saw the finished product in the long mirror, she was overwhelmed but knew the gown suited her even though she felt ridiculously over-dressed. Nerves fluttered when the assistant drew back the curtain and gently pushed Emma out for Nick to see.

Nick's eyes widened as he slowly rose. 'We'll be taking this dress,' he murmured to the assistant, and turned back to Emma. 'You look stunning. The dress is perfect, as though it was made for you and I'm buying it for you as a birthday present.' He stood back and stared so much Emma began to feel twitchy. Relief surged when she took the dress off and changed back into her own clothes.

Nick carried the bag while they walked along the pavement hand-in-hand. When they reached a café he tugged her inside for lunch. After the meal, Emma begged for some time alone.

'I would like to get my hair cut. You go and I'll meet you back at the flat.'

'Are you right to get back?'

'I'll catch a taxi. I need to learn to get around by myself. I promise I won't get lost and I've got my phone if I need help.' Reaching up Emma hugged Nick. She wanted more than a haircut; she wanted her hair styled in a more elegant manner to go with the dress and she also wanted to purchase a pair of evening shoes to match. She stood watching Nick leave before turning around and heading for a shoe shop they had passed earlier. It didn't take her long to find the shoes she wanted which gave her time to wander along the street, looking for a hairdresser who could fit her in at short notice.

Her request to look elegant had the hairdresser twisting her hair every which way to see what he would do. Emma was shown a few photographs and she listened while suggestions were made until in the end, she gave the man *carte blanche*, so long as she looked sophisticated and elegant. Never really having had anything more than a cut and blow wave before, she watched, fascinated, as her hair went through so many processes of being washed, cut, highlighted, blown dry and fluffed up. At the finished product she sat staring in awe at the reflection in the mirror. Gone, was the teenage university student and in her place sat a refined, elegant young lady. She wondered whether Nick would like the new Emma.

A short taxi ride later, she found out exactly what Nick thought. She was met with a loud wolf-whistle and she loved the approving look she received. Nick didn't have to say a word.

'I look forward to seeing the dress with the hair. It suits you like that. I must take a photo – Caro is never going to believe the transformation unless she sees it. I don't think your parents will recognise you as their daughter, either.'

The long soak in the bath Emma had yearned for, became a reality. She filled the tub with lashings of lavender scented bubbles then locked herself in with her latest novel, only emerging when she figured she would never get rid of the wrinkles on her toes and fingers in time. The fact Nick was banging on the door so he could shower and was threatening to break down the door to shower with her still there, did have some bearing on her decision to vacate the bathroom. She saw the surprise on his face when she appeared wrapped only in a towel, but wasted no time in disappearing into her bedroom, blushing at Nick's suggestive comments.

Emma took her time to dress, taking pains to apply a little make-up before slipping the gown over her head. She stared in the mirror for a long time, unable to believe the person she saw in the reflection was Emma Nicholls. The gentle knock at her door broke her stunned reverie. Taking a huge breath, she opened it. The sight of Nick in a formal dinner suit had Emma gasping, her emotions spiralling out of control. He looked downright hunky.

Nick broke the electrifying silence. 'You look exquisite. I think I might have trouble keeping all the men away from you tonight. Stand still, I must get a photo of you and email it to Caro. She's not going to believe this. Lord, but you are so beautiful.'

Moving closer he took care to not spoil her make-up as he brushed his lips across her mouth in a gentle butterfly kiss. Drawing away, he picked up a small digital camera and made Emma pose in a few different ways. She hated having her photo taken and felt like a dork as she struck each pose. Finally satisfied, he set the camera down, much to Emma's relief.

Not letting him have all the fun, Emma picked up the camera. 'And now my handsome Nicholas Hamilton it's my turn. I'm taking this photo for me. It's not often I see you in anything other than jeans. You are an incredibly good-looking man and even more so dressed in a suit.' She snapped several photos before allowing him to relax.

Released from his posing, Nick moved over to the table, picked up a wrapped package and handed it to Emma. 'Happy birthday, Sweetness. This is to complete your outfit.'

'Nick!'

'Open it.'

Slipping off the ribbon from the package she slit open the end of the silver paper. She opened out the box to find the jewellery the sales lady had adorned her with in the dress shop. Nick removed the necklace and placed it around her neck then clipped on the matching bracelet before standing back to appraise the effect.

'Perfect,' he whispered as he brushed her lips with his. The gentle caress was interrupted by a knock at the door. 'Our taxi is here.' Nick's voice was thick with emotion as he entwined Emma's hand in his and led her to the door.

Before ushering her outside, he wrapped Emma in her warm coat. They drove into the centre of London, pulling up in front of a very plush looking restaurant. Emma's coat was taken from her while the *Maître'd* stood by to show them to their table. She was pleased she wasn't as overdressed as she had thought; all the patrons were in formal evening wear befitting the upmarket restaurant. She was delighted to see a dance floor which was being used.

Nick's eyes followed hers and he grinned. As soon as they were seated, Nick ordered champagne then held out his hand in an unspoken invitation to dance. 'This is one of the reasons I chose this place, the dancing, but I hope they don't play a tango, I don't think my heart will be able to take it. I'm having a great deal of trouble keeping it under control right now. It's been thumping since the moment you walked out of your room.' He eased Emma in closer while they moved in time to the soft music where they remained until the bracket of music ended. They returned to the table where their meal orders were taken by a surreptitious waitress who seemed to appear from nowhere. Nick asked for the champagne to be opened.

'Oh, sorry,' said Nick. 'I forgot you don't drink alcohol. What would you like?'

Emma smiled. 'I don't dislike alcohol but don't drink it very often, but tonight is special. Nick, thank you so much – for all of this. I really appreciate everything.'

'Believe me, it has been a very great pleasure. Now come and dance with me while we wait for our meal.' Before he stood, they chinked glasses and sipped the bubbling wine.

To Emma, the night was perfection. The service and food were faultless, and she loved dancing in Nick's arms.

The music was soft enough, people sitting at their tables could still hear each other talk and was at a perfect level to be able to dance to. They had finished their coffee when Emma heard the unmistakable rhythm of the tango. Her smile was seductive as she glanced at Nick, grinning at his soft groan. She stood and held out her hand, swaying her hips in time to the sensuous rhythm.

This time she led him to the floor. There were no other takers for the dance, so they had the floor to themselves. When the music ended, there was an eerie silence for a few moments while Emma stood still, keeping her eyes fixed on her man. All of a sudden, the room erupted in applause and Nick drew Emma into his arms. His kiss was fierce. His mouth on hers was hard and hot. Her soft moan was followed by a gasp as her breath caught, desire spinning through her body. Emma pulled away, almost running back to their table, finding it difficult to breathe.

Back at her seat, Emma gulped down the last few mouthfuls of her champagne. She kept her eyes down while she tried in desperation to bring her frenzied emotions under control. She heard Nick slip into the chair opposite, call for the waiter and order two more coffees.

'Will you dance with me?' Emma's head shot up at the strange voice.

'Who, me?' she stammered.

'Yes, please.'

The man asked with his hand held out. Emma glanced at Nick who nodded with a smile. Good manners dictated Emma had no choice but to agree. She gave her new partner all the attention she could muster but her thoughts were with Nick and she was pleased when the music ended, and she was taken back to her man. When the coffee arrived, it was drunk in silence until Nick nodded for their bill. When they left, Nick asked if they could walk for a while.

It was freezing outside but Emma agreed, hoping the cold air would chill her still highly charged emotions. It certainly worked: everything froze, including her feet. 'Why are we walking. I feel like an icicle,' she said when she couldn't take another second of the cold.

'I'm sorry, I wasn't thinking,' he said as he turned towards the road and hailed the nearest black cab.

For the journey home, he slid his arm around her but was silent. She couldn't figure out why he shut out her attempts at conversation. Was he mad at her for dancing with the other man? Had she said or done something wrong? Everything was so new to her and she didn't have a clue about this type of society and its rules and regulations of etiquette. Once they were inside the flat, she thanked him again for the evening, reached up and brushed her mouth against his. When he didn't respond, she ran to her room and shut the bedroom door behind her. Certain she had done something wrong it took ages to fall asleep. She heard Nick walking around, following the sounds as he moved. He spent a lot of time on his computer, went to the bathroom and turned off all the lights. Her last memory before finally falling asleep was of Nick when she first saw him in his dinner suit.

Chapter Nineteen

It shocked her when Emma glanced at the bedside clock. Far out, she'd never slept in so late. She flung the snuggly doona back, leapt from the bed and made quick work of morning ablutions after which she flung on jeans, top, a jumper and thick socks. Wondering if Nick was still mad at her she wandered into the lounge and noticed an envelope with her name on the front, printed in Nick's neat handwriting. Inside she found a set of photos. She spread them out, smiling at Nick's image. While fingering the flowers he had given her, she sank her nose into the velvet blooms to inhale the sweet perfume. Coffee was next on the agenda. Recalling the heated atmosphere of the night before, Emma wondered whether she dared take one into Nick. Deciding it would be safe if she kept away from him, she made the hot brew, holding both mugs in one hand while she tapped on Nick's door. There was no response, so she pushed the door open a little to check if he was asleep. Her breath hitched in her throat at the sight of him sprawled out on his stomach, the doona covering his hips. The sight of his naked muscular back had Emma doubting her wisdom but she sucked in a deep breath, walked up to his bedside table and placed the coffee next to his clock radio. She stood gazing at him, a strange yearning emanating from deep inside.

'What, no kiss this morning?' he drawled as he turned over and settled his eyes on her face.

She jumped. 'I thought you were asleep,' she stammered with her heart hammering.

'And how were you going to wake me?' he asked with a wolfish grin.

Emma backed away. 'Thank you for printing off those photos.' The words rushed out as she fled the room, feeling her emotions spiralling up again at the sight of Nick's bare chest. Feeling uptight, she banged her way through breakfast preparations, making more noise than necessary. She couldn't understand what was wrong with her. His breakfast ready, she stood with it in her hand, wondering what the heck she was supposed to do with it.

Nick came in dressed much the same as her in jeans and a sweater with hair still wet from his shower. She thrust the plate into his hands, turned and stalked away feeling... she didn't know how she felt apart from confused. The tension was so tight she was sure it was going to snap and rebound off the walls again and again.

'Emma, come and eat at the table with me, I want to talk to you.' He glanced at her. She'd turned around but her lips were drawn tight and her eyes were studying some invisible speck on the tiled floor. 'Please?' he added before padding barefooted into the dining area, sat down and waited, smiling as she pulled out a chair and sat at the other end of the table.

'What are you so afraid of? That I will carry you off to my bed? You know damn well I would like nothing better. You tormented me last night with your dancing, and you know it.' He eyed her. 'Emma, I love you to distraction and would never do anything to hurt you. Much as I want you, to make love with you, keep you by my side forever, you're not ready.'

'What do you mean?' she was so shocked the words rushed out of her mouth.

'I could have easily persuaded you to join me in bed last night. But we both would have regretted it and I would have never forgiven myself. I know you're not ready because you keep hiding away from me. For example–Boxing Day. You feel free to run around in your bathers with Caro and Sandy, not afraid of them seeing you, because you are comfortable with them, know they are not judging you. The moment I walk out, you dive for your towel and cover up. Around here, you are the same. Last night was the very first time you have dared come out of the bathroom,' he pointed towards the bathroom door, 'With anything less on than all your clothes. How would you handle lying in my bed stark naked? Because believe me, my beautiful, adorable, Emma, when the time comes, that's how it is going to be.'

Oh, far out. Mortification hit as she glued her eyes to the floor. Cutlery clattered against china, chair legs scraped across the floor and a few seconds later she noticed Nick kneeling by the side of her seat. He reached across her lap and grasped both hands in his.

'Sweetheart, when you are ready, you will know, and I'll be waiting for you. I've waited my lifetime for you – I can wait a little longer. But no more tango until you're ready. There is only so much temptation a normal red-blooded man can take. I don't think I have any more self-control left after last night. You had me at breaking point. Now, to change the subject, would you like to see some photos of a very beautiful woman? And I'll check my email to see if Caro has seen your picture yet.'

Emma collected the plates while Nick moved into his computer room to turn on his emails. Emma joined him as he opened Caroline's response.

'Wow! That can't be our Mouse. So, who is the new girlfriend? And what did you do with Mouse?'

Nick smiled as he typed a response. 'Mouse has gone, although there is still a little shy puss creeping around my flat. So, I guess the cat ate the mouse. My new woman is Emma, and boy, can she tango.'

Emma bent down and added a bit. 'Stop talking about me as though I'm not here. How is Justin?' She turned her head sideways and deposited a kiss on Nick's mouth.

'Thank you,' she managed to whisper. 'I understand what you are saying. I promise there will be no more tango. What I don't understand is why I can't let go, because I sure know I'm in love with you. And finally, thank you for yesterday, for everything. You made my day very special.'

'The day was special for me as well. I'll show you one of the reasons why.'

After shutting down his email, he opened the photo file and brought up each photo of Emma he had taken. She plonked in a chair next to him, unable to believe the photos were of her.

'This is my favourite and the one I sent to Caro. I've printed off a copy for your parents. You are one beautiful woman and I believe the real woman emerged yesterday.'

'Nick, can you cut and paste these photos?'

'Yes, why?'

'Would you put the two of us together in one photo?'

'You mean like this?' As he opened yet another file, Emma stared at the composite photo of them both. Reaching to one side, he withdrew a picture from under a book, placing the print in front of her.

'This is for you. I already have one waiting for a frame so I can put it by my bed. This photo is also going by my bed.' He held up a photo of her alone.

'As for why you can't let go, I can't answer for you. Remember, you have been through some dramatic ordeals over the past couple of months. It's only natural you find it hard to trust men in general.'

'I trust you, Nick.'

'Thank you, I sincerely hope I never do anything to betray your trust, but I still can't answer your question for you – only you can find the answer. Now, since today is our last full day together until I return, is there anything in particular you would like to do?'

'I'm going to miss you. Can we stay home and have a quiet day? We've been on the go since we arrived.'

The day was quiet and very pleasant. Emma prepared for her new job while Nick tidied up his gear, packing the few belongings he needed, into his backpack. They sat on the lounge, with Emma wrapped in Nick's arms while they watched a film on TV, not bothering with meals but grazing on snacks when hunger pangs hit. Nick checked she had bus and train timetables at her disposal and understood which ones to catch. He went through everything in his flat, so she could work each item and left her a list of contact numbers for various trades if anything went wrong. Emma was in bed early.

It was still dark when Emma was roused from her sleep with a hot seductive kiss. 'How are you going to manage without me here to wake you?' Nick asked with a chuckle. 'I guess I'd better set your radio alarm for you.' He smiled as she yawned and stretched. 'You can't be late on your first day so get up sleepy head, breakfast is ready.'

Bacon, eggs and toast were waiting on the table when Emma emerged from her shower, dressed in a smart business outfit; one Nick had helped her purchase. He shot an approving glance in her direction and pulled out her chair. While she ate, they chatted about everyday things until it was time for her to leave. He held Emma close, kissed her then wrapped her in her parka, zipping it up and pulling the hood over her hair before ushering her out the door, wishing her all the best for her day at work.

Her lessons in the London transport system worked. Emma arrived at her new job without any hitches except for slipping on a patch of ice hidden under a thin layer of snow. After a brief meeting with her boss and being given a pile of papers, the morning dragged, with easy translation work feeling laborious. Emma was daydreaming when the phone on her desk began ringing. Delving under the pile of papers she searched for the handset and lifted it to her ear.

'How is it going, Sweetheart?'

Emma couldn't help but smile, the sound of Nick's voice sending a surge of adrenalin through her veins. 'So far, it's great. I have a pile of work Mark says he has been saving for me, but I'm enjoying it. How has your day been?' And strike me dead for lying, she added in her thoughts. She was plain miserable, missing Nick so much it hurt.

'Very lonely. I love you, Emma.'

Nick hung up, leaving Emma staring at the receiver, feeling delighted but sad. She knew who was going to be lonely when Nick flew home. Now glad of the large workload she attacked it with a renewed vengeance in an attempt to cast her thoughts of Nick aside. It didn't entirely work with the day seeming to be endless. She rushed home, running and slipping the last leg down the icy footpath, eager to make the most of every minute of their time together.

Nick must have been watching out for her for he had the door open when she reached it. Emma found herself lifted off her feet and spun around in a tight embrace. When she was finally freed and her mouth ravished, Emma changed into jeans and sweater and found a lavish meal prepared for her.

'You've been busy. This looks wonderful. Thank you.' She plonked a warm kiss on Nick's mouth.

The conversation was light-hearted, but it was a struggle for Emma since she felt uptight about the impending separation. After clearing away the dishes, Nick tugged her down next to him on the sofa and cradled her in his arms. They watched TV programmes but even though she saw the flickers and flashes, she absorbed none of the content. She felt relieved when Nick said, 'It's getting late and you need to be up early.'

Doubting she'd ever sleep, she was more than surprised when the shrill alarm from the clock radio penetrated her sleep befuddled brain, frightening her. She shot upright feeling confused. It took several seconds to search for the offending noise. How to turn it off? From the corner of her eye she noticed a movement at the door so glanced up to see a grinning Nick standing in the doorway. Dressed, he held a hot coffee in his hand, the tendrils of steam turning instantly white from the chill of the morning. Striding across the room, he showed her which button she needed to push to allow silence to reign again.

'Good morning,' he whispered while he bent and kissed her. 'That's one rude awakening I have got you back for. I haven't been game to try the iceblocks yet. Breakfast will be ready in ten minutes,' he continued as he strode out again, not giving Emma a chance to speak.

Breakfast was subdued and no amount of banter from Nick cracked a smile on Emma's face. She felt so dejected, her heart feeling leaden and hollow. Nick would be gone when she arrived home from work and the knowledge was creating havoc with her insides. She knew she was going to miss him but hadn't realised how much with the pain in her heart overwhelming.

'Emma, I promised my folks I would go home for a while. I'll email you every day and I'm only a phone call away.' Easing from his seat, he sidled around the table to Emma, drawing her up into his arms. 'Every morning when you wake and every night before you go to sleep; remember how much I love you.'

Settling her head on Nick's shoulder she hugged him tight. 'I didn't think it would be this hard to say goodbye to you. I already miss you and my heart feels so heavy. I love you, Nick.'

Nick sought out and claimed her mouth. Her kisses were wild, as though they were their last ever and she would never see him again. He moved his mouth up to caress each moist eye and finally planted a kiss on her hair before releasing her.

Emma fled to the bathroom where she repaired her face to hide the swollen redness to her eyes she hadn't realised had leaked like a colander. She sped through dressing for work adding a jacket to her outfit of smart warm slacks and pale blue blouse. A black leather bag slung over her shoulder completed her outfit. Too afraid she'd break down again, she headed straight for the front door. Saying goodbye was too hard. Her hand was on the door knob when Nick caught her around the waist. She wriggled free and had to gasp for a breath. 'Sorry, but I'm finding it hard to let you go.' Dropping his head at an angle he covered her mouth once again. Emma kissed him back with a passion she'd not given before. She jerked her head back and grabbed the door handle, pulling it open with undue force and fled.

'Goodbye, Nick,' she yelled as she ran down the pathway, tears streaming down her face.

Chapter Twenty

It was a difficult day. To hide her feelings of despair, Emma locked herself in her small office and slaved away at her work, forcing her mind to concentrate. Some translation from Chinese to English on a pamphlet of instruction about how to assemble a playpen had to be done more than once, her constant thoughts of Nick had her unable to concentrate, causing her to make way too many stupid errors. Reading the points back, she grimaced when she figured the new parents wouldn't have a clue how to connect the sides together. She tore the page into shreds and began the task again.

At the time she knew the plane was departing Heathrow, Emma sat still, staring into space with her fingers interlaced in a tight grip, her heart feeling as though it was being shredded on a cheese grater into a thousand pieces. She didn't have the gumption to go out for lunch, her hunger pangs replaced by the ache in her heart. Instead she made do with a cup of coffee in the staff room before returning to her office to work. She was the last one to leave work with no desire to go home to the empty flat.

She hated the unfamiliar emptiness when she opened the front door. Not wanting to break the intense lonely silence she crept across the darkened room and headed straight to her bedroom where she turned the light on and immediately spied a red rose on her pillow. Picking it up as though it was the most fragile thing on earth, she smelt the sweet perfume before reading Nick's note. First, she smiled at the heartfelt words, until her emotions broke down and she dissolved into tears and flung herself onto her bed, burying her face into her pillow to stifle her sobs. She cried herself to sleep, the rose clutched in one hand: the crumpled note in the other.

It was the early hours of the morning before Emma awoke. Stripping off her creased work clothes, she shivered in the unheated room then ran naked across the passage to the bathroom, the icy cold atmosphere bringing an instant flush of goose bumps to her flesh. Standing under the steaming shower jets she wallowed in the warmth trying to ease her tension. Unable to get back to sleep, she turned on the computer to see if either Nick or Caroline had sent her an email. A sad smile lit up her face when she read Nick's message.

'My dearest Emma. I've only been in the air for two hours and already I miss you like crazy. I feel like hijacking this plane to make them turn it around, but with all the fears of terrorists these days they'd probably shoot first and ask me questions later. It's going to be a long flight without you but at least I won't have all the passengers eyeing me with daggers, thinking I'd beaten you up. My heart hurts and I now wish I hadn't promised my folks I would return home. I love you, Sweetness. Nick.'

Despite the hour, Emma replied straight away, figuring Nick would be asleep on the plane. 'I'm glad your heart hurts – there is some justice in this world. I had to do most of my translations twice today – thoughts of you interfered with my brain function. I love the rose and the message, thank you. This place is so empty without you, and so is my heart – Emma.'

Nick must have had his computer on because a response came back almost immediately. 'What are you doing up at this time of the morning? You spoilt my fun. I was looking forward to the thought of the alarm waking you. Go back to bed, my love.'

'I've just had a shower and changed out of my work clothes. I fell asleep with them on. I'm about to raid the fridge for some dinner. I'm hungry – I didn't have any lunch. What would you like for dinner?'

'You.'

She paused as she fought back a fresh wave of tears. 'I love you, Nick. I'm going now. I'll open up when I get home from work tonight.' She struggled to type in her last message before shutting down the computer.

Wandering into the kitchen she pulled the fridge door open, grinning like an inane idiot when she spied the bright pink piece of paper resting in a prominent position up against a carton of juice. This message told her to play a certain track on a certain CD while she ate. Without bothering to eat, she played the song, listening to the words over and over until her pain began to ease a bit. After taking out odds and ends she tucked into what she could only describe as a mishmash of a meal.

At the office, Emma worked at a steady pace through her pile of papers to keep thoughts of Nick at bay. She hadn't returned to the warmth of her bed because she'd had her normal quota of sleep and the meal renewed her energy levels. She had stayed in the flat long enough to turn off the shrieking alarm and discovered Nick had set his own alarm to go off five minutes after hers. This caused her to take the time to email Caroline and beg her to set Nick's alarm for some ungodly hour on his first morning home, saying she needed to pay him back for some prank.

It was after her lunch break when Emma heard Nick's name mentioned. She went on immediate alert, straining her ears to hear every word even though she felt guilty about eavesdropping. She thanked the heavens her door was ajar but jolted when she recognised Jacqui's voice. Emma didn't know to whom Jacqui was speaking and didn't care. It was the words which sent a stab of pain through her heart.

'Nick was back for a while. He brought that sappy Emma with him. She doesn't know he rang me heaps of times and sends me emails every day. She is so gullible. He went back home because he couldn't stand her any longer. Next time he comes back, we're getting engaged.'

The voice trailed off as footsteps faded down the passage. Emma didn't move, couldn't move, an inner voice telling her she didn't believe a word of the woman. Nick wouldn't do anything so underhanded to her–she had no doubt. Nick was in love with her. But despite her inner logic, it still hurt–the pain stabbing deep. Giving herself some harsh self-talk, Emma dismissed the words and tackled her work with renewed vigour, never leaving her office until after everyone else had left. The last person she wanted to run into was Jacqui Stuck-up Hartford-Jones.

She opened her email the minute she walked into the flat. 'Sweetness. We will be landing in a few minutes. I didn't sleep well because the visions of you doing the tango kept moving through my brain. I'm looking forward to a good sleep in my own bed tonight. I trust your day at work was better. I've had your photo to look at most of the way; it goes some way to relieving the pain in my heart but the further I fly away from you the more convinced I am returning home was a huge mistake. Sleep well, my love. Nick.'

'Work was a bit better,' she wrote back. 'At least I didn't have to do everything twice. I found the note in the fridge. Thank you. Very funny with the alarm but since I didn't go back to bed, I was wide-awake when they **both** went off – so I guess your attempt at payback backfired on you. I will get you back though. I can't believe how empty this place feels without you. I hope you sleep **very, very** well. All my love, Emma.'

Daring to visit the ladies' rest room late the next morning when things became desperate, Emma almost bolted when she spied Jacqui's reflection staring at her from the mirror above the basin. Had the dratted woman been laying in wait for her? Emma quickly dismissed the idea as ludicrous for Jacqui wouldn't have known when nature called. She ducked into the cubicle and listened intently but heard no footsteps leaving. Knowing she couldn't sit on the loo for the rest of the day, Emma felt dour dread as she unlatched and opened the door. Jacqui was leant up against the edge of the basin. She moved to one side and waited until Emma was washing her hands.

'I need to let you know Nick and I have an understanding. We have been dating a long time now and as soon as he comes back here to live, we are getting married. So, don't go getting any ideas about him. I miss him so much, but he insisted on seeing his family because it will be a long time before he goes back home again. But I can take it because soon he will be mine forever.'

Mission completed, Jacqui turned and bounced out of the room like she was a young fawn full of spirit. Emma stared at the closing door, dumbfounded.

Not keen to go home, Emma remained even longer at work. The cleaners had begun their nightly task before Emma found the courage to leave. It was freezing cold outside, with a thick pall of mist enshrouding everything further away than the edge of the footpath. It was as though the atmosphere was brought on by Emma's sense of depression. She was pleased to finally enter the underground system, despite the dank atmosphere of damp clothes and almost unbearable noise of clattering feet, overloud busker music and constant rumblings about the weather. The walk from the station to home was made in a hushed eerie white-out.

While she prepared her evening meal, she found two more notes in the kitchen. Her heart felt confused while she read them. Jacqui's cruel confrontation had niggled away at her all day and now she was reading the most tender, loving messages. When she opened her email and read Nick's message the smile returned to her face.

'Caro has been sent to purgatory for being a party to your prank. I had barely managed to go into a very deep slumber when I was so rudely awoken. I think maybe I'm going to live to regret falling in love with you, little vixen. I am now suffering from the worst jet lag ever, but I still love you to pieces and miss you heaps. Your photo is by my bedside so every time I feel pangs of loneliness, I reach out and touch you. It is nowhere near as good as the real thing, but better than nothing. How was work?'

'The work I do, I enjoy. It is interesting, and I have almost worked my way through the pile Mark left for me. I did warn you I would get you back – and I did mention something about you sleeping very well. The clues were obscure, I know, but clues, nevertheless. I promise I have nothing else planned – yet. Nick, if your feelings for me ever changed, would you be honest straight away and let me know? I love you so much it hurts. Emma.'

Emma was woken in the early hours of the morning by the phone ringing. She stumbled out of bed to answer it. Having remembered to switch on the central heating when she had arrived home, the flat was cosy. 'Sweetness, I've just woken up and read your message. My love, I will always be honest with you, you don't even have to ask. The way you have wangled your way into my heart, there is no way on earth I will ever change my mind about you. I do recall I mentioned something about marrying you. I haven't changed my mind. Now I'm waiting for the love of my life to make up her mind. Emma, what brought on your question?'

Emma felt her heartbeat begin to thunder at the sound of Nick's voice. But how to answer him without letting him know what caused her to ask the question. She had slipped the question in, hoping he would write a reply. What if Jacqui's statements were true? But how could they be?

'It was only a conversation at work.' Not wanting to elaborate she sought what she could say to change the subject. 'Do you realise what time it is over here? I do believe you are getting back at me.'

'Sorry, I didn't even look at the clock. My sleep pattern is way out of kilter, thanks to you and your pranks. Your message alarmed me so much I had to phone. It's so good to hear your voice. How are you, Sweetness?'

'Apart from very lonely and missing you, I'm fine.' She crossed her heart for lying. 'I'm wide awake now and won't be able to go back to sleep so will be really tired by tonight, but it is worth it to talk to you. I love you, Nick. Please don't ever forget it?'

'Not a chance. I'm sorry I woke you. Try to go back to sleep. Goodnight, my love.'

When Nick hung up, Emma felt stupid for doubting him but there was still a niggle of concern stabbing away at her innards: a niggle she tried to shove away.

After completing her basket of work late the next morning, Emma went in search of Mark, seeking more. She was approaching Jacqui's office situated half-way between her own and Mark's when she noticed the door was wide open and Jacqui was talking on the phone. She couldn't help but overhear part of the conversation as she walked past.

'Nick darling, this is the second time today you have rung. Do you miss me so much?'

Emma didn't hear any more. With her heart jammed somewhere between her stomach and her mouth, she fled towards Mark's office, her tense knuckles pressed up against her mouth. She paused outside Mark's closed door to try to gather her wits and wipe the distraught look she felt sure must be obvious, from her face. When she was bidden to enter, she forced the corners of her mouth up into what she felt sure looked like a plastic smile, crept in and handed over her completed work.

Muttering compliments about how he was impressed with the quality and the speed in which Emma had finished, Mark spent some time going over each item with her. He dictated answers to two letters she had translated. 'Can you translate these into French?'

'Of course.' Emma returned to her office, happy to have more work to concentrate on and take her thoughts away from Nick. She took a long roundabout route through the lunchroom, out a back entry, down two flights of fire escape stairs and back through the building entrance to avoid going anywhere near Jacqui.

Over the weekend, Emma found several more messages from Nick, all written on bright coloured pieces of paper; messages which went a long way to calm her shattered emotions. Some were humorous, others more serious, two more asked her to play certain songs but they all ended with the words, *always remember how much I love you, Sweetness.* They were placed in obscure places: her shoes, in a book, poking out of the TV guide, the washing powder, in pots and pans, between plates and she even found one in the washing machine, albeit, after she had used it and her white underclothes came out a pale lime green and covered in hundreds of tiny pieces of shredded paper pulp.

She wrote an email to Nick, 'You now owe me several sets of white underwear. I didn't find your vivid green note until after I had done my washing. My whites have turned into lime greens.'

It wasn't until an hour later her housecleaning was interrupted by the phone ringing. 'What size,' he spluttered with laughter. 'I'm sorry,' he added sounding more sober and darn it his voice sounded downright sexy and husky, 'I would like nothing better than to be buying your underwear, as skimpy and sexy as I can find.'

Emma felt her face heat with embarrassment. 'Don't bother, I'd prefer wearing my iridescent green ones as no-one is ever going to see them in any case, especially you and it is none of your business what size I am.' As she hung up, she heard distinct guffaws of laughter.

There were several email conversations over the weekend along with two more phone calls from Nick and by the time Emma returned to work on Monday, she had renewed belief in his love for only her. But during the next week it seemed Jacqui was in constant phone contact with Nick. Emma had heard and seen Jacqui's mobile phone ring with Jacqui answering it, in the staff room, in the passage and in the office. Every time she said hello, it was accompanied by the word *Nick* and was followed by gushing, romantic murmurings. Emma did her best to avoid the woman until Jacqui stepped into her office and shut the door.

'Nick suggested it wasn't such a good idea for you to be living in his flat. People might get the wrong idea about you and think you to not be a nice person living in an engaged man's flat.' Her poison barb reaching its target, Jacqui left as quick as she had arrived.

Distraught, Emma said nothing in response; she couldn't find the words or get them past her constricted throat. How Jacqui knew where Emma was living, was something she wasn't game to ask.

By Saturday, Emma felt like a complete quivering wreck. With her self-confidence taking a severe nose-dive to such an extent she ceased answering her mobile phone when she knew it was Nick ringing and ignored the landline in the flat. Since none of his friends and colleagues knew Nick had even returned for a short time, she figured the only person to be ringing his unit was the man himself and she couldn't find the gumption to speak to him. What had tipped her over the edge of believing or disbelieving Jacqui was the fact she knew where Emma was living. Knowing she had never mentioned her abode to a single person at work, there would have been only one-way Jacqui could have found out.

She read all Nick's emails, poured her heart out to him in her replies but didn't press the send button on any of them. She felt drained, empty and numb with a relentless ache in her heart and her stomach felt as though it were a tight ball of painful tension.

Things were no better the first day back at work after a tension filled weekend. Within the first hour, Jacqui headed towards Emma in the passage, went to dodge one way but managed to bump into her, dropping a pile of papers as she brushed against Emma. Full of apologies, Emma crouched down to pick them up, glancing down as she scooped up the pile. What she saw sent sharp stabs of sheer agony through her body. They were emails addressed to Jacqui with Nick's email address on top. She wished she could read the words but with Jacqui standing in front of her, didn't dare be seen snooping. She forced her face into some semblance of normality, but it felt like a stone mask as she handed the papers back. The flood of tears she held back until she locked herself in her office, remaining there until it was time to go home.

Emma left early, buying a paper on her way home to scour the *To Let* columns. Over a meal which tasted like cardboard, she circled those places she thought were suitable and she could afford. With her hand hovering over the phone she was in two minds about whether to go ahead. Finally she rang to make appointments to see each. Pushing away her uneaten food, she searched the bookshelves and cupboards until she found a local map book, marking each location with pencil to see how far they were away from work and how close each was to transport.

Each day at work, Jacqui would somehow contrive a way of Emma seeing the latest email from Nick, despite Emma's almost ridiculous efforts to hide. The number of times Emma overheard phone conversations with Jacqui always mentioning Nick's name while saying romantic words to him, was astounding. Each evening, Emma viewed the flats. Most were disappointing, being nothing more than dingy, miniscule squats but in despair she signed the lease on the last one she found, not really caring any more. The fact it was a tiny, one bedroom flat with a poky kitchenette, a lounge big enough for only a two-seater settee and the squishiest bathroom she'd ever seen, all at the top of five flights of stairs with no elevator, held little significance. The ceilings were mouldy and there was no central heating. There were very few things it had going for it except basic furniture was included in the rent, it was on the opposite side of the city to Nick's flat and she could move in, in a week and a half.

Arriving home too late in the evening to bother with food she knew she couldn't eat in any case, Emma read Nick's imploring emails, begging her to tell him why she didn't answer his phone calls or emails. She answered every single one in long responses, letting out her anguish and pouring out her deepest thoughts and feelings, but she didn't press the send button on any of them. The ache inside her heart swelled to such proportions she thought it would burst. She fell asleep feeling emotionally exhausted and when she awoke the next morning her feelings of misery and loneliness welled up again. She knew by the haggard image she spied in the mirror how she was losing weight. It didn't surprise her since she had lost interest in food and eating. Her face was wan with dark circles under her eyes becoming more and more noticeable.

Emma spent the weekend scrubbing and cleaning the flat, leaving every surface spotless. She packed her clothes, leaving the blue dress and jewellery hanging in her wardrobe, and enough work clothes in a separate pile to last the final few days before she moved.

On Wednesday when she arrived at work, Emma found a large buff coloured business envelope on her desk. Her fingers shook as she slid the flap open. Inside she found a whole pile of emails addressed to Jacqui, from Nick. Emma didn't bother to read them because she knew, by the agonising pain stabbing in her heart she wouldn't be able to concentrate on her job. She shoved the envelope into her bag and carried them home where she read them through a haze of tears, her confidence and belief in Nick shattered.

An intense anger enveloped her as she ripped the sheets of paper into several pieces and dumped them into the already overflowing bin outside the front door. The state of the bin reminded her she was supposed to wheel it to the roadside early the day after tomorrow for collection. Too humiliated and angry to eat, she had no dinner but flung herself onto her bed and cried herself to sleep knowing she had lost the man she loved with every fibre of her being.

The following day at work was a real effort. Emma had a few dictations to translate and type. She locked herself in her office, making a monumental effort to concentrate. When she had completed her tasks, she returned them to Mark. His look as he eyed her was curious. 'What's wrong, Emma?' He demanded.

'Nothing,' she lied. 'I'm a bit tired. I was feeling a bit off colour for a few days and didn't sleep very well. But I'm fine now. I'll catch up on my sleep over the weekend.'

She sent up a silent prayer of gratitude that Mark took her at her word as he handed her the next few tasks. 'There is no real hurry so take it easy. I don't expect the work for a couple of days.'

Emma placed the completed work on his desk before she left much later than usual. Not bothering with the heating system when she entered the flat, she ate the remaining items of food in the fridge for her dinner. An apple, a small chunk of cheese and hot milky chocolate to use up the remaining milk was more than she eaten at any one time since Nick had left. Dreading going to bed, she huddled under a thick quilt on the settee before forcing herself to pack the last few items. It was after midnight before she completed her packing and cleaning. Emotional and physical exhaustion had taken their toll. She fell into bed, but sleep eluded her until the early hours of the morning when sheer exhaustion dragged her into oblivion.

Chapter Twenty-One

There was an unusual noise when Emma opened her bedroom door. She glanced up and spied movement from the corner of her eye.

'Nick, what are you doing here?'

Emma stood rooted to the spot, her pulse beating at what seemed, a thundering pace along the underside of her jaw. He looked so wonderful: so angry. She wanted to fly into his arms but didn't dare.

'What I'm doing here, Sweetness, is trying to fathom out what the devil is going on. You won't answer my emails nor my phone calls, you look terrible, as though you haven't slept or eaten since I left.' Nick's voice sounded cold but why? It was her who was angry and hurt and disappointed. He took a few steps towards her but suddenly stopped.

'Sweetheart, what happened? For two weeks, your answers came back almost before I had sent my emails, your phone only rang once or twice before I heard your wonderful voice. You thrilled me with your words but suddenly – nothing. So, I figured the only way for me to talk to you and get some answers, was in person.'

'I'm sorry, Nick.' Emma said in a quavering voice which didn't sound anything like hers. She paused, glanced up and added, 'I have to go to work.' With her foot, she pulled her bedroom door closed behind her to hide her packed bags.

Like a panther, Nick moved to block her path. 'What's wrong, Sweetheart? Please talk to me?' His tone was far gentler as he reached for her. When he managed to reel her against him, she trembled at his touch and melted into him, but common sense came roaring to the forefront and she struggled to free herself, willing her eyes to not leak. She jerked her head away and shot towards the door.

'I'll miss my bus. I have to go.' Emma called as she fled. 'I'll always love, you, Nick,' she added under her breath.

Output of work was non-existent. Every time Emma set her mind to the paper in front of her all she could see was Nick's angry face and a new bout of tears turned the typed words into a blur of squiggly lines. Instead of reaching for a pen, her hand found tissues, which turned into sodden shreds. Inside, it was as though a huge vacuum had sucked out her innards yet at the same time there was a ten-tonne block of concrete pressing into her chest. Too afraid of being seen with swollen red eyes, she stayed put when her break time arrived. By lunch-time an over-full bladder sent her a definite message, but she couldn't figure out how her body could possibly have any fluid left.

She poked her head out of the door and seeing no-one, crept along the passage to the ladies. Her heart lodged itself in her throat when she opened the door, terrified Jacqui would be waiting to pounce again with her nasty vitriol. A sigh escaped when the room was empty. Washing her hands involved soaking her face under copious hands-full of water and patting it dry with paper towels. She was almost back to her office when she stopped dead in her tracks. Nick was striding towards Jacqui's door.

'Oh, God, no,' flew from her mouth in a harsh whisper. Now she knew for sure that everything Jacqui had said was true. Why else would he go to her first? Why couldn't he come to Emma and be honest? Break it to her before he went to see *her?*

Emma fought back threatening tears. She wanted to confront him but knew she wouldn't. She couldn't. Not after those emails where he had gloated about hanging her on a string, boasted about how easy it was to sucker her in and string her along, how stupid she was for believing him, how unsophisticated, naïve and simple she was. She had to get out of here. No way could she stay in this building.

She felt her ice-cold heart snap, the icicle shards stabbing her in agonising pain. Creeping backwards she felt her way along the wall until she found her boss's door, opened it and fled inside, not bothering to knock or wait to be summonsed in.

Mark glanced up at the intrusion and frowned. 'What is it, Emma? Are you all right?'

'Mark, I have to go – now – please? I'll explain on Monday.'

Looking completely perplexed, Mark stood but Emma backed away to the door, pleading with her eyes. 'Please, Mark?' she begged.

'Of course, Emma, if it's so urgent. If there's anything I can do to help, let me know.'

Without a word, Emma raced to her office, grabbed her bag and fled the building via the fire escape.

It was impossible to see through the haze of moisture blurring her sight as she fled the building. She took no heed of which way she went, interspersing jogging with running and quick strides, stepping onto the roadway when she found her passage blocked by mobs of people. She took little notice until she was breathless. Dodging around a group of people looking at hand-held screens, she was caught in steadying arms when she stumbled down a kerb. Glancing up she thanked her saviour but realised she wasn't where she thought she was going. Seeking out something to recognise she recalled the building in front of her. She was in Covent Garden, miles away from Nick's flat and in the opposite direction. Needing time to think about what the heck she was supposed to do next, she entered the nearest eatery and wove her way through the tables to find her favourite spot when she was feeling insecure – right at the back, in a corner; unseen and hiding. She ordered a meagre salad and large coffee, lingering over both and toying with her food while trying to think. She had her new flat to go to, but the keys were in her bag, in Nick's flat, along with all her belongings.

She was still sitting huddled in her chair at closing time, when she had no choice but to leave. With thinning crowds, she ambled towards Nick's flat until her sore feet and the freezing cold sleet had her hailing a cab to drive the rest of the way. She asked the driver to wait while she collected her luggage. Too afraid to go inside, she stood on the front porch checking for any lights or sounds coming from inside. Satisfied Nick was either asleep or not there, she tried not to make a sound as she turned the key in the lock, paused when it clicked open and dared to push the door ajar a few centimetres. Not wanting to make any noise, she removed her shoes, leaving them in the doorway before creeping her way across the lounge to her room. She opened the door and, in the darkness, felt around for her cases but they weren't where she'd left them.

'Looking for something?' queried a quiet voice behind her.

She squealed in fright as her body jerked from the ground and whirled around. The lights flashed on.

'Nick?' she squeaked out.

'Since it's my flat, who else would it be? Unless you were expecting someone else–maybe a new boyfriend? Is that why you were leaving? To move in with someone else?'

'I wouldn't do such a thing to you,' shot from her mouth without giving her a chance to think.

'No, you wouldn't, and nor would I do it to you. But it seems my faith in you is a lot stronger than your faith in me. You doubted my word and the thought pains me a great deal. Come with me, I want to show you something.' Not giving her any opportunity to escape he grasped her wrist and gripped tighter as she fought to free herself while being gently towed into his study where he had both his computer and laptop set up and running. After literally forcing Emma into the swivel chair he pulled up a stool behind her, reaching either side of her shoulders while he operated the mouse on the laptop.

Emma was trapped. The scent of his skin sent her senses on a spiral, her emotions on fire. Her nerves were electrified when his arms brushed against hers. He was so close she could feel his breath fan her hair, which was covered in moisture from the dampness outside. A quiver ran down her spine giving her a desperate urge to turn around and wrap her arms around his body to warm her.

'Emma, look at the screen. These are all the emails I have sent to anyone over the past four weeks. Have a look at the dates and the names next to each.' Ignoring her indrawn breath at his mention of emails, he scrolled down the list slow enough for her to read the names, pausing at any names associated with his work to explain who they were. When he reached the end, he leant closer and whispered in her ear, almost caressing her, his lips were so darn close.

'There are sixty-five emails addressed to one adorable Emma Nicholls. I think every single one tells her how much I love and miss her. She read every one. This mark up here tells me.' Nick reached over, brushing his chest against her back as he pointed. A gasp of pleasure slipped out. 'How many are addressed to Jacqui Hartford-Jones? Would you like me to go through them again?'

'But she showed me…' Emma began, her voice breaking. 'You must have deleted them.'

'Okay. Let's pull up all my deleted emails.' After playing around with the mouse, the list flickered onto the screen. 'Point to all those addressed to Jacqui,' he instructed as he moved down the list at a snail's pace. A loud banging at the door interrupted them.

Emma jumped from her seat but couldn't move with Nick's arms trapping her against his body. She sucked in her breath and closed her eyes then sank back down, ensuring there was no physical contact. 'The taxi – I asked him to wait. I forgot about him.'

'Stay there.' His words were stern, yet his voice was tender as he left her to pay off the driver.

'I'm sorry, Nick,' she whispered when he settled down behind her again.

'You have nothing to be sorry about, you did nothing wrong. Now please turn around.' He spun Emma to face the computer screen again. She was sure he brushed against her with his arms on purpose, but it was sweet torture.

'Sweetness, I didn't write those emails to Jacqui. She wrote them herself. Watch this and I'll show you how she did it.'

Sliding the laptop aside he dragged the keyboard over from his main computer system. Within minutes he had generated and printed off an email addressed to Nick from a phantom writer. Next, he opened a drawer and pulled out a pile of paper. Emma gasped when she saw the stuck together pieces of paper.

'And in case you were thinking it, I wasn't snooping, my love. I heard the rubbish truck this morning and checked to see whether you'd remembered to put the bin out in your rather hurried exit. The lid flew open as I rushed them down the steps and these came out. I spent the morning doing jigsaw puzzles. Things started falling in place rapidly. Let me show you something else I discovered which intrigued me.'

She was rigid while Nick opened her email address to show all her unsent responses. 'You did answer all my emails, but you didn't send them.'

'But I deleted those,' she protested.

'Sweetness, one of the things I get paid very good money for is retrieving lost data from computers. Yours were easy because you only deleted them once. These took my particular interest.'

Very slowly, he clicked open each of his emails and Emma's unsent responses. He read out each one aloud. 'This one is my favourite. My darling, Nick,' he whispered in her ear. He followed it with a soft kiss on her neck, below her ear lobe, sending a quiver down her spine. 'I love you so much.' This time he rained several lingering warm kisses along the nape of her neck, not ceasing when he heard her indrawn breath. His next target was her other ear. 'My heart feels like it is bursting every time I think about you.' His arms slid down her side and around her waist while his lips settled on her ear lobe giving her a soft, provocative nip.

'Do you want me to go on reading, Emma?'

'No.'

'Or would you rather this? I flew twelve thousand miles thinking only about this.' Turning her around to face him, he leant forwards and with a very gentle touch, ran the pads of his thumbs along her lips. 'I kept thinking about the softness of your mouth, the wonderful smell of lavender from your skin, the feel of you in my arms, how I like your soft contours pressed up against me.'

His lips took the place of his thumbs in a kiss which started off as nothing more than a gentle brush while he explored every part. The kiss deepened to become more searching until the loneliness of four weeks apart turned the kiss into a long passionate embrace with Emma held tight against his body.

When he drew away Nick stood, easing Emma up with him, never once releasing his hold. With outstretched fingers of one hand, he held her head cradled against his shoulder. 'I never believed it was possible to miss someone as much as I have missed you. I couldn't believe it when you stopped answering my emails and calls. It devastated me to the extent I haunted your parents, trying to find out what had happened, but it seems you kept all this from them as well. Emma, I would never, ever think about hurting you by having any kind of relationship with another woman.'

Now knowing for sure she had got things very wrong, Emma pulled away and plonked down again, pointing to Nick's stool. 'Can we talk?' she asked.

His arms eased away as he perched on the edge, but he kept hold of her hands with his thumbs making seductive circles in her palms.

'I'm so sorry for doubting you but Jacqui was so insistent as well as persistent. She started the first day after you left, having conversations with you on her mobile phone. The second day she followed me to the toilets and told me how you two had dated and had an understanding and you had only gone home as a final farewell because you were planning on getting married when you came back.'

'She what?'

'I didn't believe her at first.'

'How I wish you had never believed her at all but now I understand your question about me being honest with you if I ever changed my mind about you. You were fishing for information.'

'I was warned to keep my hands off you. It built up a bit more every day. She'd walk past me talking on her phone –

always saying your name and whispering romantic things. Every day her phone would ring, and she would answer it and start off a romantic conversation with you, sometimes several times a day. Nick, if it wasn't you ringing, how did she do that?'

He lifted her hand to his mouth and planted a lingering kiss into her palm. It might have been a hardly-there touch, but her toes curled. 'There are a couple of ways. The easiest would be to have two mobiles. Just as you have numbers saved and you scroll down and press one button to connect, she could have had the number preset in one phone in her pocket and all she would have to do is press the dial button and the other phone would ring. There are other ways of doing it. Keep going.' With one hand he swept an escapee tendril of hair from her eye but dropped his hand to hold hers again when she wanted more.

'Then the emails began. She dropped a few papers on the floor when she walked past me. I guess now, it was on purpose. It had your email address on top and I guess you can figure out what it said.' Her voice sounded humble and contrite, even to herself.

'The next day when I had to deliver some files to her, she showed me her computer screen when I went into her office. The email was from you, telling her how gullible I was. She was relentless. I tried so hard to keep out of her way, so I didn't have to face her. I even hid in my office with the door locked from the inside and wouldn't go out for lunch. I remained behind after work, but she would always find me. Hints followed, about it not being a good idea for me to be living in your flat. It would make people think I was not a very nice person. I don't even know how she found out where I was living. She never let up. I found the pile of emails on my desk yesterday morning.'

A loud sigh escaped his lips as Nick lifted his hands to her shoulders and drew her close, so her head was resting against his chest. 'Let me finish for you, Sweetheart. Your self-confidence plummeted when you began to believe all her lies. The little mouse who allowed Greg to bully her, returned. He's back in jail by the way. The mouse began hiding in corners and creeping around the walls, hoping no one would notice her. She worked extra hard at her job to try to rid her mind of her anguish. She came home every night refusing to socialise with anyone, scrubbing and cleaning until she was so tired, she would fall asleep from sheer exhaustion. She never ate because her appetite had gone. She couldn't switch off her over-active brain. Am I close?'

He didn't wait for an answer but instead ran his outspread hands up and down her back before cupping her backside. 'How I wish you had said something to me. I would have, no, should have told you what Jacqui was like. I only ever dated her once before I discovered how possessive and nasty she was, but I never imagined she would go to these lengths, especially to a newcomer.'

'I saw you at work today, going to her office but you didn't come to me, so I knew all she said was true.'

'Oh, Emma, I'm sorry. I was white with anger for what she had done. I had to confront her, get the anger out of my system before coming to you. I also confronted Mark for he had promised to keep an eye on you. When I came looking for you, you had gone. Mark told me how desperate you were to leave.'

Drawing her out of the chair, he swapped seats with her to shut down both computers before grasping her hand and leading her into the lounge where he settled at one end of the sofa, easing her down next to him. Taking it slow, he lay her down with her head in his lap where he brushed her hair from the side of her face. 'Tell me something, Emma. Where were you going to move to?'

Her breath hitched. 'I found a small bed-sit. I was supposed to move in today. I signed a lease. I didn't know what else to do. I'm so sorry, Nick. I feel so bad, but I was so confused, and it hurt so much I couldn't think straight.'

His long fingers continued a rhythmical caressing of her skin. 'We can sort everything out but if you still have a need to move out, to be independent, I won't prevent you from going but before you make a decision consider this. Before I left home, I went to see your parents. They gave me their blessing if I could convince you to marry me. After only a week back home, I had decided exactly where I wanted to live. It was with you. If you want to pursue your career, it's fine by me. If you want to live here, or Paris, or back home – wherever – I want to be there with you. Sweetheart, I'm so much in love with you, please will you marry me?'

Not daring to move and unable to believe what she was hearing, Emma lay still. Suddenly the tears of torment and relief she had been holding back for so long welled up while the huge raft of different emotions finally culminated. Sitting up she wriggled into Nick's lap seeking the security she knew only he could give her while ignoring the steady stream of hot tears she had absolutely no control over.

As she sobbed, Nick held her to him, allowing her to release all her pent-up anguish. They remained in the tight embrace until Emma was spent and fell asleep in his arms.

Chapter Twenty-Two

When Emma woke her head felt like the stuffing from a pillow, all fuzzy with no lucidity. She tore off her rumpled clothes before remembering she had nothing else to put on. As she stumbled from bed, she noticed her still packed bags inside the door. Tugging one open she hunted around for a warm fleecy tracksuit. It was going to be awkward facing Nick but knew it would be all right. She tip-toed out to see Nick sitting in his favourite lounge chair reading a novel. He hadn't seen her, so she snuck over to him and put her mouth close to his ear. 'I didn't answer your question last night. Yes please, Nick.'

It took him a few moments for the significance of the words to sink in. With an ear-splitting grin on his face, he turned, grabbed hold of the hands belonging to the voice and swung the rest of the body around until Emma was perched in his lap and his mouth was firmly settled over hers. When they finally surfaced, one hand snaked over to the glass-topped table by his chair. She heard his fingers pad around, rustling papers and knocking into things until he held up his mobile phone. Using one hand, he scrolled down his saved numbers and pressed.

'Hi, it's Nick,' he said and handed the phone to Emma. 'Congratulations, honey.'

'Mum, how did you know?'

'Nick said he would ring us the moment you said yes. Has he given you the envelope?' asked Jeannie.

'What envelope?' asked Emma as she turned to look at Nick, who had a very smug grin on his face and was waving an envelope around in the air. Recognising the insignia from her university Emma grabbed it. 'My results. Hang on Mum, I'll hand you over to Nick.'

Swapping the phone for the envelope she leapt from his lap and tore the end from the envelope. Opening out the few sheets of paper while Nick accepted the congratulations of his future parents–in–law, Emma scanned her results sheets and the accompanying papers. Dumbstruck, she plonked down in a chair.

'Oh, oh,' said Nick into the phone. 'She either failed miserably or has done brilliantly because her jaw is dragging on the ground.' After removing the papers from shaking hands, he called out the results to Emma's mother. 'My goodness, no wonder she's speechless. Every subject has a high distinction, she's been awarded first class honours and let me see, has been awarded a prize, no make it two, good grief, three prizes! Graduation is in May, will Emma be attending, it asks? Most definitely. We'll both be home in

May. Nick handed the phone back to an astonished Emma, who spoke at length with both of her parents although she was so stunned, she didn't have a clue what was said.

When she hung up, Nick suggested a celebration dinner that night. 'Allow me to take you somewhere special to celebrate your brilliant results and more important, the fact you have finally agreed to marry me. I can't believe you said yes.' He paused for a moment. 'You did say yes, didn't you?'

She smiled as she nodded and received another heart stopping kiss.

'Go and have your shower and change while I make a booking. My second phone call will be to my parents to tell them the wonderful news. After your shower we are going shopping. By the way, Caro and Sandy both passed everything as well and if you haven't looked at a clock this morning, it's nearly lunchtime.

Emma fought to decipher all the information she had been given but followed instructions. She returned in time to speak with Nick's parents who were delighted with the news. Caroline was out with Justin, but Emma had no doubt she would be in contact the moment she heard about their engagement.

Shopping consisted of Nick ushering Emma into a jeweller, insisting no other man was going to be getting any ideas about stealing the love of his life from him. She was so confused by the variety and style of engagement rings she insisted Nick choose. She was disappointed when he sent her to a nearby café to order a late lunch while he made the final decision. The disappointment dropped to devastation status when he wouldn't show her the ring, saying she would have to wait for the right moment.

At Nick's request Emma wore her blue dress and when she emerged that evening, Nick's eyes smouldered. They returned to the restaurant Nick had taken her to before he had gone back home. The pre-ordered champagne was in an elegant silver ice-bucket waiting for them.

'I believe congratulations are in order, allow me to wish you all the very best on your engagement?' the waiter said while he poured the icy cold bubbles into the crystal champagne flutes. 'And to you ma'am, on your achievements in your studies.' Stunned, Emma guessed Nick must have said something when he had booked the table. She couldn't help the beaming smile spread across her face as she thanked the waiter.

Nick raised his glass. 'Congratulations on your brilliant results. I know how much work you need to put in to achieve such consistent high marks. Caro said you would do well and how she and Sandy gave up competing with you after first year. They were happy to pass, but they both did well, nevertheless. There was quite a sprinkling of distinctions for them both. I'm going to be a very proud man when you go up on the stage at your graduation – and make no mistake about it – we are going to be there. To you, my love.' The moment after Nick sipped on his champagne his face turned serious.

'I'm not sure whether you heard me tell you Greg Saunders has been caught and is in jail. Which means you don't have to stay here if you want to go home.'

'I heard you but wasn't really in the space to talk about it last night. I'm not so sure I ever want to discuss him. How was he caught?'

'Well, he was kind of foolish. It seems he had been searching for you. For a while he thought you were still hidden in our house so kept watch. He confronted me one night. Mind you he had a dirty great big knife waving in front of me at the time.'

Emma drew in her breath in alarm, the memory of the knife sending a shudder of fear through her body.

'I presume it was the same one he used to threaten you. You never told me it was so enormous. The thought of what could have happened to you had he had the opportunity to use the thing, gave me nightmares for a few nights. He demanded to know where you were. It pleased me he didn't know you had gone overseas. I told him you had found employment and had moved to where you were working. He wasn't too happy when I wouldn't disclose exactly where it was, so he attacked me to force the information from me.' Nick watched as Emma felt the blood drain from her face.

'Sweetness, I do recall I said he would get a shock if he ever attacked me. I studied self-defence while I was at high school and in university. I still go to sessions as a way of keeping fit, so it gave me a great deal of pleasure to defend myself and let me tell you, I was not very gentle. I gave him a pasting and when I kicked him, very hard, in the part of his anatomy you threatened to shoot off, I informed him it was a gift from you. He was incapable of walking when Steve's men came to pick him up. The knife will be used in evidence at his trial, which is in late April – so we will have to go home in any case. Now how about far more pleasant things; come and dance with me?'

Pushing his seat back he held out his hand. Still reeling, it took her a few rounds of the floor to relax and melt into Nick's arms.

'It seems I still have a lot to learn about you, Mr Nicholas Hamilton. But I'm delighted you gave him my present. I was so tempted to shoot him there, but he was not worth the jail term. Thank you. And I don't want to go home yet. I'm enjoying my job; it's what I worked for. But what about you, you were going to spend six months home with your parents?'

'That was before I met you, my precious love. Now my priorities have changed. I'm staying with you. Mum and Dad understand and are very happy and I figure we'll be home for at least a month with the trial and your graduation. I think they were glad to get rid of me because I wasn't very good company. I was pining for you. Could I make another suggestion?'

'Let me guess, how about we get married while we're home? Yes, I would love to.' Emma smiled at Nick's astonished face, then reached up and kissed him.

'So, mind reading is another of your talents is it?' he asked as he led Emma back to their table to eat the entrée which had been served.

During the main course, Emma brooded over the subject of Jacqui until she figured it needed to be cleared. 'Nick, what was your relationship with Jacqui?'

'There was no relationship. When I was working for Mark, installing their computer system, they had a staff function. I was invited and attended alone and ended up having a couple of dances with Jacqui, as well as with a few other women. She seemed to attach herself to me. I took her out on one date, and I have regretted it ever since. It was probably the worst time I've ever had on a date. She showed her true colours and became possessive and overbearing. Several time she asked me to accompany her to various functions, but I always declined because I didn't like her very much. We didn't even share a kiss.'

'Why did she treat me with such venom?'

'She is a bully and you were vulnerable. If you'd had the confidence to stand up to her after the first incident she may have backed off. But she could see she was getting to you, which gave her power over you. If she couldn't have me, she wasn't about to let you have what she couldn't have. She's much like Greg. He bullied you, and being the gentle-natured person you are, you accepted it to keep the peace. He also became possessive of you and he wasn't about to let me have what he was denied. Only with him it became an obsession, which became physically violent, because he couldn't handle the loss of power. Mentally, he is a sick man but also a very dangerous one. I doubt Jacqui would have resorted to violence. She enjoyed the power she had over you, probably because she was jealous of you. See what effect you have on people. Caro and Sandy think you are the greatest person on this earth, and you have bewitched me, caught me hook, line and sinker.'

With a beguiling smile Nick stood and beckoned Emma to the dance floor. By the time they reached the floor, the music had changed and Emma heard the unmistakable rhythm of the tango. Remembering her promise, she stopped on the edge of the floor.

'No, I promised there would be no more tango dancing.'

'And I insist you break your promise. Let's make it a fun dance and not so intense. Please, my beautiful little witch?'

She hesitated a while longer but finally agreed and moved onto the dance floor. She tried her best not to be so seductive with her movements making the dance more the fun they used to put into it at boarding school with the girls. But it was different dancing with Nick opposite her and she felt the pit of her stomach tensing up into a coiled emotional ball. Once again, they had the floor to themselves with all eyes on them. It didn't matter how unseductive Emma tried to make her movements she still felt the intense emotion with her eyes drawn to Nick's sexy stare. She was shocked to see the depth of emotion in his eyes, because he had been the one to insist on making it less intense. When the dance drew to the end, Nick sidled up to her, wrapped one arm around her waist while he kept his eyes locked onto hers.

The moment the music stopped Nick dropped to one knee still holding her left hand. Drawing a ring from his shirt pocket he slipped it on her ring finger in full view of the entire restaurant. He stood, drawing her into his arms as he rose, locking his mouth onto hers and giving her a very long, ardent kiss.

Emma felt the coil in her stomach spring open in a surge of raw emotion and was left gasping when Nick lifted his head to a rousing standing ovation. His smile was wide as he lifted Emma's left hand to proudly show the audience.

Knowing she was incapable of moving anywhere by herself she was glad when Nick wrapped one arm around her waist and guided her back to their table. Before sitting, he lifted her left hand and kissed where he had placed her ring.

'You planned all this,' spluttered Emma, her emotions running a wild ride through her body.

'I wanted to make it a memorable occasion. I love you, Miss Emma Nicholls and am immensely proud you have agreed to become my wife. I am very much looking forward to spending the rest of my life with you by my side.' Nick filled their glasses before handing one fizzy flute to Emma. 'To us, Sweetheart.'

The crystal glasses chinked as the two stared at each other.

'To us,' whispered Emma before taking a sip.

Their waiter approached the table and handed Nick a camera. Emma's eyes popped in astonishment while Nick reviewed the photos on a camera she now recognised. How did he manage to do all this?

'Very nice, thank you. You have captured the relevant moments perfectly. I think my gorgeous fiancée is beyond sweets or coffee, so if I could have my bill, I think I had better take her home to recover.' Nick grinned at her, refusing her request to see the images. 'I'm going to print them off first. I want to see your face when you see the finished product. Are you happy to leave now, I was being a bit presumptuous there?'

'Yes, of course, because I think I need to have a few severe words with you.'

'I look forward to it.' Nick laughed while he signed his credit card slip and stood and held out his hand for Emma. She was further embarrassed on their way out when several women stopped her to inspect her ring: the ring she had barely noticed herself coming down from her shocked state. Now she had a chance to study it under the scrutiny of the other women, she noticed the large central pink diamond, surrounded by smaller white diamonds. It wasn't one of the rings she had looked at with Nick. She glanced up at him.

'The pink represents the unleashed fire I keep seeing hidden in your eyes. It is also an Argyle diamond, so it comes from home.'

'It's beautiful, Nick. Thank you.' She felt unashamed as she swept her mouth over his before they moved away from the last table.

Chapter Twenty-Three

While Emma changed for bed, Nick went to his computer with a promise of attaching the photos the waiter had taken. When Emma took him a cup of coffee she stood behind him, leant over and picked up the already processed photos.

'Oh, Nick, these are fabulous. This one I must have for myself. The waiter captured the look in your eyes. Heavens, I can feel ...' Emma stopped, not wanting to reveal the intensity of the feelings Nick's eyes had invoked in her.

'Feel what?' Nick had turned around and was watching her. She dropped her eyes to mask them from his scrutiny. 'I can wait, my love,' he whispered but she knew what he meant.

Unable to handle her deep emotions, Emma silently left the room and retired to bed, her body on fire with the feelings the look in Nick's eyes in the photo had unleashed on her again. She lay in deep thought, unable to relax enough to sleep while listening for movements as Nick worked, following him in her mind when he walked through the flat and readied himself for bed.

She heard soft music coming from his CD player and smiled when she recognised the tune. He was being a devil; the music was a tango and she knew it was deliberate to stir up the emotions in her.

The music went on and on, one tango after another. Darn man was probably killing himself laughing but she figured a way to pay him back with a high rate of interest. She stripped off as she gyrated to his room in time to the music. She opened the door. He was lying on his stomach, so she crept to the side of his bed.

'Nick?'

'Yes, my love.'

'I've always believed the tango has two parts. Part one is the dance on the dance floor.'

'And part two?' he questioned without moving.

'Is what I would like you to teach me. Please look at me, Nick.'

He turned over and stilled, staring. Sitting up he opened out his arms. 'Sweetheart, are you absolutely sure about this, because you are about the most beautiful thing I have ever had the good fortune to see, and you are driving me crazy with wanton desire.'

Feeling hesitant but knowing she was ready to take the next step, Emma knelt on the floor by the bed and slipped her fingers into his proffered hand. 'I wouldn't be here right now if I wasn't certain.'

Never once taking his eyes from hers Nick threw back the edge of the doona with one hand and eased her from the floor with the other. He ran his warm hands down her arms while he planted soft kisses on the nape of her neck. She thrilled at the shudders she felt go through his body before he reached around her and tugged her to lay next to him.

The heat of Nick's body and the brush of his skin on hers caused her to shiver in delight. He explored her mouth until she felt a strange and wonderful warmth spiralling up from her toes and spreading out.

As he moved his mouth down to her neck, her arms crept around his shoulders and back. The fingers of one of his hands wandered down between her breasts and around her abdomen, caressing, sweeping, barely touching.

Emma involuntarily clutched tighter as she let out a loud gasp of pleasure, gripping him when the feel of his fingers on her breasts sent an explosion of blissful sensations pulsing through her body. She thought she would die when his mouth moved to her tight aroused nipples and his moist tongue curled around each in turn, to be followed by his fingers gently kneading and awakening even deeper sensations from deep within her body.

Pulling his head back as far as Emma's tight grip would allow, he studied her face while his hand swept lower to play with her tight curls. His mouth moved back to reclaim hers while his hands grasped her around the waist. He twisted to lie on his back, pulling Emma on top of him. His warm hands wandered up and down her back as his kiss deepened, his fingers forever caressing her skin.

Emma didn't know where the need came from, but she had an overwhelming desire to do the same to him. Rolling back on her side she allowed her fingers to roam of their own volition, seeking and searching for every inch of his skin, exploring every plane and hollow and loving the sensation of the hairs on his chest and the indrawn gasps of pleasure she was able to elicit from Nick until he could take no more.

His kiss was passionate while he reached over for protection and paused for a moment while it was rolled into place. It felt like forever as Nick caressed and cuddled and touched until she was writhing with a need she knew about but had never experienced, until now.

She felt the brief searing pain when he breached her innocence. He must have felt her tense for he paused to give her body time to adjust but it was instantly followed by pulsating waves of sheer pleasure.

It took a while for the ecstasy to ease. Nick lifted his body from Emma, gathering her to him as he rolled onto his side, her head on his shoulder. He spread his fingers out, one hand in the small of her back and the other cradling her head as he held her close. His kiss was tender and soft.

'Oh, God, Nick. Part two is so much better than part one,' Emma whispered against his neck. She felt Nick's body shake with suppressed laughter.

He lifted his head and glanced down at her, smiling. 'It was worth the wait for you to come to me on your own volition, my darling, Emma. It will be even better next time; there will be no pain. There was absolutely nothing I could do to avoid the initial pain for you, Sweetness.'

'How could anything be better than that?'

'I promise it can get better. Now go to sleep and let me enjoy the pleasure of sleeping with you in my arms.'

Upon waking Emma leant on her elbows to study the still sleeping man lying next to her. She was about to lean over and kiss him when his eyes opened.

'Good morning my wonderful, Nicholas. I've been watching you, wondering what I've done to deserve such a caring, gentle and kind man as you.' She leant down and pressed her lips to his mouth.

'I'm not sure I like the way you use the word 'deserve'. Everybody deserves to be treated with respect. I believe respect to be the essence of a good partnership, and I hope it is what our marriage will be, a partnership where we can respect each other's desires, wants, needs. I would like us to share all aspects of each other's lives, but not to the extent we become demanding or owning. By ownership I mean you will never be treated as though you are an item I own. I don't believe one person can own another. Greg treated you as though you were a possession of his, for you to obey his every bidding, something I don't agree with. Jacqui thought she could own me. Neither gave a thought to the other's wishes. Greg never considered your feelings. Look at how he didn't like to dance and therefore wouldn't let you dance. Such behaviour, to me, is ownership. Take your rifle to me, if I ever act in such a manner.'

He bent and kissed the smile on her face. 'We both have free wills. There will be times when you want to do something which doesn't interest me and vice versa. I will respect your desires as I hope you will mine, but I would never expect you to give up your life to follow my interests. Look at our parents. Mum has an interest in art which Dad doesn't. He doesn't stop her from pursuing her interest and she doesn't mind that he does other things. From what I've seen of your parents, they treat each other with the same kind of respect. I would very much like us to be the same. And now my delectable fiancée, what would you like to do today?'

'Spend a quiet day with you. Get up my nerve to face Jacqui at work tomorrow and learn how to stand up to her.'

'I like the first bit, my body is jetlagged and as for tomorrow, you have nothing to worry about. While I was waiting for you to return home the other night, Mark rang me. Jacqui has been fired. After questioning some of the other staff it appears you are not the only person she has been bullying. It was a little more dramatic with you because you were so vulnerable. Now, I'm going to have a nice hot shower and send at least one photo to Caroline, from last night. Come and pick one out with me. I might be game enough to show you something you are going to have words with me about.'

Nick laughed at Emma's curious face while he climbed out of the bed and left her there.

By the time he emerged, refreshed, Emma had coffee made. She handed Nick his and left for her turn in the bathroom. Nick followed and leant against the door jamb. 'You could have joined me you know. The shower was built to be big enough for two and I haven't tested it out yet. I've been waiting for the right woman.'

When she sent him a withering glare he laughed before leaning into the room to grasp the door knob and pull the door shut.

'What are you so smug about?' Emma asked when she spied his grin as she handed him a coffee.

'Caroline first, then I'll show you.'

While Nick brought up each photo on the screen, they studied them. Emma felt her blood surging when she saw the photo of Nick's face again.

'Print this one for me, please? This one is special. I know you are looking at me and I know exactly what you are saying with your eyes. I want this one for my bedside.' She planted a kiss on his cheek as he pressed the print button.

The photo they sent to Caroline showed Nick kneeling in front of Emma, placing the ring on her finger. Emma asked him to also send it to her brother, so her family could see it. After they had been through them all, Nick opened a different photo file. He turned to study her face as he clicked the mouse to open the file.

'Oh, God,' she spluttered when she saw the photo of her asleep, with a soft, satisfied smile on her face. It was obvious she was naked and in Nick's bed. The doona barely covered her nipples. She had one arm draped above her head and the other across her stomach. Her hair was messed and her face rosy from the thorough kissing she had just received.

'I think I'll have this blown up and hung on the lounge room wall. I'll call it Emma's Awakening.'

'I don't think so,' retorted Emma. 'Where is your camera, that needs deleting?'

'Too late, I've already printed it and saved it in my memory bank. How about this one?' Nick grinned. The second photo was equally as revealing but taken from a different angle.

'Nick! How many of those did you take?'

'Only four.'

'Four! You'd better show me them all and I warn you, they'd better not get sent to anyone, especially Caroline. I need some target practice.' She eyed Nick with her threat.

'Believe me, Sweetheart, these are only for my memory album – they are something I never want to share with anyone other than you. And what a memory it is. The night my lovely Emma seduced me, the night she came to me of her own free will, the night she was ready for me, the night she made such sweet love to me.' He interspersed every phrase with a soft kiss on different parts of her face, paused long enough to shut down the photo file before sweeping her into his arms as he continued showering her with hot, fervent kisses.

'Sweetness, come and dance with me, and let me show you how much better part two can be?' Grasping her hand, he led a very willing Emma back to his bedroom, via the lounge room where he set the tango CD on to continuous play.